DIAMONDS

DIAMONDS

by

Alan
Michaels

St. Martin's Press
New York

Copyright © 1980 by Alan Michaels
All rights reserved. For information, write:
St. Martin's Press, Inc., 175 Fifth Avenue, New York, N.Y. 10010.
Manufactured in the United States of America

Library of Congress Catalog in Publication Data

Michaels, Alan.
 Diamonds.

 I. Title.
PZ4.M62136Di   [PS3563.I268]   813'.5'4   79-25275
ISBN 0-312-19923-6

To my brother-in-law, Seymour Wagner,
who is also my friend.

List of Characters
(in order of appearance)

YANKEL KUVITZ—first courier

JULIAN HECK—Samuel Heckowitz's son

MAX GUBER—Sam's lifelong friend

MAREK KORDITZ—Sam's friend

CHIAM BORSKY—Sam's friend

SAUL URISHENSKY—a Russian Jew

MARINA URISHENSKY—Saul's wife

KLUGIN—a Russian courier

MAJ. SERGEI DIMETROV (SAUL KASS)—KGB agent assigned to find Samuel Heckowitz

COL. IGOR MARROSOV—KGB bureau chief

HARRY VOGEL—diamond dealer

PAUL FOURNIER—Sam's illegitimate son and French intelligence agent

SHULAMITH GIBORI—Israeli intelligence agent

JACOB LEVITAS—second courier

ANTHONY DALIS—New York Police Department detective

PETER CHILDS—CIA agent

MR. CALLUCHIE—a member of the Mafia

MR. SPINELLI—a Mafia Don

HERSHEL BEGIN—disco owner

CARLO FUENTES—KGB hit man

AVIGEOR—Israeli intelligence agent

MME. FOURNIER—Paul's mother

LUANA—Indonesian prostitute

SAUL LUBLIN—Amsterdam diamond dealer

CYNTHIA KOSS—Julian's girlfriend

SAUL M. LEGRIS—Paris diamond dealer

1

YANKEL KUVITZ WAS A TALL MAN with a grizzled beard, a prominently hooked nose and sad, deep-set green eyes. He wore a long black frock coat, a white shirt buttoned at the neck. No tie. And a black, wide-brimmed hat. A cigarette dangled from the left side of his mouth. He pushed the down button and waited patiently for the elevator.

The hallway was dark, with the exception of the small patch of light coming from an overhead fluorescent fixture at the elevator station and a thin sliver of yellow light escaping from under the door of the office he had just left. All the other offices on the floor and, no doubt, in the building were locked for the night.

He raised his eyes to follow the upward movement of the elevator on the indicator panel above the door. Ordinarily he would leave the office of Lebowitz & Sons, where he worked as a diamond appraiser, at about five thirty, never later than six. And on Friday, almost always at four, in order to be home before the beginning of the sabbath, which would begin at sundown and last a full twenty-four hours.

Other than illness—his own or that of anyone in his family—the only departure from his schedule would occur when he would be called to meet the men he had just left. And that, thank God, he commented to himself—not daring to even think the name God, but substituting instead, in the manner of an orthodox Jew, the four Hebrew letters *YHWH* that stand for God—did not happen too often. Yet, whenever he was called by those men still in the office, he felt an enormous sense of pride. For their call marked him as a very special person. Even more, it gave him the opportunity to help other Jews.

The elevator stopped and the doors opened. He stepped

into the empty car, turned and faced the doors. The elevator was old and slow. Its cables made growling sounds that during the day were muffled by hubbub in the building. But it was now past seven o'clock and a deep silence filled the hallways and offices.

On reaching the lobby, he pulled up the collar of his coat to shield himself from cold, blustery wind. Though it was only the last week in November, the weather for the past two days had become wintry. By tomorrow, or more precisely late tonight, he'd be in San Juan. But only long enough to transfer the two hundred thousand dollars' worth of diamonds he was carrying to a man named Roberts, who would take them later in the day to another man in another city. Eventually, the diamonds would find their way into the right hands . . . Kuvitz walked toward the door, his footsteps echoing loudly in the deserted lobby.

The night guard, a black man with a billy club and handcuffs, sat at a bridge table and asked him to sign out. Kuvitz nodded, and with a few deft strokes wrote his name.

"Cold outside," the guard commented, getting up to unlock the door.

"Let's hope it won't be a bad winter," he said. Though he spoke with a heavy German accent, he had no difficulty with the English words.

"Last winter was bad enough," the guard said.

Kuvitz walked out of 16 West Forty-seventh Street, pushed his hands deep into the pockets of his overcoat and made his way toward Sixth Avenue, to hail a cab for the Pan Am Terminal at JFK Airport.

Crowded during the day, the street was now deserted. It hardly looked like one of the great diamond centers of the world. On it and a few streets to the north and south, millions of dollars' worth of diamonds and other gemstones were bought and sold each day. But at night, with only the street lamps and a few window lights to illuminate it, everything looked mean and shabby. The windows of the various dealers were filled with darkness. The trays of glittering diamonds were stored in huge vaults for the night and returned to the windows each business day.

The wind tore down the street, blowing from west to east, making him bend into it. A piece of newspaper blew against his right leg and wrapped around it. He stopped, pulled it off and let the wind take it.

Kuvitz continued to walk toward Sixth Avenue, wondering if the rapid change of climates he would experience in the next few days would affect his health. Usually when he returned from Florida, where every winter he visited his brother, he came down with a cold.

He saw a man cross the street at the corner and come toward him. Suddenly he realized someone was also behind him. Nothing to become excited about, Kuvitz told himself. Nonetheless, he quickened his pace. The sooner he reached Sixth Avenue, the safer he'd be.

Whoever was behind him quickened his pace too, while the man coming toward him seemed to have slowed down.

"Jew," the man behind him called. "Jew bastard!"

Kuvitz started to run. Sweat poured down his face. He made for the northeast corner of Forty-seventh Street and Sixth Avenue. He heard two loud pops, like the cork exploding off a bottle of champagne. He was thrown to the ground. The pain made him cry out. He couldn't breathe.

They were bending over him. He could see their shoes. They were going through his pockets. Blood began to fill his mouth.

"Got it!" one of them said. An instant later, they were gone.

Kuvitz tried to move but couldn't. He looked toward Sixth Avenue, where the lights were already beginning to blur. He died slowly without asking God why his life had been taken from him. He knew; he was a Jew.

2

THE CAB STOPPED IN front of the Kirsh Brothers Funeral Home on Coney Island Avenue in Brooklyn. Julian Heck handed the driver a twenty-dollar bill.

"It's seventy-five cents more for the tunnel," the driver said.

"That's okay," Julian answered, taking his change and giving the driver a generous tip. He left the cab and for several moments stood at the curb side. After an absence of eight years, he had returned to bury his father. He took a deep breath and hoped the service and burial would be over quickly.

In the lobby, a man in a black suit asked him the name of the family.

"Heckowitz, Samuel Heckowitz," he answered, aware of the weeping coming from a nearby room.

"At the end of the hall. The last room on the left." the man said. "Here, take one of these." He handed Julian a black *yarmulke*.

Julian's first impulse was to wave it away. Instead, he took it, thanked the man and put the skullcap on the back of his head. He hated the *yarmulke* and everything connected with it. He had worn a small knitted one as a boy. After his bar mitzvah, he had one made of red velvet decorated with designs in goldlike thread, held in place by two long bobby pins. Two years later, at the age of fifteen, he had rebelled and had torn the *yarmulke* off his head. He had refused to continue going to the yeshiva . . .

"The room is at the end of the hall," the man repeated.

Julian flushed, suddenly aware that he hadn't moved. He nodded and started down the hallway. A tall, broad-shouldered man, his natural swarthiness had been made darker over the years by the southern California sun. He had bright gray eyes and very black hair. Often asked if he were Italian, he would laugh and answer that he was a Rumanian gypsy. Seldom did anyone think he was a Jew; not even the women he slept with, because most men were circumcised.

There were several rooms off the hallway; grief poured out of all of them. This was the second time he had been to this funeral home; thirteen years before, his mother had died after a long bout with bone cancer. Her memorial service had been held in a room along the hallway, though he couldn't remember which.

Julian stood at the entrance to the chapel. It was a very small room fitted with two rows of highly polished benches. The walls were decorated with fake windows of stained glass, each depicting a scene from the Old Testament with an appropriate quote in Hebrew. After so many years of not looking at the language, he was surprised he could still make out some of the words.

There were six men in the room, including his father's oldest and closest friend, Max Guber. Max and his father had come from Bialystok, a small city in Poland, and had survived the years in Auschwitz together. Though their voices were of different timbre—his father's had been a deep bass— they spoke with the identical eastern European accent. Guber was a short, rotund man with a cherubic face, a bald head and brown eyes. Julian had always liked him. His son had become a doctor, and the daughter had married a lawyer. With the exception of Guber and another man, the others were bearded, wore black frock coats and wide-brimmed hats. None of them wore ties. They glanced briefly at Julian and looked away.

Julian felt very much a stranger. He looked toward the pine casket. Though he couldn't see his father's face, he could see a portion of *tallith* in which the body was wrapped.

Guber came up to Julian and, offering his hand, said, "I'm glad you could come."

"He was my father," Julian answered, looking toward the body.

"Come, I'll introduce you to the others. They were all his friends."

Julian hesitated.

"Come, come," Guber said. "They know all about you." Julian slipped out of his coat; draping it around his shoulders, he followed Guber.

The men shook his hand and offered their condolences. Each one had something good to say about his father. They spoke in Yiddish. Two of them said he was one of the kindest men they had ever known. Julian had the absurd feeling they hadn't known his father and were talking about someone else. The last man Guber introduced him to was Marek Korditz, who was a clean-shaven, handsome man with expressive eyes and sensuous lips. He wore an expensive dark-blue business suit. "Your father was a good man," Korditz said. "He'll be missed by many."

"But not missed enough to bring a *minyan* here," Julian answered, remembering ten men were needed to say the ritual prayers for the dead. With the exception, perhaps, of Guber, he didn't think his father would be missed by anyone. The rest of them were in his eyes phonies, and he would not have been at all surprised to learn that Guber had given them a few dollars to come to the chapel. As for Korditz, Julian couldn't make up his mind; not that it mattered one way or another.

"I didn't let them close the box. I thought you'd want to take one last look," Guber said.

Julian walked to the casket and looked down at the body of his father. The cosmetician had given the face a look of quietude it had never possessed in life. But that impression was only momentary. Sam's face, even in death, was that of a predator. A hook nose, deep-set eyes, and high cheekbones gave it a hawklike appearance. The lips were thin and the chin jutted forward pugnaciously. There was one small wart under his left eye. That he had been a hard man had been

6

obvious in everything he had done. But he had also been a frightened man, an insecure man. He had always kept a suitcase packed in case of sudden flight. Julian could not make up his mind whether his father had been a predator.

Julian could remember being awakened by shouts in the night coming from his parents' room. Within minutes, his father would come rushing out, and regardless of the weather, Sam would leave the apartment to prowl the streets of Brooklyn. Hours later he'd return, exhausted. It took Julian years to understand that Sam's experiences in Auschwitz had made him an insomniac with a lifetime of nightmares.

Once Julian had asked him about the war and Auschwitz. They had been walking in Prospect Park, near the lake. The sun had been shining and many rowboats had been out that day. . . .

Sam stopped. His face was twisted with agony. He gripped Julian's shoulder so hard that the boy wanted to cry out but dared not. "They have a name for it now," Sam said. "They call it the Holocaust, as if a name could explain what happened." He shook his head. "Nothing could ever do that— not all the books written about it. Nothing could explain the stink of burning bodies, or the stink of the living." He spoke so loudly, people nearby turned to look at him. "My mother and father, my three sisters and four brothers were burned at Auschwitz before my eyes. . . . That's what it was like!" Then, letting go of Julian's shoulder, he glared at the people who were looking at him and continued to walk, as if nothing had happened. . . .

Julian felt almost as if he were looking at the body of a stranger and not the man who was his father. The blood tie did not preclude an emotional one and there was an undeniable tinge of regret that forced him to clear his throat. But they were strangers. His father had lived in a world that coexisted with Julian's but was so very different that the inhabitants could not communicate. And the death of one did not serve to bring them any closer; they were still strangers.

"He was very proud of you," Guber said, putting his

7

hand on Julian's shoulder. "Whenever one of your plays was on TV, he'd watch it, even if it meant breaking the sabbath laws."

"My son, the TV writer," Julian answered. "It doesn't have the same ring as my son, the doctor, or my son, the lawyer. But even he couldn't argue with the success."

"It hurt him when you left," Guber said, removing his hand from Julian's shoulder. "He didn't say much about it, but from the little he did say, I knew it hurt him."

"He had his Auschwitz. I had my Vietnam," Julian answered. "Auschwitz changed him forever. Nam did the same to me. I could not be a lawyer or a doctor. I couldn't be what he wanted me to be. Did he tell you we came to blows?"

Guber put his finger to his lips. "He only said you argued and the next day you left."

Again Julian looked at the body of his father. "He struck me across the face, and I struck him back. He told me to get out of the house. I spent the night with a friend. And the next day I withdrew the money I had in the bank and went to Hollywood." And then he added, "I never really knew him."

"Few people did," Guber responded.

Julian moved away from the casket and Guber followed. They sat down on a bench in the front of the chapel. "When I was a kid, a teenager," Julian said in a low voice, "I'd have this fantasy about Sam. I'd say to myself, 'Somewhere there's another family that belongs to him. A son, maybe a daughter, and a wife.' And you know, now I hope I was right. He should have had someone who loved him."

"That's *narishkeit,*" Guber responded, using the Yiddish word for foolishness.

"At least it would have given him a son," Julian said.

"You're his son," Guber told him. "I should know. I was there at your *bris;* I was the *sondach,* I held you."

After a few minutes the rabbi entered. He asked Julian to accompany him into a small room, where they would be able to talk about his father.

"I have nothing to say about him," Julian answered.

"Make your service as brief as possible." The rabbi looked questioningly toward Guber, who nodded.

The top of the casket was put into place and fastened down with wooden pegs. The rabbi mounted the pulpit and recited the various prayers. The service was over in a matter of minutes.

"We'll go to the Washington Cemetery in my car," Guber said as the casket was wheeled out of the chapel and put into the rear of a waiting hearse.

"Are we the only ones going?" Julian questioned.

"The rest of the men have their businesses and their jobs to go to."

"Even when one of their dear friends is about to be buried?" Julian asked sarcastically.

"For the living, life goes on," Guber answered with a shrug.

"Yes, it does. And that was something my father couldn't understand," Julian said as he walked alongside Guber to the car. Guber positioned his tan Volvo behind the hearse and switched on his lights.

Julian asked about Guber's children and wife. "Manny, my son, has a son of his own," Guber said. "And Rose has two girls and a son. But my wife, God rest her soul, has been dead for the past two years."

"I'm sorry; I didn't know," Julian responded, with a sudden vision of a woman with a pouter-pigeon body who always had a smile on her face and baked delicious cakes and bread.

"How long have you been gone?"

"Eight years," Julian answered, looking out the window. Guber didn't comment.

"We spoke on the phone," Julian said, breaking several moments of silence. "He called me a few times a year."

"Did you ever call him?" Guber asked, easing the shift into drive. He followed close behind the hearse.

"Not too often," Julian admitted. "I didn't have much to say to him even when he called me."

They stopped for a light on Coney Island Avenue.

"He never mentioned he had any trouble with his heart," Julian commented.

"He wouldn't," Guber answered. "He only told me because that afternoon—he died at night—he said he wasn't feeling well. When I asked him what was wrong, he touched the left side of his chest and said the pump wasn't going smoothly."

They began to move along Avenue J.

"You know, in all the years I knew Sam, I never heard him complain about anything," Guber said.

"Maybe he enjoyed suffering."

Guber shook his head. "Believe me, he didn't. He liked to laugh and was a great practical joker."

Julian shook his head. "My father's name was Sam Heckowitz. The man you're talking about had to have a different name."

"It's the same man," Guber said. "It's the man in the pine box in the back of the hearse we're following. You didn't really know him. But I did, and I assure you it's the same man."

Julian could tell from the tone of Guber's voice that the man was angry with him. But he had to say what he felt, what had been and still was the reality of his relationship with his father. "I never knew that side of him. To me and to my mother, he was cold, forbidding and hard."

"And with all that, with the exception of the last argument between you, was he a fair man?"

Julian thought for a few moments before he answered, "Yes, he was a fair man."

Guber nodded. He didn't say anything else.

They drove along Bay Parkway and through the gates into the cemetery. Close by, along MacDonald Avenue, was the elevated subway that continued all the way out to Coney Island. Whenever a train passed overhead, sparks flew out from under the wheels and the whole structure swayed. It was impossible to hear anything except the roar of the train.

The hearse stopped in front of a small white administration building. The driver went inside.

Guber let the engine idle. "There aren't too many plots left here," he commented. "In the old days, it was one of the few cemeteries where a Jew could be buried. Now there're places out on Long Island and in Jersey."

Julian had nothing to say. He did not approve of cemeteries. In his will, he had left instructions that he was to be cremated. And as for this particular cemetery, it held the sad memory of his mother.

The driver returned to the hearse and they began to move slowly along the narrow roadway to where his father had years before bought a grave for two. Julian and Guber waited in the car while the casket was placed in the grave. After a few minutes, the driver of the hearse waved to them.

"It's time to go," Guber said, opening the door. Julian walked alongside Guber.

When they reached the grave, Guber said, "I didn't ask the rabbi to come here. I wanted to say the last prayers over him myself. I hope you don't mind."

Guber took a half-step forward. His right foot rested on the earth that had been dug out of the grave. In soft Yiddish, he said, "No fine words between us, old friend. We go back a long way. You were my father and my brother and my strength when I no longer had any." Guber paused and wiped his eyes. "If ever one man loved another, I loved you. Sleep well, old friend. You've earned it." Again, he wiped his tears and, turning to Julian, he said, "Now you can say *Kaddish.*"

Julian was watching Guber so intently that he was taken completely by surprise. He shook his head and stammered, "I don't believe."

"Neither did he," Guber said, looking back at the open grave. "At least not in the way you might think. But he was a man and a father, and every Jewish father wants his son to say *Kaddish* for him."

Out of respect for Guber's loyalty, Julian moved alongside the man and, in unison with him, he haltingly recited the prayer for the dead. The words felt strange in his mouth, yet he felt it was right to say them.

"I know what would have pleased him," Guber said. He picked up the shovel and handed it to Julian. "It is the last thing you'll do for him." Julian lifted up a shovel full of earth and dropped it into the grave. He gave the shovel back to Guber and stepped away from the grave.

Guber repeated the motion. Then he set the shovel down, took up several small rocks and placed them on the portion of the gravestone that marked the place where Miriam Heckowitz, Sam's wife and Julian's mother, was buried. "It is part of the tradition," Guber said, rejoining Julian.

"Yes, I know."

"And you don't like tradition?" Guber asked as they got back into the car.

"Not if it gets in the way of other things."

Guber guided the car out of the cemetery before he said, "Your father wasn't one for tradition, though he respected it."

Julian didn't want to discuss the matter. As far as he was concerned, his father had rammed tradition down his throat until he had gagged. It was obvious that Guber had a great many illusions about his old friend, and he saw no reason to disturb them.

"Where are you staying?" Guber asked.

"At the Roosevelt."

"I'll drop you off. It's not far from the exchange."

"Are you sure it won't be any trouble?" Julian asked.

"No trouble at all."

They turned onto Ocean Parkway. Guber remarked that the parkway had recently been widened and more benches placed along islands.

"Sometimes," Julian said, "I used to ride all the way to Coney Island along the bicycle path."

"I know; your father used to tell me. He was always afraid you'd get hurt."

"I could take care of myself," Julian said.

"He knew that too."

They crossed Church Avenue and went onto the Prospect Expressway. "This might not be the right time to ask," Julian said, "but I'd like to know if my father left a will." He turned slightly toward Guber. "Sooner or later, I'd have to ask."

"No need to apologize. What was Sam's is now yours. You're his continuation. That's the way of things. It's tradition," Guber said archly. Julian shifted his position, uncomfortable with Guber's response.

"There are two bankbooks and a number of Israel bonds. Altogether, it's worth a hundred thousand, give or take a couple of thousand. Not a great fortune, but still substantial."

"No diamonds?" Julian questioned with surprise. "He always carried thirty to forty thousand dollars' worth of stones in a small brown purse."

"There aren't any diamonds," Guber answered.

"That's hard to believe. He had more faith in their value than he did in money."

"I told you what he left," Guber said.

"Don't you think it strange that he didn't leave me any stones?" Julian asked.

Guber shrugged. "Sam did things his way, and there was never any questioning why."

They stopped to pay the toll for the Brooklyn Battery Tunnel, prevented from talking by the noise. But as soon as they emerged from the tunnel, Julian said, "He must have kept some stones with friends. He usually kept one or two parcels with a friend."

"Sam never talked about such things," Guber said. "I only knew about the bankbooks and the rest of what he left because he gave me a sealed envelope a week before he died. He told me that if anything should happen to him, I was to open the envelope and give whatever was inside to you. I think he knew he was going to die."

They went up the East Side Drive. Julian looked out the window at the East River. A tanker riding low in the water made its way toward upper New York Bay.

"I spoke to him about a month ago," Julian said, referring to his father. "He never mentioned anything about not feeling well. He told me he had had a good trip to Paris and he was thinking of going back there to live."

"Sam wasn't a complainer. But I know he was tired. I told him to take a few days off. But he just shrugged."

The smell of the Fulton Fish Market enveloped them. Julian shook his head. "I remember when I was a boy, maybe six or seven, Sam took me to Sheepshead Bay to buy fish off the fishing boats when they came in. It was during the summer. My mother stayed home. We rode the Rogers Avenue trolley.

"Anyway, we were walking along the docks looking at the fish. I don't remember exactly what happened between my father and one of the men who worked on the boats. But there was an exchange that quickly developed into an argument. They were shouting at each other. I was frightened out of my wits. Then suddenly the man called my father a fucking Jew bastard, and he leaped from the deck of the boat to the dock, brandishing a good-size knife.

"My father pushed me aside, and in a very even voice, he said, 'I chew up bums like you and spit them out.' And before I realized what was happening, he had rushed forward, grabbed hold of the man's wrist, twisted it backward, forcing the man to drop the knife. He drove his fist into the man's stomach, doubling him up and making him puke. But he didn't leave it at that. He picked up the knife and threw it with such force that the point sank deep into the boat's deck. Then he took me by the hand, walked over to the next boat and bought fish."

Guber laughed and struck the steering wheel with the palm of his left hand. "Sam was like that," he said. "He wasn't afraid of anything or anyone."

"I haven't thought about that for years," Julian admitted.

"You'll find yourself remembering other things in the days ahead," Guber said.

Julian shrugged. "Sometimes it's better not to remember."

Guber nodded, then asked, "What are you writing now?"

"A two-hour special based on the book *High Terror.*"

"Sam was proud of you," Guber said again. "But he was upset when you changed your name to Heck. I told him you probably had to do it for business reasons."

"I just didn't want his name anymore," Julian said.

Guber sighed deeply but didn't comment. They left the Drive at Forty-second Street. "I'll turn up Madison," Guber said, "and let you off at the corner of Forty-fifth."

"That's fine," Julian replied. He was silent for a few moments before he said, "I'm going to stay in New York for a while. I can't believe my father didn't leave any stones with his friends. He always did it."

"You can ask around, but I don't think you'll find any."

"What about his friends—the men who were at the chapel—he might have left something with them."

"Ask," Max said. "It'll do no harm. But don't expect anyone to say, 'Here's what your father left. Take it.' "

"What about the small fact that it doesn't belong to them?" Julian challenged.

"But it doesn't belong to you, either," Max answered. "No one but your father would know who the stones belonged to. Many of them could have been on consignment from other dealers. And, may he rest in peace, Sam can no longer tell us which."

"Well, I'll just see if I can change that," Julian said resolutely.

"You sound like Sam," Guber replied with a laugh. "Once he got it in his mind to do something, he went and did it."

"Maybe he did give me something after all—his stubbornness."

"You're too hard on him," Guber said softly.

Julian looked away.

They turned into the heavy traffic on Madison Avenue.

"By the way," Julian said, looking at Guber again, "have the police made any progress in their investigation of the recent killings in the diamond center? I followed the story in the newspapers. I thought it might have something for a TV script, but the stories stopped."

"Bad business," Guber commented in a low, angry voice. "Very bad business."

"Somebody is doing the fingering," Julian said.

Guber remained silent. A few minutes later, they reached the corner of Madison and Forty-fifth Street.

"Thanks for the ride," Julian said, opening the door. He offered Guber his hand. "And thanks for everything else you've done."

Guber shook his hand and said, "Why don't you meet me for dinner on Friday night? We'll drive out to my daughter's house. She knows you're in New York and she'd be delighted to see you."

Julian was about to refuse, but because he felt he owed Guber something, he said, "All right. I'll go."

"You come to my office about four o'clock. That'll give us plenty of time to leave before sundown. . . . Twenty West Forty-seventh Street . . . I'm in room eleven twenty-one."

"I'll be there," Julian said, shaking Guber's hand.

"Good. We'll have a good dinner and talk."

Julian stepped away from the car and closed the door. He was tired and at odds with himself for accepting Guber's invitation. He didn't want to spend an evening listening to Guber tell him directly, or indirectly, what a wonderful man Sam Heckowitz had been. . . .

3

A WIND-DRIVEN RAIN pelted the window where Dr. Saul Urishensky stood looking out on Gorki Street. Below him was a street lamp whose yellow aureole diminished rapidly in intensity from its center to its circumference.

Urishensky was tall and broad-shouldered, with a close-cropped beard and black hair and eyes. He stared at the street for a long time. The window reflected his wife, Marina, seated at the table, her eyes on him. Not far away from her was a man known to them only as Klugin. The two of them looked like figures in an Impressionist painting, both blurred by the rain on the window.

"I was given a month's holiday from the Biological Institute," Urishensky said. "Two weeks have gone by and nothing has happened." He turned from the window and glared at Klugin. "I don't know how much longer I can remain cooped up like an animal."

"I don't make the decisions," Klugin answered with a shrug. He was a handsome man in his late thirties. "But I do know something went wrong on the other side."

Urishensky shook his head. "That won't do," he told Klugin. "Obviously something went wrong or we wouldn't still be here." He moved toward the table and placed his hands on it. Leaning forward, he said, "I'm a geneticist. I don't know anything about politics. Don't tell me something went wrong. We risked our lives to come here. Can you imagine what would happen to us if the KGB got wind of the fact that we were about to defect?"

"I assure you that you are safe," Klugin answered unctuously. "Everything has been arranged for your departure. Why, you are even registered in the Krosovit Hotel in Yalta, where you're vacationing. No, my dear friend, you must not worry about your safety."

"I'm worried," Urishensky persisted. He straightened up. "A Jew is always worried about his safety in Russia."

"But you're in East Berlin, a few streets away from the border."

Urishensky shook his head. "Those few streets might just as well be a distance of light-years if I cannot walk across to the West."

"You will. You will cross to the West. But you must be patient. Certain things happened that are out of our control . . . . All right, if it will make you feel better, I will tell you what little I know."

"Please, tell us," Urishensky said.

"Someone was killed," Klugin explained. "I don't know who it was or when it happened."

"Oh, my God!" Marina exclaimed. She looked up at Urishensky. With tears in her eyes, she said, "I don't think we'll ever get out. We'll never be free."

"We will get out," he answered. Then to Klugin he said, "You tell your friends that if we're not allowed to leave soon, we'll return to Moscow. I can't subject my wife and child to this kind of tension. I must know once and for all whether I'm going to be allowed to go to the West."

"You're hardly in a position to demand anything," Klugin answered.

Urishensky took a deep breath. He did not want to become angry at a man who, with one phone call, could destroy him and his family forever. "It is very difficult to wait for something to happen," he said in a much softer tone.

"I wouldn't know about that," Klugin replied. He turned and, opening the door, left the apartment without saying good-bye.

"The bastard!" Urishensky exclaimed. *"I wouldn't know about that,"* he repeated, mimicking Klugin's voice. He went to the window and looked out. Klugin hurried down the front steps, passed through the circle of light and went up the street, quickly disappearing into the darkness and the rain.

"Klugin was angry with us," Marina said.

Urishensky shrugged. He had been dealing with the Klugins of the world his entire life. They hated Jews simply for being Jews. If they were in a position to give pain and anguish to a Jew, they gave it with complete indifference, or with the certain knowledge that God would look more kindly at them when they finally stood in His presence or that they were helping the state overcome a disease. But if the opportunity came their way to make money from a Jew or by associating with one, they never hesitated to do that, either. They had the best of either possibility whenever they had to deal with Jews.

"What will happen to us if we go back to Moscow?" Marina asked. She was very pale and her lips trembled as she spoke.

Urishensky went to her and lifted her into his arms. "I will be officially reprimanded," he said, "nothing more than that."

"Can you be sure?"

He nodded, knowing he was lying. He knew he would be severely punished. Perhaps sent to a penal colony in Siberia, or a mental hospital? Perhaps executed?

"Maybe we should go back before it's too late," Marina suggested.

"Another few days," he said gently. "We will wait another few days."

"I'm frightened," Marina whispered.

"So am I," Urishensky admitted, holding her tightly to him. "More frightened than I've ever been in my life. But we must wait."

4

THE SIGN ON the door read: Max Guber, Diamonds &
Gem Stones: By Appointment Only, 322-6493. Guber opened
the door to his office, entered and immediately began to remove his coat.

Rose, a gray-haired woman of sixty, looked up from her
desk. She was a combination receptionist, secretary, book-
keeper, and since Guber's wife had died, the person who worried about him most. "Borsky and Korditz are waiting for
you," she said, cocking her head toward the inner office.

Guber didn't give any indication of hearing her. He was
in a dark, angry mood. Burying Sam had filled him with
ineffable sadness, and meeting Julian had upset him further.
No, that wasn't it; he could tolerate the meeting. What he
couldn't take was Julian's attitude toward Sam.

"Any calls?" he asked brusquely.

"A man named Paul Fournier, from Paris. He was calling for Sam, God rest his soul. I told him that Sam had died
of a heart attack."

"Fournier?" Guber questioned.

"He was very upset," Rose said.

"I don't remember anyone with that name."

Rose nodded. "I do. Sam sometimes called him from
here, but the charges were always billed to his credit card."

"Do you have the number?"

"No. Sam had it written down on a piece of paper. He
never spoke very long. Usually he'd tell him he would be in
Amsterdam or wherever he was going on such a day. Then
he'd hang up."

"Are you sure that was all he said?"

"Yes."

Guber scratched his beard. Fournier was, like a great

many other things in Sam's life, a secret. "Have you men-- tioned Fournier to Borsky and Korditz?"

"Why should I do something like that? The call didn't concern them."

Guber nodded. "Good," he said. "Now send down for three black coffees and tell Izzy in the luncheonette it would be nice, for a change, if the coffee was hot." He started toward the door of his private office.

"Max," she called.

He stopped and looked over his shoulder at her.

"Maybe if you cried a little, you'd feel better," she said.

"A little won't ease the pain," he answered. "I loved him."

"And he loved you."

"Yes, I know that," Guber said. He took a deep breath, pulled back his shoulders and entered his office.

Korditz was sitting in a leather chair reading the *Times* business section, while Borsky was looking out the window. The office was small. There was a red velvet couch on one wall, a desk in front of the window, the leather club chair occupied by Korditz, a large safe against another wall, a coat tree close to the door, and a pen and ink drawing of an old man with a *tallith* draped over his head.

Guber hung his coat and jacket on the coat tree. He rolled up his sleeves, baring the tattooed number on his left forearm. "I had to park on the other side of Sixth Avenue," Guber said, going to his desk. "Traffic was very heavy."

Borsky moved away from the window and Korditz folded the *Times*.

"What kind of son is that Julian?" Borsky asked, speaking in Yiddish. "He sends his father to the grave in as much time as it takes to snap his fingers."

"It wasn't right," Korditz said. "He didn't even tell the rabbi anything about Sam. Why the hell did he come back here for the funeral?"

Guber looked at one and then the other. They were in- volved in a duet of complaints against Julian. "Enough," he shouted, slamming his hand down on the desk. "Now is not the time to talk about Julian. We have more important things to talk about."

"A son that doesn't sit *shiva* for his father is no son," Borsky told them.

"He should have announced he would be sitting *shiva* in his father's house," Korditz said.

"I'm going to speak to my rabbi about reading him out of the congregation," Borsky announced. "I don't think he should be allowed to be a Jew. I think he should be excommunicated. He's not one of us."

Max leaned back into his chair and pursed his lips. He could do nothing to stop them from talking. He'd have to wait until they wound themselves down.

"Well, what do you think about it?" Borsky asked.

"I think what Julian does or does not do isn't anyone's business. He's not your son."

"A blessing," Korditz said.

There was a knock on the door. "That's Rose with coffee," Guber announced.

"Why didn't you order sandwiches too?" Borsky asked, as Rose handed each of them a container of black coffee.

"I just told her to get coffee," Guber said.

"Why not sandwiches?" Borsky pressed.

"Because I knew I'd lose my appetite as soon as I heard the two of you gab about something that doesn't concern you. If Julian doesn't want to sit *shiva* for Sam, that's his business, not yours and not mine. We have other problems."

Borsky and Korditz fell silent. Guber stood up and went to the window. He held the container in his hand and now and then drank from it. The street below was crowded. Late fall was a busy time for the diamond dealers. As soon as Thanksgiving was past, the Christmas buying began in earnest.

"I spoke to Kuvitz's mother," Borsky said. "I told her some of Yankel's friends have put together a little fund in his memory."

Guber turned from the window. "Have the police made any headway in their investigation?" he asked.

"None," Korditz answered. "The killings get into the newspapers and then every crazy anti-Semite comes prowling around here at night looking to kill a Jew and make a fortune doing it. Yankel was the fifth to be killed. If they don't stop soon, we're going to have to stop what we're doing. The men are frightened."

"I'm frightened too," Guber said. "But we can't stop. Sam wouldn't let us stop, God rest his soul, if he were alive. We've got to continue. I know it's going to be harder without Sam, but it will have to be done."

"Sam knew his way around," Borsky commented. "He knew everyone. None of us knows the people he knew."

"We've got to get somebody to take his place," Guber said, trying hard to remember if Sam had ever mentioned Fournier. Had he worked with Sam, and if so, would he still be willing to work with them, though Sam was dead?

"Can't be done," Borsky responded, leaving the couch.

"It'll have to be done," Guber said to him.

"Jacob Levitas has agreed to make the delivery in Amsterdam," Korditz said.

Guber nodded.

"The price has gone up," Borsky said.

"How much are our friends asking this time?" Korditz questioned.

"A man between the age of twenty and forty will now cost twenty-five thousand; a woman, twenty; and a family of three, forty-five thousand. But Doctor Urishensky and family will cost us a quarter of a million. He's being held in East Berlin with his wife and child. They would have let him out if Yankel had made the delivery."

"And I suppose all the stones must be graded blue-white and none over two carats?" Guber asked.

"That's what the man on the phone specified," Borsky said. "It's always the same."

Guber drained the coffee from the container and dropped it in the wastebasket. "We'll give him what he asks for. Urishensky has to be gotten out."

Korditz nodded. "We know it's what Sam wanted."

"I made the same promise to his father in Auschwitz. It took us years to locate and identify Urishensky. After the war, his mother remarried and the boy was legally adopted by her new husband, Yussal Urishensky."

"If diamonds can buy him out, then we'll buy him out," Borsky said.

"Tell the rest of our people that Jacob will make the pickup late Friday afternoon. He'll be in London the following morning."

"Everything will be ready for him," Korditz answered.

Guber leaned forward and placed his elbows on the desk. "So that it doesn't come as a surprise, better let everyone know that Julian intends to look for the diamonds he thinks Sam had."

"Then he has no idea what Sam had been doing for the last few years?"

"We don't need him sniffing around," Borsky said. "He's a troublemaker, I can feel it in my bones. How can a man like Sam, may he rest in peace, have a son like that?"

Max made a swift cutting gesture with his right hand. He didn't want them to start talking about Julian again. "Let him sniff around. After a while, he'll get tired of sniffing and go back to Hollywood. In the meantime, I'm going to have dinner with him on Friday, at my daughter's in Glen Cove. Forget about Julian and remember to have Jacob pick up stones from everyone on the list."

"I told you everything was ready," Korditz said, lighting a cigar. "Do you think the man on the phone knows what happened to Sam?"

Guber bolted up. "We all know what happened to Sam." His eyes became slits. The blue vein on his temple throbbed. "Sam died of a heart attack."

Borsky nodded.

Max glared at Korditz. "He died of a heart attack," Korditz agreed in a low voice.

Max breathed deeply and said, "That damn coffee was too strong. I have heartburn from it."

Korditz was the first to leave. He said, "If I were you, Max, I'd go home early today."

"I was thinking about doing that," Guber answered.

A few minutes later Borsky left, telling Guber, "You call me if you need anything."

Guber thanked him. Finally alone, he said in a low voice, "Well, Sam, I never thought you'd finish it yourself. Never." Guber stood up and went to the window.

"Lots of men are tired. The world is full of tired old men. I'm tired. But you couldn't wait until your time came. You had to do it yourself. You had to take your own life. Even at the very end, you had to do it your way."

The long shadows of the afternoon filled the street. Only the upper portion of the buildings were bathed in sunlight. Still speaking aloud, he said, "To make everything kosher, Sam, to make it seem like you really died from a heart attack—it cost me." He took out his handkerchief, wiped his eyes and blew his nose. "It cost me. But after all these years, I figured I owed you a decent Jewish burial. Rest in peace, old friend, rest in peace. No one will ever know your secret."

He sat down again. He crossed his arms on the desk and, lowering his head onto them, he began to sob.

After a while, Guber looked up and saw Rose standing in the doorway. "You said crying would help," he told her, blowing his nose again.

"Has it?"

"No," he answered with a shake of his head. "It's hard to take. We went through so much together. He was always the strong one."

"Go home early," Rose said gently. "Have a good dinner, watch some TV, take a couple of drinks of schnapps and go to sleep. Tomorrow, life will look better; the world will be a brighter place."

Guber stood up.

"Go on," she urged. "I'll close up."

Guber pushed his sleeves down and buttoned the cuffs. He put on his jacket and coat. "Did you know we lived on the same street in Bialystok?"

"Yes, he told me that many times."

Guber left the office feeling very old, tired and terribly sad. Part of him had died with Sam. Had Sam come to him, he might have prevented him from committing suicide. . . .

Guber shook his head. If Sam had made up his mind to take his own life, nothing would have changed it. That was the way Sam was; that was his strength and his weakness.

5

FOURNIER APPROACHED THE Crypt Memorial de la Déportation slowly. Behind him was the soaring gothic splendor of Notre Dame, whose illuminated towers and flying buttresses glistened in the misty rain.

Fournier was a tall, slender man of middling height with deep-set blue eyes and a sensitive mouth above a firm chin. He wore a black rain hat and a black loose-fitting raincoat. Within a few meters of the memorial, he stopped and turned completely around. A figure emerged from the deep shadows on the left side of the cathedral.

Fournier glanced at his watch. It was exactly nine o'clock. He continued toward the crypt. Within a few minutes, he was looking at the two hundred thousand names of Jews who were turned over to the Nazis by the French during World War II. The starkness of the place seemed more intense in the night rain.

Suddenly he became aware of a woman's perfume. Tea Rose, he thought. "It's hard to look at these names," she said, "when you know it need never have happened." Her voice was soft and she spoke French with a slight foreign accent.

He hadn't expected the Sheruti Bethahar to send a woman. All his previous contacts had been with men. He nodded and responded with the countersign. "France has never been able to make up its mind about Jews."

She smiled at him.

"Samuel Heckowitz died of a heart attack in New York," he said, looking at her. She was a petite, dark-complexioned woman with long black hair, braided and piled under a green rain hat. Her eyes were gray and very bright. "Is there any doubt about the cause of his death?" she asked.

Fournier shrugged. "I don't know," he answered. They began to move slowly along the walls where the names of the dead Jews had been cut into stone. "He looked very tired the last time I saw him."

"You did warn him that the KGB had become involved?" she asked.

"Yes. And he said, 'Sooner or later that was bound to happen.' "

"And your own involvement with them," she asked, "is it the same?"

He nodded. "They're concerned about the traffic," he said. "They're as confused by the recent killings as we are."

"I have seen enough," she told him. "These names make me sad."

They left the crypt together and Fournier said, "My car is parked on the rue des Ecoles."

She arched her eyebrows. "Are you offering me a lift?"

"No," he answered. "That would be a breach of security. I merely told you to let you know which way I would be walking. But I will offer you dinner. I haven't eaten yet, and I'm hungry."

"I accept," she said.

He took hold of her arm and asked, "What do I call you?"

"In French or Hebrew?"

"French will have to do for now," he replied. That she had accepted his dinner invitation pleased him. The news of Sam's death had depressed him. He had known Sam all his life. And though he was dating Gabrielle, he did not want to share his grief with her. She had once met Sam and had not really liked him.

Suddenly he realized the woman at his side had not answered his question. He looked at her. "I'm thinking," she said. "Maybe by the time we finish dinner, I will have thought of a name."

The restaurant he chose was called Les Trois Bouleaux, the Three Birches, a small place off the rue des Bernardines. There were only six tables, each with a candle in an old wine bottle covered with wax drippings.

"They only serve a single entree," Fournier explained. "It's written on the blackboard at the side of the kitchen door."

"Baked mackerel with vegetables," she said. "Then I guess that's what I'll have." Fournier ordered the house white wine, which he told her was very good.

"Tell me about Mr. Heckowitz," she said. "I've heard he was an extraordinary man. Many of my colleagues say that if there were more Jews like him, then the Holocaust would have never happened."

"We were friends for as long as I could remember," Fournier said. "But he was a sad man, a very sad man."

"He had a family in the United States, didn't he?"

"Yes. A son named Julian. He's a successful writer for TV. Sam's wife died twelve years ago. When I was younger, I used to think that he and my mother were lovers. I know she loved him. She couldn't wait until he came over from the States. But I tell you this," he said, "if they weren't lovers, they should have been. The only time I ever saw him smile or heard him laugh was when he was with her."

The waiter brought their food, warning them about the hot plates.

"And what about your family?" he asked.

"Two brothers and one sister," she answered, "all in Israel."

He poured another glass of wine for her and filled his own. "I'm going to miss him," he said. "He was one man who was able to look at life with an equal mixture of fear and love. You know, he wasn't very religious, yet everything about him was unmistakably Jewish, even his clothes."

"You're not Jewish, are you?" she asked.

Fournier shook his head. "I was raised an atheist. My mother is a lapsed Catholic."

"And your father?"

Fournier shrugged. "I never knew him," he said. "My mother never spoke about him, other than to say once that circumstances prevented them from marrying. Fournier is her name." He drained the wine from the glass. It was unlike him to talk about himself or anyone close to him, especially since he had become a member of the Service de Documentation Extérieure et de Contre Espionnage. But Sam's death bothered him.

"Would you mind if I asked a question? I'm sorry," she said, "that was stupidly put. You need not answer, if you—"

"Ask the question."

"Why did you come over to us?"

He took another drink of wine before he said, "Sam is the reason."

"I don't understand."

"A few years ago," Fournier explained, "I happened to be in the back of Notre Dame. Sam was in Paris. I saw him, but he didn't see me. He went into the memorial. I followed him. He moved from panel to panel, reading the names. He wept, choking down the sound of his weeping but unable to stop the tears. Finally, when I could no longer stand to see him in such pain, I went up to him and said, 'Come, it's time to go.' He turned to me and said, 'I knew them. I knew all of them.' He took hold of my hand and said, 'It's a terrible thing to have known so many dead. But I knew them, Paul, I knew them.' I led him out of the crypt and into a beautiful spring day. I took him to a small café and we drank a bottle of wine. He didn't speak for the better part of an hour. Then he said, 'While I was in Auschwitz, I did everything I could to stay alive, but afterward I was ashamed of myself for not having died. But now—now I have a reason for having survived.' Then he told me how he and several other men were bringing Jews out of Russia. Then and there I decided to help him. The best way to do that was to join your side."

"You loved him that much?" she asked.

"Respected him," Fournier said.

Each had a cup of espresso laced with cognac; neither wanted dessert. When they left the restaurant, the rain had stopped and the sky was full of ragged clouds. A strong wind had come up and it had turned colder.

"You haven't given me your name," Fournier said.

"In Hebrew, it's Shulamith—Shulamith Gibori."

"Shulamith, the woman whom Solomon loved," he said. "Abishag."

"So you know the Old Testament."

"And the new also," he said, taking hold of her hand. He had enjoyed her company. "Are you sure I can't drive closer to where you live?"

"It's better if you don't."

"Do you want me to walk back to the crypt with you?"

"That won't be necessary," she said.

Suddenly Fournier stopped. With a single motion, he brought her around to him and kissed her. He said, "I would like to see you again."

"It's not allowed," she replied, and yet she didn't move away.

"Tomorrow night at eight in Galignani. It's a bookstore on the rue de Rivoli."

"I know it."

"Will you be there?" he asked.

"I can't promise."

"Promise."

"I will try," she answered, easing out of his embrace. "I will try." She turned and hurried away.

He watched until she turned the corner of the rue des Bernardines. By the time he reached his car, he was whistling softly to himself.

6

Sergei Dimetrov was suffering from the effects of jet lag and a mild case of sinusitis, which always occurred when he spent long periods of time flying. He sat alongside the desk of Igor Marrosov, senior cultural advisor with the Soviet mission in New York and operations chief for the KGB in the northeastern portion of the United States, extending from New York to Maine and as far west as Chicago.

Marrosov occupied an office with a window overlooking the street on the second floor of the mission's building. The office was painted a light green. Facing a large sepia photograph of Vladimir Ilich Lenin was an ordinary black and white print of Leonid Brezhnev. Because Marrosov functioned in the capacity of senior cultural advisor, there were many books and brochures relating to cultural activities in the Soviet Union on the shelves of the bookcases and the several small tables. Classical music was piped in during working hours.

Marrosov did not appreciate it when his superiors in Moscow sent another agent into his territory without first informing him. And he most certainly did not like the idea that Dimetrov was the one they had chosen. But he managed a smile. "You caught me unprepared for another agent," Marrosov said, lighting up a Cuban cigar. "I have a full staff, and unless headquarters has given me another assignment, I am not sure you will—"

"Excuse me, comrade," Dimetrov interrupted, "but I am reporting to you as a matter of courtesy. My assignment here is totally independent of your mission."

"But not out of my control," Marrosov said, leaning his right elbow on the desk. He was a heavyset man with a thick neck and round face. His eyes were brown and very bright.

"I'm afraid so," Dimetrov answered. "I have a letter here that gives me complete autonomy."

"May I see it?"

Dimetrov handed him the letter. "As you see," he said, "your men and facilities have been put at my disposal, should I require them."

Marrosov nodded and returned the letter. "Your assignment must have a high priority with the people at headquarters for them to give such authority."

"I wasn't told," Dimetrov answered, knowing full well Marrosov would understand he was being warned not to ask any more questions.

Marrosov puffed savagely on the cigar. He most certainly didn't like Dimetrov any better now than he had when they had first worked together in Hanoi in the late sixties and early seventies. Dimetrov had been one of the few KGB men who had spent time in the field with the Vietcong and later with the North Vietnamese Sixty-Fifth Infantry Battalion, against elements of the American First Marine Division. Even then he had a reputation for getting things done. But Marrosov, and several others in the KGB, had believed Dimetrov to be trying to live up to his father's astounding reputation as a World War II hero.

"I will make every effort not to disturb your daily operation," Dimetrov said.

Marrosov nodded. "Where will you be staying?" he asked.

"Not far from here, at the Plaza."

Marrosov raised his eyebrows. "That is capitalistic extravagance in the extreme. There are hotels more in keeping with our ideological concepts here in New York."

Dimetrov smiled.

"You could even stay here at the mission, or at our facility on Long Island. A car would bring you to the city every day and return you to the compound at night."

"Your offer is most generous," Dimetrov said, "but for this particular assignment, the Plaza is the right place." And with a chuckle, he added, "I can stand to live in 'capitalistic extravagance' for short periods of time."

Marrosov glared at him, said nothing and puffed violently at his cigar. "Will you be checking in—"

"Comrade, you must understand. I came to see you as a matter of courtesy. But I am under no obligation to do even that." He spoke in an even tone but with absolute authority in his voice. He did not want Marrosov to mistake his purpose.

"Yes, yes, I understand." Marrosov flushed. He wasn't used to being told to mind his own business by someone of lesser rank. Dimetrov was only a major, while he was a full colonel; yet with that letter in Dimetrov's possession, he could completely sidestep Marrosov's authority.

"Should I need anything," Dimetrov said, extending his hand, "I will call you."

"Please do."

They shook hands and Dimetrov commented, "Now all I want to do is sleep and get rid of my sinus condition." He stood up. He was a rangy man with strong features and green eyes that tended to shade to gray when he was angry. "There's no need to escort me out. I know my way." He went to the door. Turning to Marrosov, he said, "Had I been given the choice of refusing this assignment, I would have. But I was not given the choice."

"There are times," Marrosov answered with a nod of his head, "that headquarters tries to place a square peg in a round hole, so to speak."

"Believe me, comrade, I feel very much like a square peg," Dimetrov responded, opening the door. Immediately afterward, Marrosov picked up the phone and ordered one of his agents to follow the tall, thin man.

Dimetrov walked to Fifth Avenue, hailed a cab and told the driver to take him to the Plaza. He spoke English without an accent, and if the situation required it, he could speak fluent French, German and excellent Vietnamese.

"This is some gorgeous weather for this time of the year," the driver commented. "By this time last year, we already had snow on the ground."

"Yes, I remember," Dimetrov lied, rubbing the area between his eyes to ease the pain. The smoke from Marrosov's cigar had aggravated his sinus condition. He couldn't blame the man for being resentful. After all, he was in his territory.

Dimetrov would have preferred a different assignment. He did not like the idea of becoming involved in an investigation that would surely lead back to officials in the government. But the KGB was certain there was a definite traffic in diamonds for Jews. Certain men in the government were being bribed to issue exit visas to Jews.

Dimetrov did not agree with the official policy that prevented Jews from leaving Russia. The country would be better off without people who didn't want to be there. But he could not countenance illicit traffic in Jews or any other people. The individuals willing to accept bribes had to be found and punished.

For the purpose of the investigation, he had come to the United States with a French passport on which he was listed as a jeweler with a residence in Paris. He had been given a dossier on a Jew named Samuel Heckowitz and was told by his superiors that Heckowitz was involved in the exchange of Jews for diamonds.

Most of the information came from captured German documents and dated back to the time when Heckowitz was in Auschwitz. Even then, according to the documents, Heckowitz had been trading diamonds for Jews. He had bought himself the position of *kapo* from the SS guards with diamonds, though it had not been known how he had come to have them.

More recently—within the last eight years—Heckowitz had made frequent trips to Prague, Warsaw and East Berlin. Each of these cities, and Amsterdam, Paris and London, were, according to the dossier, places where the final exchange transactions had been concluded. Heckowitz had been traced to an address in Brooklyn. It was Dimetrov's plan to become involved in a business relationship with Heckowitz and eventually become part of the organization that made arrangements for the illegal movement of Jews out of Russia.

Two days before leaving Moscow, Dimetrov met with the head of the Jewish Department, which was under the control of the Fifth Chief Directorate. He was told that the department had reason to believe that neo-Nazi groups had been responsible for recent killings of diamond dealers in New York and other cities. The department did not know if the dead men had any connection with the traffic of Jews for diamonds.

The cab stopped in front of the Plaza. Dimetrov paid the rate shown on the meter. After an angry look from the driver, he remembered the tip. It always took him awhile to adjust to these Western practices.

Reaching his room, Dimetrov removed his coat and jacket, dropped down on the bed and closed his eyes. His head was pounding. He reached up, loosened his tie and opened his collar button.

He would have preferred an assignment in Africa or the Middle East, but instead he was trying to track down a group of greedy, stupid men. He shook his head. The movement made him wince and drove all thoughts about the assignment from his head, leaving only keen awareness of the throbbing . . .

7

JULIAN RODE THE SUBWAY to Brooklyn, changing at Nevins Street from the Lexington Avenue to the New Lots Avenue. The trains were almost empty. They seemed to be far dirtier than he remembered. The outsides of most cars were either covered with huge surrealistic splashes of color or with obscene graffiti, much of which was directed against the police. Several protested the building of more nuclear power plants. He was surprised by the number of swastikas and anti-

Jewish comments he saw. It twisted his stomach into a knot when he read: "A good Jew is a dead Jew." He suddenly found himself wondering what his father's reaction would have been.

Julian left the train at the Nostrand Avenue station and walked upstairs, into a day gray with the promise of rain. He crossed the street and went down Nostrand Avenue toward Carol Street. The neighborhood had changed in the years he had been away. Once predominantly Jewish, with a large concentration of Hasidim, now it was predominantly black and Hispanic. Where there had been a kosher butcher shop there was one that sold goat's meat. Fruit and vegetable stores featured West Indian produce.

He turned into Carol Street. The building where his father had lived was near Rogers Avenue, at the other end of the street from the shopping area. It was a yellow brick structure, six stories high. The apartment was on the second floor front, on the right hand side, in the corner. His parents had lived in the building before he had been born, and even after he had left for Hollywood, his father had chosen to remain in the apartment, though it had four rooms. He had thought the bother or trauma of moving had kept his father from seeking smaller quarters.

Julian no longer had the keys to the lobby door or to the apartment. He rang the superintendent's bell and was buzzed into the lobby.

A door opened.

Julian turned and explained, "I'm Mr. Heckowitz's son. I don't have the keys to the apartment."

The superintendent was a chunky, dark-complexioned man with gray hair. He nodded. "I have keys," he replied. He said something in Spanish and closed the door. "I am sorry about your papa. He was a nice man—always asked about my children."

Julian mumbled a thanks. They went up to the second floor on the elevator. Its walls, too, were covered with graffiti, some of which were crude drawings of nude women.

The superintendent proceeded out of the elevator. The

hallway was as dingy as Julian remembered it. The yellow walls were dirty and in places either covered with another color or had plaster completely broken away, exposing the lath underneath. He passed a window overlooking a narrow courtyard where, as a boy, he had played with the other children who lived in the building or in other houses nearby. Between the courtyard and the street was an underground passageway in which, late one summer evening, he and a girl had explored each other's bodies.

Julian smiled at the memory. He wondered if children of opposite sexes still dared each other to expose themselves or played doctor, as he and his friends had, in order to verify that girls were different from themselves. Probably the youngsters of today became aware of the differences at a much earlier age. When he had first gone into the tunnel with a girl, he must have been about eleven.

The superintendent stopped at the door. There were two locks, one above the other. Julian could only remember one of them.

"I give you the keys," the superintendent said, "so you won't have to ring my bell when you come here."

Julian thanked him. "As soon as I go through my father's things and dispose of them, I'll let you know."

"There's a month on the security. . . . You have plenty of time."

"If I need more time, I'll pay another month's rent," Julian said.

"Keep the door locked," the superintendent cautioned. "And if the downstairs bell rings, don't buzz the person in unless you know who it is. Strangers come and rob, or maybe mug some of the tenants."

"I'll be careful," Julian answered.

The superintendent walked back to the elevator and Julian stepped into the apartment, closing the door behind him. He stood very still, his heart beating very fast. The apartment was musty. He had never expected to return, and surely not for this purpose.

From where he stood, in a narrow alcove, he couldn't see

37

any of the rooms. He took a deep breath, reached around and double-locked the door before walking into the foyer.

His father had changed nothing. Because the shades were drawn, the room was filled with grayish light. He looked into the two bedrooms. His own was filled with an assortment of old newspapers, magazines and several empty cardboard boxes, his bed pushed against a wall. His father had probably used the room as a storage area.

He stood in the doorway of the master bedroom. The big double bed was unmade. Two pillows were stacked one on top of the other, blue quilt pulled off to one side at the foot of the bed. The shades were drawn. His eyes went back to the bed. He remembered his mother's fragile body resting against the pillows. Her face was very pale; her lips were bloodless and her blond hair was faded to the color of straw. Her eyes glazed from morphine, she could seldom speak two successive words.

Julian shook his head to displace the image, which slowly oozed out of his brain. When it was completely gone, he raised the shades, unlocked and opened the windows. He returned to the living room, raised the shades and opened the windows there. Then he took off his coat and jacket and set them down on the couch. As he rolled up his sleeves and opened his collar, it occurred to him that he probably would have to tip the superintendent to get rid of the furniture.

Even with the shades up, the day was sufficiently gray to require that the lights be turned on. Julian began to go through the drawers in the highboy. He found nothing but clothes: shirts, socks and underwear. A number of the shirts were new.

Julian moved to the night table. He opened the bottom portion and saw his father's gold-fringed *tallith* and blue velvet *yarmulke*, worn only on Passover and Yom Kippur, really the only holidays that his father had observed. Even as he held the *tallith* and *yarmulke*, Julian could not understand the dichotomy in his father's thinking. Sam had insisted on a kosher home and that his son be sent to the yeshiva. He even had gone so far as to become a follower of Rabbi Ben Yoish

Kalb, one of the many Hasidic rabbis in the neighborhood. Yet Sam hadn't believed in God. He had once heard him say to Guber, "I spit in the face of God. . . . Yes, I, Sam Heckowitz, spit in His face. . . . Let Him hold me to account for that and I will hold Him to account for the millions who called to Him in their hour of need, and to whom He turned a deaf ear. Max, He must first answer to me, if I am ever to believe again." His face was distorted with rage when he spoke. With his fist clenched, he beat on the kitchen table, repeating over and over again, "He must answer to me, if I am ever to believe again."

Thinking that Guber would probably appreciate having them, Julian set the *tallith* and *yarmulke* aside. Then he opened the night-table drawer. It was crammed full with letters, papers and Sam's passport. The number of trips his father had made abroad, especially to France and several of the countries on the other side of the Iron Curtain, surprised him.

He put the passport down and picked up a handful of letters. Many came from Israel, others from Holland, England, France, and there were several from Poland, Hungary and Rumania. Most were written in languages Julian couldn't even recognize; all except two were at least a year old. The two that were relatively recent had been written in what appeared to be German. With the intention of asking Guber if he was familiar with the language, he put the letters in his breast pocket. Like his father, Guber read and spoke at least a half-dozen different languages in addition to English and Hebrew. Guber had once told him, "Auschwitz was, in a strange way, a kind of school. . . . You learned to survive, often by being able to speak to an inmate or a guard in a language that was not your own."

He continued to rummage through the drawer and found a small brown purse: the kind his father would have used to carry diamonds. He ran his fingers over it, his heart beating faster. Opening it, he dumped the contents into the palm of his hand. There were one emerald-cut, two pear-shaped stones and four settings. His father had disliked emerald-cut diamonds.

Holding the emerald-cut stone up toward the light, he said aloud, "Paste. Fucking paste!" The pear-shaped stones turned out to be paste, too. And the settings were gold-plated brass. "Goddamn it!" Julian exclaimed, throwing the three pieces of paste and the settings across the room. "He always had some stones on him; always." Overwhelmed with frustration, Julian pulled the drawer out of the night table and dumped its contents on the floor.

He reached down and picked up several of the photographs. There were some of his mother when she was younger and well. There was another of the family. Sam looked stiff and uncomfortable. There was a photograph of Guber with his wife and children. And there was one of a young woman with a small boy, both of them unfamiliar to Julian.

He picked up the other photographs. Many were shots of him taken while he was in Nam. There was one in particular that he lingered over. He was in the center of the picture, kneeling. On either side of him was another Marine. The three of them were dressed and armed for combat. The man on his right was Salvatore Calluchie, the one on the left Carl Truck.

Sal had been born and raised in the Bay Ridge section of Brooklyn. His family had ties to the Mafia. Carl, part Cherokee Indian, had spent all his life on a small farm not far from the town of Shawnee, Oklahoma. The three of them were "good buddies."

Julian pursed his lips. A sudden ache came into his throat. The picture had been taken hours before his two friends had been blown away in a firefight with a North Vietnamese unit. Sal had taken a round in the chest, and Carl had been ripped apart by a grenade.

Julian brushed the tears from his eyes. When he had returned to the States, he had visited each of their families before going home. Every year since, on Easter Sunday and Christmas Day, he telephoned their families.

He'd never told any of his friends about Sal and Carl. Those who hadn't been in Nam would never understand what it had been like, and those who had been there had their own ghosts; they didn't need his. Julian slipped the snapshot into his shirt pocket and took a moment to wipe his eyes and blow his nose.

There were more photographs of him. Then he came to a picture of a man standing in front of what was obviously a European café. The man was tall; he was smiling. There was something vaguely familiar about him.

Julian made a pile of all the photographs. Later he would decide which he wanted. Some he would keep, if for no other reason than to show his children what their grandparents had looked like. He remembered having asked his mother and father that question, and they had told him the Nazis had destroyed the photographs as they had destroyed the people.

He continued to go through the drawer. Most of the papers were bills or receipts. Many of them were for diamonds that Sam had taken on consignment from other dealers in the exchange.

Julian found a piece of paper with the name "Fournier" on it, followed by "Paris operator 83." The handwriting wasn't Sam's. He placed the piece of paper in his breast pocket with the two letters. He would ask Guber if he knew who Fournier was.

Finished with the pile of papers, he put them all back into the drawer and returned it to the night table. Resuming his search of the highboy, he found his father's citizenship papers, a marriage certificate and his father's loupe.

He went into the kitchen, surprised to find only two bottles of ginger ale and a quart of milk in the refrigerator. There wasn't any canned food in the cupboard. Sam must have eaten all his meals out.

He walked into the living room and looked around. There was a painting on one of the walls of a fox pretending to be asleep while plump chickens were nearby, too curious for their own good. But nothing in the apartment made any sort of a statement about who and what Sam Heckowitz had been.

Shaking his head, he turned and was about to go back

into the bedroom for his jacket and coat when the downstairs bell rang. The loud, shrill sound startled him.

The bell rang again. He went to the intercom and asked who it was.

"Mr. Saul Kass. . . . Are you Sam Heckowitz? I've come to speak with you."

"Second floor," Julian said. "Come up to the second floor." He buzzed the man into the lobby.

Julian unlocked the two locks, opened the door and waited for Kass to come up. Eventually the elevator door opened and Julian called out, "Down at the other end of the hall."

The man came toward him with determined strides. He was a tall, thin man, well-dressed, with a strongly masculine, weatherbeaten face. He extended his hand and said, "Mr. Heckowitz, it is a pleasure—"

"I'm Sam's son, Julian," he said, shaking Kass's hand. "Please come inside. I was just about to leave the apartment."

Kass looked around. "I called several times, but there was no answer."

"My father died of a heart attack a few days ago. He was buried yesterday."

Kass frowned and shook his head. "I came over from Paris yesterday," he said. "I'm terribly sorry to hear Sam is dead."

"Did you know my father well?"

"We did some business now and then. I saw him during his last visit to Paris, about three weeks ago."

"Then you're a diamond dealer, too?"

Kass smiled. "Not to the degree that your father was. By comparison, I'm rather inexperienced."

"Sam knew his diamonds," Julian agreed with a nod.

"Your father gave me this address. He said that when I came to New York, I should be sure to visit him, and so I did."

Julian walked into the bedroom and picked up his jacket and coat. "I was going through his things," Julian explained to Kass, who stood in the doorway. "Would you believe he didn't leave a single diamond?"

Kass shook his head and made a sympathetic clicking sound with his tongue. "I would have thought that he'd have put more faith in diamonds than in anything else."

"He didn't," Julian said, as he slipped on his jacket and coat. "I've had enough of this place today. How did you come here? By subway?"

"No, I rode a cab," Kass answered.

"Would you mind if we shared one going back to Manhattan?"

"Not in the least."

Julian left the apartment and locked the door with both locks.

Kass withdrew an inhaler from his pocket and took two deep breaths, inserting the inhaler into one nostril and then the other. "I am sorry," Kass apologized, "but whenever I fly for a long period, my sinuses act up."

"I know the feeling," Julian commiserated.

"By tonight I'll be fine," Kass said.

"It'll be quicker if we walk down the steps than if we wait for the elevator," Julian said.

"Are you also a diamond dealer?" Kass asked.

"No. I write for TV, and live in Hollywood. I'm only here because of my father's death."

They stepped outside. The wind was stronger.

Julian said, "We stand a better chance of getting a cab if we walk up to Eastern Parkway and Nostrand."

"I'm completely in your hands," Kass said, looking across the street where a black Cadillac was parked. There was a man behind the wheel and another one next to him.

"I wonder who they are." Julian said. "That's not the kind of car that's seen around here unless there's a funeral or a wedding."

To draw Julian's attention away, Kass said, "I've always had the desire to write. Yes, I think if I someday have the opportunity, I will write a book."

"I might do the same," Julian said with a smile. "But

right now I make good bread—some might even call it cake—writing for TV."

"Cake? Bread? Please excuse me, I have some familiarity with American slang, but those words are new to me."

"Bread is money, and cake—well, that's lots of money." Kass laughed.

At a hack stand they found an empty cab.

"You know," Kass said, "I owed your father, may he rest in peace, a dinner. I'd appreciate it very much if I could discharge that debt by buying you dinner while I'm in New York."

"Hell, why not. Call me at my hotel . . . the Roosevelt, room eighteen ten. If I'm not there, leave a message at the desk."

"Do you want to go to your hotel?" Kass asked.

"I'll get out at Third Avenue and Thirteenth Street. . . .There's a bookstore on Broadway and Thirteenth that I want to visit."

Kass pretended to change his position. He took the opportunity to glance out of the rear window. The black Cadillac was close behind them. "Your father was a remarkable man," Kass commented, turning toward Julian.

"I wouldn't know," Julian answered, with a sudden feeling of regret.

8

DIMETROV RELAXED against the back of the seat and used the inhaler. He looked into the rearview mirror; the black Cadillac was two cars behind.

He was more annoyed with Marrosov's lack of subtlety than with the fact that he had ordered him followed. Dimetrov would have been surprised if Marrosov hadn't taken any action to discover why he had been sent to New York. It was an indication of the paranoia that was rife in the organization—and not only in the KGB, from what he had discovered from several different sources. The same situation existed in the American, British and French intelligence operations as well. All too often such distrust would get in the way and jeopardize the work that had to be done.

The cab continued up Third Avenue and swung west on Forty-seventh Street. Traffic moved slowly. Dimetrov considered getting out of the cab and walking, but it had started to rain.

That Sam Heckowitz had died was going to make his assignment much more difficult. Heckowitz was the only lead he had, and it wasn't going to be easy to find another one. If Julian had been a diamond dealer, he would have had one. But that might not have been true either, if Julian's relationship to Sam had been the same.

Though Dimetrov had heard stories about the hostility that sometimes existed between a son and father, this had been his first encounter with it. Julian most certainly resented Sam, and Dimetrov couldn't help but wonder if Sam had had the same feelings toward Julian. The information in Sam's dossier gave no hint at the man's emotional life.

Dimetrov was certain Julian knew absolutely nothing about Sam's activities. If he had any knowledge, he would not have gone looking for diamonds. Sam had done very little buying and selling of stones, probably just enough to make his expenses. All his energies had been devoted to the movement of diamonds in a two-way traffic system of his own devising, according to the information given to Dimetrov in the dossier. Headquarters was certain about Sam's involvement with the traffic of Jews for diamonds, but less certain about his reported connections with the Mafia.

The cab had reached Park Avenue and was stopped by a red light. "It's the damn trucks that bollix up the traffic," the cab driver complained. "They oughtta unload at night."

Dimetrov agreed, pleased at correctly guessing the meaning of "bollixed."

It took another seven minutes before the cab pulled up to the curb at Forty-seventh Street and Fifth.

Crossing to the south side of the street, Dimetrov entered the International Jewelers' Exchange. He had been given fifty thousand dollars to buy stones with, and should he require up to an additional fifty thousand, he had been authorized to use funds from the mission's general operating expenses. His knowledge of gemstones, and diamonds in particular, was one of the reasons headquarters had given him the assignment. He was an amateur gemologist.

There were dozens of diamond dealers in this exchange. Some occupied only a few feet of space; others were large enough to have several showcases. Those adjacent to the windows overlooking the street had, in his opinion, the very best location.

The aisles were crowded with buyers and sellers. There was a raucous cacophony. Everyone seemed to be shouting something. Within minutes, Dimetrov heard his native language, as well as German, Yiddish, Hebrew, French and Polish.

Most of the dealers were Jews. Some were bearded and wore their hair in ringlets. They wore long, black frock coats, no ties, and black, wide-brimmed hats. Others were more Americanized.

Besides diamond dealers, there were men who sold only ropes of gold and silver and those who dealt only in watches. Every counter was illuminated by very bright lights, and those where diamonds were sold had one or two trays lined with black velvet on which to show a prospective customer one or more stones.

Dimetrov singled out a small dealer named Harry Vogel, whose counter was near the end of the fourth aisle. Dimetrov made several trips to the counter, looked at the goods displayed and walked away, only to return again after a few minutes.

The third time he came back, the dealer, a man with a dull red beard and green eyes, put down a container of coffee, walked up to him and said, "Either you want what you see, or you don't want it. But make up your mind, mister, because you're making me nervous, giving me a nervous stomach. So, make up your mind."

"That one there," Dimetrov responded, pointing to an engagement ring, "the third from the left."

"What about it?"

"I might be interested in it," Dimetrov answered.

"Your interest I'm not interested in," Vogel said. "If you want to buy it, that's a different matter. Do you want to buy, or are you just interested?"

Dimetrov suppressed a smile and said, "Show me the ring."

"You want the ring or the stone?" Vogel asked, squinting at the prospective buyer.

"The stone, but if the setting—"

"Platinum," Vogel said, unlocking the case and taking out the ring. "It's two and a quarter carats and blue-white. A fine solitaire."

Dimetrov picked up the ring and examined it.

"It's worth five thousand, if it's worth a penny. You go to any appraiser on the street and you'll get it in writing, and probably for six thousand." Vogel walked back to where he had set his container of coffee and took several sips before he said, "Listen, mister, you hold in your hand a gem."

"It's an old European cut," Dimetrov commented.

"I'm selling you a gem, and you're telling me what I already know. Listen, mister, it's yours for forty-five hundred."

Dimetrov took out his loupe.

"You a dealer?" Vogel asked.

Dimetrov nodded and looked at the stone through the loupe. It was clouded with yellow on the right side. "Cash, two thousand," he said, returning the loupe to his pocket. "Not a dollar more."

"Where you from?" Vogel asked, moving closer.

"Paris . . . Name is Saul Kass," he said, extending his hand.

Vogel shook his hand. "On a buying trip?"

"Yes. I was going to do business with Sam Heckowitz, but he died of a heart attack just the other day."

"God rest his soul," Vogel said. "He was here for many years. A good man."

"Yes, he was," Dimetrov added with conviction.

Vogel uttered a deep sigh. "But God was merciful to him. The heart attack came while he was sleeping. He probably didn't feel a thing."

"God was merciful," Dimetrov echoed.

After a respectful few moments of silence, Vogel said, "This is a bad time of the year to come here and buy. Too close to Christmas. You can't get value. It's a seller's market."

"It's the only time I could make it," Dimetrov answered.

"Well, are you going to take the ring?"

"At my price."

"Listen, Mr. Kass from Paris, I wouldn't give that stone to my brother for less than three thousand."

"Two," Dimetrov said.

Vogel shook his head, picked up the ring and started to put it back into the showcase. Then he changed his mind. "I'll give it to you for twenty-seven hundred."

"Twenty-four."

"Twenty-five hundred and it's yours. At that price I'm losing money."

"I'll take it," Dimetrov said.

The handshake between the two men sealed the deal.

"I'm at the Plaza Hotel," Dimetrov said. "I will be by tomorrow with the cash."

Vogel smiled broadly. "Cash is best."

Dimetrov picked up the ring again. Taking out his loupe, he pretended to examine it again. "In Paris," he said, "the dealers only talk about the killings." He looked at Vogel.

The man shook his head.

Dimetrov put the ring back on the black velvet cloth. "We're afraid it could happen to one of us," he said.

Vogel crossed his lips with his finger. "Gangsters," he whispered. "Most of us know it's the work of the gangsters. Mafia."

"Haven't the police done anything?"

"Who knows. . . . But you ask most of the dealers—they'll tell you the same thing."

"What about the others who don't think it's the work of gangsters?" Dimetrov asked.

"Most of them say it's the PLO, and some think it's Germans, neo-Nazis."

Dimetrov lingered a few minutes longer with Vogel and wandered off to make three additional purchases. The other dealers told him the same thing, though the last man thought there was a strong possibility that someone on the street had killed the last two men.

By the time Dimetrov made his last purchase, it was one o'clock. He stopped at a Chinese restaurant and lingered at the bar, listening to the conversation that swirled around. All of it had to do with diamonds, various other kinds of gems and precious metals. When he moved over to a table, he sat alone and ordered a number five from the special luncheon menu, which included won ton soup, shrimps in lobster sauce, an eggroll, a small portion of fried rice and tea, all for five dollars.

Dimetrov enjoyed himself, and for a while did not think about his assignment.

9

FOURNIER ARRIVED at Galignani fifteen minutes before eight and took the time to browse. He wanted to buy two or three books to give to his mother when he saw her on Sunday. He had not yet told her about Sam's death and did not look forward to it. He was sure she would become emotional, and that wouldn't be good for her. She suffered from high blood pressure, and the doctor had insisted that she not be subjected to unnecessary stress. But there wasn't any way that he could keep it from her. The letters and money would abruptly stop coming, and then she would know.

Fournier found a historical romance entitled *A Flame on the Wind,* written by an American and translated into French. He was about to look for another when he saw Shulamith enter the shop. Without hesitation, he went straight up to her and said, "I'm glad you came early. We'll have more time together."

"There are two people who want to talk to you," she said.

He stiffened.

"I'm sorry," she whispered, putting her hand on his arm. "It will only take a short time."

"I want to pay for this book," he told her. "Are they outside?"

"Around the corner on the rue Saint Honoré."

Fournier paid for the book and asked the clerk for a plastic bag. He left the store with Shulamith at his side. Neither of them spoke. His quick stride was long and determined.

"In the gray Peugeot," she said.

Fournier went straight to the car. The rear door opened and he slipped into the seat next to a man who wore a wide-brimmed gray felt hat. Shulamith sat in the front.

Only after they had pulled away from the curb and joined the flow of traffic did the man at the wheel speak. He apologized for the inconvenience of the meeting. "But it will take only a short time," he said. "Until now," he went on, "my superiors have been able to live with your peculiar relationship to France and to Russia. We even know, for example, that your own organization actually made it possible for you to become a double agent."

"If you know that much, I don't understand what more you need to know," Fournier replied.

"We also know—"

"Suppose you stop telling me what you know and tell me exactly what you want to know." He had no intention of letting them think he was frightened.

"It is difficult for us to understand how a man is able to serve three masters."

"That's your problem," Fournier answered. "I have no intentions of explaining myself to you, or for that matter, to anyone."

"And that's your final word on the subject?"

"Yes," Fournier answered. Then, moving his eyes to Shulamith, he asked, "Do we still have a date?" She nodded.

"If you would pull over to the curb and let us out, I'd appreciate it."

"The name of the Soviet agent assigned to the task of stopping the traffic is Sergei Dimetrov," said the driver. "We want to know everything we can about him. Shulamith will be your contact."

"How did the KGB get onto Sam?" Fournier questioned.

"We're not exactly sure. The message seems to have originated in Israel. But we can't trace who sent it."

"Anything else?"

The driver pulled over on a small street in the vicinity of Sacre Coeur. He turned around. Even in the darkness, Fournier could see he was a young man, perhaps in his late twenties.

"Just so that you don't ever have any doubts about which master you serve," he said matter of factly, "there is something we want you to know. It will make your choice much easier, if the time should ever come when you'd be forced to make a choice."

Fournier edged slightly forward, but the man next to him pulled him back.

"Sam was more than just that kind old Jew from New York," the driver said.

"If you're going to tell me he was my mother's lover, I guessed that years ago."

"He was your father," the man said.

Fournier glanced at Shulamith. He felt as if his breath had suddenly been choked out of him. But he managed to ask, "Did you know?" She shook her head.

Tears came to Fournier's eyes. He nodded and said, "When I was a little boy, I often wished he was."

"You can leave the car now," the driver said.

"One more question."

"Go ahead."

"Would you know if his . . . I mean my half-brother is aware of me?"

"Not to our knowledge," the man answered. "And until certain other matters are settled, I suggest you keep your relationship to him a secret."

"Yes," Fournier answered. "I'm not sure he would understand anyway."

"You know him?"

Fournier shook his head. "Only from what Sam told me," he said. He reached over to the door lock and opened it. "Are you coming with me, Shulamith?"

"Do you still want me to?"

"Yes," he answered. "Yes, I want you to come with me." He opened the door and left the car.

Shulamith joined him. Fournier took hold of her arm and they began to walk. "Which way?" she asked.

"Up toward the cathedral," he answered. "I just have to walk for a while."

She pressed his hand against her breast.

10

"Listen," Julian said, walking as far from the night table as the telephone cord would permit, "I don't want you to come to New York. I'll be back in a few days." He was speaking to Gloria Fleming, his current lover. He never considered a relationship to be anything more than temporary; she was fun to be with and a good lay. But she happened to have been with him when Guber had called to tell him about Sam's death. For some reason that Julian couldn't understand, she seemed to think that her presence at that particular time gave her a proprietary interest in him, which he was rapidly beginning to resent. He was sorry now he had returned her call.

"You don't have to shout at me," she said. "All I wanted to do was make you feel good. You said you were depressed and—"

"I'm depressed, and nothing you can do here is going to change that."

"There are some things," she answered with a laugh, "that I know will make you feel better."

"Save them for me. When I return, we can spend a few days in bed. But now I have things on my mind," he said, walking to the window. Though it was only three in the afternoon, many of the offices in the building across the street had their lights on.

"You know," Gloria told him, "I miss you."

"We'll have a ball when I get back," he said. "I've got to run. I'm going to meet one of my father's old friends for dinner."

"You sound uptight."

"I am. Now will you hang up?"

"Will you call me tomorrow?"

"If I can. Now hang up."

"I really do miss you."

"For God's sake, hang up!"

As soon as he heard the click on the other end of the line, Julian felt relieved. Deciding not to call her again, he set down the phone and went into the bathroom to wash his face. He had spent most of the afternoon and much of the preceding few days going to the dealers his father had known, hoping that whoever had his father's diamonds would be honest enough to turn them over to him.

Over and over again he had been told that Sam had left nothing. But Julian couldn't accept that. If he knew anything about his father, he knew the man would have left diamonds with someone. Like most dealers who had no stall, Sam had conducted his business from his pocket. He had often left his goods in the safe of one of his friends for a weekend.

Julian returned to the bedroom and took a few moments to adjust his tie. Then he went to the window and looked out. All day it had been cloudy and raw. He was no longer used to the bone-chilling cold of early December in New York and wondered whether to buy a heavier coat. He left the room without making up his mind.

As soon as he reached the street, Julian walked over to Fifth Avenue. Most of the stores were brilliantly decorated for Christmas, though Thanksgiving was still a recent memory. He stopped to look at a display in a men's shop. He passed the TAP office and looked at the posters of Portugal. He thought about the possibility of going on a vacation when the script for *High Terror* was done. He'd combine a visit to Portugal and Spain, not having been to either.

He continued to walk, stopped, and turned around to go back to the TAP office and ask for a schedule and information on the rates. Then suddenly he realized a man was looking at him. The man moved too quickly to be seen clearly.

Julian frowned. Several times during the past few days he had had the feeling that someone had been watching him, but he had dismissed it with a shrug. There wasn't any reason he should be followed.

Instead of returning to the airline office, Julian crossed Fifth Avenue and on Forty-fifth Street went into a bar named the Quiet Man. He found a stool in the corner near the door and sat down. From where he was, he could see whoever came in without their seeing him. He ordered a Chivas neat. Two men came in and sat down at the bar. The bartender knew them.

Julian looked around. There were photographs and drawings of John Wayne on the opposite wall. Many of the stills came from the film *The Quiet Man.* He had never been a John Wayne fan. To him, Wayne had tried to be in real life the two-fisted, hard-drinking hero he had played so many times. Wayne had come to believe in the reality of the fantasy. But that was an easy thing for anyone living in Hollywood to do. It was an occupational hazard for the people involved in motion pictures or television.

A woman entered. She glanced at Julian and took a stool close to where he sat. She ordered a very dry martini; then looking straight at him, she commented, "It's a good day for sleeping and whatever."

Julian nodded and dropped two singles on the bar for the drink and a tip. "I have to meet a friend," he said. "But you're right, it is a good day for sleeping and whatever." He left without waiting to hear her reply.

The gloom of the day and the time of the year combined to deepen the darkness. The cars and trucks had their headlights on. All the shop windows were illuminated.

Julian walked to the corner, stopped and looked over his shoulder. No one followed. He crossed, went up to Forty-seventh Street and quickly found the building where Max had his office. There was a private security guard in the lobby who was too busy talking to a young woman to notice anyone going in or out. Julian rode the elevator up to the eleventh floor.

The door to Guber's office was locked. He placed his finger against the bell. A disembodied woman's voice asked who he was. Julian identified himself and was immediately buzzed in.

"I'm Rose," the woman said. "I knew your father, Sam, may he rest in peace."

Julian nodded and glanced around the room, trying to recall if he had ever been there before. Now and then Sam had taken him to the exchange. Not often.

Rose said, "Your father would tell me when one of your shows was on. If it was not *shabbus*, I always watched it. He was proud of you."

Julian felt the color rising into his cheeks.

"Your father was a real *mentsh.*"

"Thank you," Julian said.

The door to the inner office opened and Guber beckoned

to Julian. "If I didn't come out and see who came in, she'd never tell me. I'd sit in that office worrying whether she was being raped and I was going to be robbed."

Julian smiled.

"Listen to him talk," Rose said. "All he thinks about is rape and robberies. You'd think a man as old as he is would think about other things."

"Go home, Rose," Guber told her. "Julian and I will stay awhile longer." He stepped back into his office, waited for Julian to enter and then closed the door. "Take off your coat and sit down. We'll wait till Rose has gone; then we'll have a drink of schnapps. On a day like this, it's good."

Julian dropped his coat on the couch. "Know anything about diamonds?" Guber asked, gesturing toward the desk where there were several on a black velvet cloth. "After all, you're the son of a diamond dealer."

"Not too much," Julian answered, looking intently at the diamonds. Most of them were large stones.

"Choose the best of the lot," Guber said.

Julian raised the palms of his hands. "I'm a writer, not a diamond dealer."

"Try," Guber urged.

"Only if you promise not to laugh."

Guber nodded.

"May I have your loupe?"

"Already I know you're no amateur," Guber said with a smile.

Rose opened the door and announced she was leaving.

"So go," Guber responded.

Julian said good night.

As soon as Guber was sure Rose was gone, he unlocked the bottom drawer of the desk and brought out a bottle of twenty-five-year-old scotch and two paper cups just big enough to hold a shot. "If she saw me drink, she'd tell my daughter." He filled each cup and put the bottle down to one side. "There's more if you want it," he said, handing Julian one of the paper cups. "I'd drink a toast to Sam, may he rest in peace, but he'd want me to drink to life, so *le'chayim.*"

"*Le'chayim,*" Julian repeated, downing the scotch in one gulp.

"Another?"

Julian shook his head. "I stopped for a drink before I came here," he said. He was about to mention that someone might be following him but changed his mind and instead busied himself with the diamonds. He placed the stones in a straight line. One by one, he examined all of them. Several were markedly flawed, either with yellow as a result of iron, or with carbon spots that his father had called niggers. He looked at each stone twice and then held up the second one in the line. "This is it for my money," he said, handing the diamond and the loupe to Guber.

Guber studied the diamond for several moments. "What do you think it might weigh?" he asked.

"Less than a carat, probably three-quarters."

"Just eighty points . . . Not bad for someone who doesn't know diamonds. I'd have chosen this stone, too. It's got the best color of the lot."

Julian smiled, pleased with himself. "Sam used to play a game with me," he said. "He'd come home on a night when he had a lot of stones in his purse and spread them out on the table. Then he'd say, 'You pick the best one.' After a while, I learned what to look for."

"He taught you well," Max commented. "If for some reason you can't write anymore, you can always become a diamond dealer."

"No, thank you!" Julian exclaimed.

Max shrugged and began to place the diamonds on small sheets of paper made with a pale blue translucent lining, and folded them into envelopes. He worked quickly, by color and then by weight.

Julian changed his mind and poured himself another drink. He was vaguely uneasy at having played the "diamond game"—Sam had named it that—with Guber. Again he felt that he had made a mistake when he had agreed to have dinner with Max.

"Well, that's that!" Guber said, placing the last of the

packets of diamonds in the safe and locking it. He came back to the desk and poured himself another drink.

Julian took out the letters he had found in his father's apartment. "Can you read these?" he asked, pushing the two letters across the desk.

Guber scanned them, concentrating on one in particular, before he looked up and asked, "What do you want to know?"

"Does either mention anything to indicate that Sam might have left something with them?"

"Sam had a lot of friends in Europe and Israel," Guber answered, moving the letters back toward Julian. "Neither letter had anything to do with business. One was from a friend in Holland and another from someone in Germany."

Julian removed a scrap of paper from his wallet. "Does the name Paul Fournier mean anything to you?" he asked, handing the paper to Guber.

"Fournier?"

"That's Sam's writing," Julian said. He removed two photographs from his breast pocket and placed them on the desk.

"Who are they?" Guber asked.

"I don't know. But take a good look at the man."

Guber put the scrap of paper down on the desk and picked up the photograph of the young man. He held the palm of his hand against the lower part of the face and then the upper. "Must be someone from your father's side of the family," he said.

"All of them were killed."

Julian extended his hand and placed his finger on the scrap of paper. "Is the man in the picture Fournier?"

Guber shrugged. "How should I know?"

"And the woman and child—"

"I don't know who they are. But I told you before," Guber said, "Sam knew a great many people. The man in the picture looks something like you."

"That's probably why when I first saw the picture I thought there was something familiar about him."

"He never mentioned Fournier to me."

"What if Fournier had some connection to my father?" Julian questioned. "He could be holding some of his goods and if he is, I want it."

"It's time to go," Guber said, putting the bottle of scotch back into the drawer and locking it. Guber remembered that Fournier had called the day of Sam's funeral. He picked up his drink and finished it. He had no intention of saying anything about Fournier, or anyone else for that matter.

"I went to Sam's friends," Julian said, "and asked if he left anything with them."

"*Bubkes,* right?"

"They offered me their condolences."

"You can't say I didn't warn you," Guber told him.

Julian picked up his coat and put it on. "I don't intend to give up that easily. My father did leave me—"

"One hundred thousand dollars isn't exactly nothing."

"Listen," Julian said, "I want everything I can get. Sam didn't give me a damn thing when I was a kid. . . . I don't mean money. Then I needed—I needed him to get away from Auschwitz and take me to a ball game or some other damn place. He never gave me the things that most fathers give their sons, and now I want the fucking money and the stones."

"Maybe he couldn't. Maybe he gave all he could in the way that he could."

"Nothing with nothing," Julian answered, following Guber out of the office. They walked through the dimly lit hallway to the elevator.

"There's a man here from Paris who did business with my father," Julian said. "Maybe he knows Fournier?"

"What's his name?" Guber asked, having difficulty keeping the sound of his voice from cracking. Sam hadn't been overseas in the last few months.

"Saul Kass. Do you recognize the name?"

Before Guber could answer, there were three sharp reports.

"Gunfire," Julian said.

"Oh, my God!" Guber exclaimed. "Hurry upstairs. Take the stairs."

Julian ran, flung open the door and bounded up the steps. Guber pounded after him. Two floors up a man was sprawled on the floor near the elevator. Blood soaked through his long black frock coat.

"It's Jacob Levitas!" Max exclaimed. Dropping to his knees, he took hold of the man's hand and felt for his pulse. "He's dead," he said, looking up at Julian.

"I'll phone the police."

"Use the office," Guber said, handing him the keys. "Remember to turn off the alarm. The switch is on the right wall."

As soon as Julian was gone, Guber went through Levitas's pockets. The purse was gone. He stood up and stepped back. Wide-eyed with fear, he looked down to the other end of the hallway. The light was too dim for him to see anything. His eyes moved slowly back to Levitas's body. More diamonds would have to be collected, and someone else would have to be found to deliver them. He raised his eyes upward and silently asked God to give him strength. "Like Sam," he told the Almighty, "I am weary; very weary."

"The police are on their way," Julian said as he came through the door leading to the stairwell.

Guber nodded. He couldn't stop his hands from trembling. "I'd better go and call my daughter and tell her we won't be coming for dinner," he said.

"Go ahead. I'll stay here."

"I don't know anyone by the name of Saul Kass," Guber said. "But maybe Sam did."

"Go make the call," Julian urged.

"I'm going," he answered, walking slowly toward the stairs.

Julian watched him. His father used to walk like that: slowly and with a roll, almost as if he had sea legs. But he hadn't. The roll had come from a broken leg that had never healed properly. Julian had never known how and where Sam had broken his leg.

11

ARM IN ARM they walked toward Sacre Coeur. Neither spoke. Fournier was filled with a melancholy joy. He had always wanted Sam to be his father, and now that his secret yearning had come true, he was deeply sorry he had never really told Sam how much he loved him.

"I suddenly feel like a small boy again," Fournier said. "A small boy in a man's body with a man's understanding."

"You're not angry with me?" Shulamith asked.

He shook his head. "No."

She pressed his arm tightly against her. They walked up the steps of the terrace in front of the cathedral.

"I want to do something," Fournier said, leading her into Sacre Coeur. He went directly to the first altar he saw, placed a few coins in a box, took a candle and lit it. "For you, my father, for you," he said. For a few moments he stood and watched the flame. It flickered and seemed as if it were about to go out. Fournier cupped it with his hand. The flame steadied and took hold. He smiled. Turning to Shulamith, he said, "I don't think it matters much whether it is in a church or a synagogue, as long as a son pays his respects to his father."

"It doesn't matter," Shulamith responded.

Once out on the terrace again, Fournier said, "This is the first time I've gone inside."

"Me too," she told him.

He led her to the stone fence. The night was very clear, and Paris was a jeweled city. Off to the right was the Eiffel Tower, and almost directly in front of them was Notre Dame. Here and there along the Seine, patches of light turned the dark water into gold or silver.

"Tell me," Fournier said, "how you became involved with Sheruti Bethahar."

"A professor at the university worked for them and recruited me."

"And you weren't afraid?"

"I was terrified," she admitted. "But I felt that I had to do whatever I could to help my country."

"For myself," he said, answering her question before she asked it, "I enjoyed the danger and the power."

"My people don't trust you," she told him.

He shrugged. "That's their problem."

"I suddenly feel cold," she said, pulling up the broad collar of her coat.

They went down the steps and Fournier hailed a cab. "Rue O'Andione, corner of rue Maspero," he told the driver.

"Where are we going?"

"To my apartment," he said.

She looked at him and then faced the window. "Neither my people nor yours would approve. If mine found out, they would send me home." There was a breathy quality to her voice.

"Then we must not let them find out."

She didn't answer. He put his arm around her shoulder and drew her close to him. She smelled of tea roses. "You could say no," he told her.

"I should say no," she whispered, "but I won't."

Fournier held her close until the driver pulled up to the curb.

"Where are we?" she asked.

"The Passy district," Fournier answered, as he helped her out of the cab. "Across there are the Gardens of Ranelagh. And I live up the street." She wrapped her arm around his.

"These are chestnut trees," he said, gesturing toward the trees lining both sides of the street. "In the spring and summer, they're very beautiful."

The building where Fournier lived was a short distance from the corner. His apartment was on the second floor of a four-story walkup. He unlocked the door, switched on the light and moved aside to let her enter. "It's nothing more than one very large room," he said. "Here, let me have your coat."

Shulamith walked toward the fireplace. "Does it work?" she asked.

"If it didn't, I'd probably freeze to death during the winter," Fournier answered. He placed two large pieces of kindling on the andirons and some wood shavings underneath them. "You light it," he said, handing her a box of matches. She struck a match, knelt down and set fire to the shavings.

Fournier stood close to her. The firelight gave her dark complexion an orange glow. He reached down and moved his fingers over her face. She took hold of his hand and kissed the palm.

"Would you like something to drink? Wine?"

"No," she said, standing.

He brought her to him and kissed her.

She trembled and returned the kiss with a passion equal to his own. "You see," she said, moving her lips from his, "I want you as much as you want me." He nodded approvingly.

She slipped out of the white sweater she was wearing and removed her tweed skirt.

Fournier watched her.

When she was completely naked, she reached up to the top of her head and loosened the braids. Within moments, her black hair spilled down below her shoulders.

"You're beautiful," he said.

She smiled at him, went to the large brass bed, turned down the covers and slipped into it. Fournier undressed and lay down next to her.

They faced each other and their mouths opened; their tongues touched. Then Fournier caressed her hair. Shulamith trembled.

He moved his hand over her breasts. He kissed her neck, and then the nipple of each breast.

"I like that," she said.

"So do I." He moved his hand over her love mount and

the insides of her warm, silky thighs. She reached down and played her fingers over his penis and under his scrotum. "I didn't think you'd be circumcised," she said.

"I always thought it was strange," he answered. "But it's done in some hospitals here if the parents want it."

She sat up, and without a word Shulamith put her lips on his penis. A surge of pleasure went through his groin. "Stretch out," he said, enabling him to use his tongue on her sex. She had a pungent muskiness that made him want to devour her. Shulamith pushed her body against his mouth and gently moved her hand over his head.

When he sensed she was close to a climax, Fournier stopped. "I want to go inside you," he said.

They faced each other, and Fournier slipped into her.

"That feels good," she said. "Very good."

Fournier moved slowly, bending low to kiss her breasts, and then her mouth. Their tongues touched. Shulamith moved faster. She reached down and caressed his scrotum. He moved his hand across her buttocks and down the crack between them.

"Yes," she told him in a throaty voice. "Yes!"

He felt the tenseness come into her body and he quickened his thrusts. Deep in her throat, she made low sounds of pleasure. Suddenly she let out a wordless cry. Her body heaved against his, tightened and shuddered. Several times she tensed and relaxed.

Fournier held back no longer. He came with a deep growl of satisfaction.

After a while, she said, "Now I would like some wine."

Fournier touched her breasts. "Sunday I want you to come with me to meet my mother," he said.

"Yes," she answered with a nod. "I'd like that."

12

GUBER LIVED IN A THREE-ROOM APARTMENT on Washington Avenue in Brooklyn. The two windows of his living room overlooked the Botanical Garden. In the spring, he could see the sudden burst of pink from the rows of Japanese cherry trees; and later in the season, when the summer heat hammered down on the city, the roses bloomed. But now the flowers were gone and the trees were bare, except for the evergreens.

Guber stood at one of the windows in the living room. The Botanical Garden was dark. In the distance, a few street lights marked Flatbush Avenue, separating the garden from Prospect Park, where no one in his right mind would venture at night. Once the park at night had been a place for lovers, but in recent years, it had become a jungle.

He shook his head, went back to the end table and poured himself another scotch. The questioning by the police and then by Detective Anthony Dalis had drained Guber of any desire to sleep. Dalis led the team of detectives assigned to investigate the killings in the exchange. He had discovered that a door to an office at the far end of the hall had been forced without setting off the alarm. He had said that whoever had killed and robbed Levitas had made his escape through a window in the office that led to the fire escape. Guber paced between the windows and the doorway of a small foyer. He glanced at his watch. It was three o'clock in the morning. There wasn't much time left for sleeping, since he hadn't slept past six for many years. He went back to the window, turned and looked into the room. He felt constricted by its smallness. As soon as Urishensky was safely brought out, Guber decided to go on vacation. Maybe he'd go to Florida and visit friends. Maybe he'd give up the apartment, sell the business and retire. His children had been after him for years to retire. But neither of them had any idea he was using his business as a cover for the exchange of diamonds for Jews. He had had enough of that, too. And now that Sam was gone, it wouldn't be the same kind of operation. Sam, not he, had really held the operation together.

"Sam," he said aloud, "you shouldn't have left me holding the bag." As soon as he spoke, his thoughts switched to Julian. "And you should have left a few stones for your boy."

Guber downed the scotch. "A few diamonds you should have left, not letters and names." The name Fournier began to tease his memory. He faced the window. After he and Sam had been freed from Auschwitz, they were sent with several hundred other survivors to a displaced-persons camp in France, near the city of—the name escaped him, though he was sure that if he looked at a map, he'd be able to recognize it. At the camp there was a Frenchwoman who worked in the library. Guber had always believed that Sam had had an affair with her. Years later, when he had asked Sam if his suspicions about the Frenchwoman had been correct, Sam had pretended to have forgotten the entire incident.

"A Fournier calls from Paris and a Kass comes from Paris," Guber said, "and you, Sam, are beyond their reach." He poured himself another scotch, knowing he was drinking too much and would regret it afterward.

He couldn't recall if the librarian's name was Fournier. But the woman in the photograph with the small child looked like her, as far as he could remember. And there was a striking resemblance between the man in the other photograph and Julian.

Guber dropped down into a club chair whose tan upholstery on the arms was badly worn and whose springs had given way years before. "Left holding the bag," he said, closing his eyes. He often fell asleep in the chair, especially if, for some reason, he couldn't fall asleep in bed, or awoke during the night and was unable to get back to sleep.

He was still confronted with the problem of bringing Urishensky out. A new shipment of diamonds would have to be gathered. Some of the previous contributors might not want to risk having their stones go to thieves a fourth time. And then there were the people on the other side—the Russians. They might become too frightened by what was happening and refuse to make the exchange.

Guber was beginning to feel the discomfort of heartburn. He rubbed his stomach and made a face. Slowly he pulled himself to his feet, went into the kitchen and prepared himself a bicarbonate of soda. He drank it, waited a few moments, burped several times and felt better. As difficult as it might be to gather another shipment of diamonds, it would be twice—perhaps ten times—as difficult to find someone to deliver them. The men he knew would be too frightened to do it, even if they had made previous deliveries.

Guber let the cold water run and drank a glass. He went back to the windows in the living room. If Sam were still alive, he would have done it, as he had many times in the past when the danger had been too great to send anyone else.

Suddenly Guber realized that Julian was available. He smiled. Julian was so anxious to find diamonds he was certain Sam had left that he'd go anywhere if he thought he could get them.

Guber was pleased with himself. He didn't appreciate Julian's attitude toward Sam, and maybe Julian would learn something from the experience. Sam would approve, even if it meant putting Julian in some danger. Guber raised his empty shot glass and silently toasted his dead friend.

13

JULIAN SPENT SATURDAY in his father's apartment. With the aid of the superintendent of the building, he was able to dispose of most of the furniture. When he returned to his hotel, he found a message from Kass. He returned the call and they agreed to meet for dinner Monday evening at seven, outside Brentano's bookstore on Fifth Avenue.

"Since you're a native," Kass said, "I'll let you choose the place."

"In eight years, a lot of changes have taken place."

"I insist," Kass said.

"All I can do is try," Julian responded. "If the food is bad, blame the eight years, not me."

Late Saturday night Julian left the hotel and made the rounds of the singles bars. He had more than one opportunity to pick up a woman, and though he bought a round of drinks for several of the women he spoke to, he wasn't interested in taking any of them back to his hotel room. By one o'clock in the morning, he was tired and started back to the hotel from the Teddy Bear, a small but lively bar on East Seventy-eighth Street and York Avenue.

With no taxi in sight, Julian decided to walk up to Second Avenue. It had turned colder, and the light topcoat he wore wasn't warm enough. He turned up the collar and dug his hands into his pockets.

Julian hadn't given much thought to the shooting that had taken place, though he had been deeply concerned about Guber and had phoned him from his father's apartment. The shooting, as far as he was concerned, was as much the fault of the police as it was of the man who pulled the trigger. He had told Detective Dalis that and much more during the hours they had been together after Levitas had been killed.

"I assure you," Julian had commented, "if the dead men were Wasps, you and your men would be patrolling every damn hallway on the street twenty-four hours a day. But because they're only Jews, you don't do anything."

"I'm sorry you feel that way," Dalis replied.

"I bet you are," Julian said with a mocking grin. . . .

At First Avenue, Julian waited for the light to change. As soon as it did, he crossed. Just as he reached the other side, he had the feeling that someone was behind him. He glanced over his shoulder. A man was beginning to cross.

Prickles raced down Julian's back and he quickened his pace. He was certain he was being followed.

Sunday was dreary and cold. Back at his father's apartment, he sifted through the bills and letters he had found during his first visit. He placed them in a large paper bag and dropped the bag into the incinerator, and returned to Manhattan by subway.

He napped for an hour and then went to the Metropolitan Museum of Art, now certain he was being followed. From time to time, he saw the man who was following him, though always from a considerable distance. Julian tried losing him in the museum. Very quickly a perverse game developed between them. Julian hurried through the galleries, sometimes doubling back in an effort to escape, while the man worked just as hard to stay close by. Julian was beginning to think that possibly two or three men were keeping watch over him.

By the time he returned to the hotel, Julian was nervous enough to phone his agent, Carl Bodwin, in Hollywood to have someone to talk to.

"When are you coming back here?" Carl asked.

"As soon as I wrap up my father's affairs," Julian answered.

"Listen, I have to give the studio people *High Terror*—"

"I'll have it on time," Julian told him. They spoke a few minutes longer; then Carl said he was going out.

Julian apologized for calling on a Sunday and hung up. He went down to the hotel restaurant for dinner and spent the rest of the evening in his room watching TV. Finished reading the paperback edition of James Jones's novel *Whistle,* he switched off the light and thought about the man who had followed him. He found himself wondering if the man might know something about Sam's diamonds.

After a while, Julian drifted off into a restive sleep, dreaming about Sam and the time Sam had taken him to the Diamond Exchange for the first time. He was wearing his blue *yarmulke.* The subway brought them near the exchange. Sam knew everyone. The men shook Sam's hand, saying, "A son you have, and we didn't even know you were married." They laughed and Sam nodded. He never laughed, though sometimes he smiled. Sam took him by the hand—

The phone rang, cutting into Julian's sleep.

He picked up the phone and cleared his throat. "Who is it?"

A woman said, "If you want to find your father's diamonds, be at the information booth on the main level of Grand Central Station at ten o'clock in the morning." The phone went dead.

Julian switched on the light and looked at his watch. It was 3 A.M.

He didn't fall asleep again until after five. He was up at eight, and by nine, he walked into Grand Central Station through the Vanderbilt Avenue entrance.

People were moving in almost every direction. There were at least a half-dozen men and women waiting near the information booth.

He was very early. He walked down the steps and moved to the right. The person who would contact him had the advantage of knowing what he looked like. Julian felt as if he were a character in one of his own suspense dramas. He was sweating, and there was a terrible tightness in his stomach.

He stopped at a coffee stand and asked for a glass of apple juice. As he drank, he looked toward the information booth. One by one, the people who were standing there left with the person for whom they had been waiting.

He paid for his juice, took his change and began to walk

around the information booth in a wide circle. No one he saw looked in the least bit suspicious, or if he allowed his imagination to run riot, everyone did.

At three minutes to ten, he walked directly to the information booth and stopped. He stood there pretending to be nonchalant, but always looking at the large clock on the wall above the corridor leading to Forty-second Street.

Ten o'clock came and went. He wiped his brow and sucked on an antacid tablet. Someone was making a fool out of him. Perhaps one of the men in the exchange to whom he had spoken about his father's diamonds had decided to tweak his nose?

He waited a full ten minutes before walking to the escalator. He was angry. Then suddenly he was bumped from behind.

"Why the fuck don't you watch yourself?" a man said.

Julian whirled around. Before he could speak, he received another bump.

"Asshole, wake up," the second man growled.

Too stunned to answer, Julian watched them race up the escalator. Furious, he went up after them. But when he reached the top, they were already gone. He stopped at the newsstand and bought a *Times* and a *News*. So far, the story of Levitas's murder had not appeared in the newspaper.

He passed a Zum Zum coffee shop and decided to stop for coffee and a piece of farmer's cake. He sat down, gave the waitress his order and, reaching into the pocket on the right side of his jacket for the small notebook he always carried, he found a white envelope. Immediately Julian understood why the men had bumped him. Probably the second man had planted the envelope. Julian tore open the envelope and took out the piece of paper. The message was formed out of words cut from a newspaper and Scotch-taped onto a piece of white typing paper.

Go back to California. Don't become involved in things you don't understand. You will not be warned again.

Julian refolded the piece of paper and replaced it in the envelope. He picked up the cup of coffee that had been set in front of him and began to drink. Whoever sent the message was trying to frighten him off. They either had his father's diamonds or knew where they were. They didn't want him to come after them. But that was exactly what he would do. If they thought they'd be able to frighten him off, they were wrong.

He set the coffee down and using his fork, chipped away at the farmer's cake. No longer nervous, he felt the knot in his stomach dissolve. He was very calm and more determined than ever to claim his father's diamonds. He'd continue to ask questions in the exchange, continue to make himself visible. Perhaps, if it was absolutely necessary, pretend to go into the business himself. But he was going to get what was his.

After he finished the coffee and cake, Julian picked up his newspapers and left the restaurant. He was going back to the exchange. In time, he was sure he would recover the diamonds. But he had to be patient; he had to be able to outwait men who were used to waiting; he had to be able to outfox men who had managed to outfox Hitler's death camps. And he would do it!

14

JACOB LEVITAS WAS BURIED on Monday in the New Montefiore Cemetery. Because he came from a large family and had many friends, there were twenty cars in the funeral procession. His mother, father and recently acquired wife were hysterical at the grave side. The wife, a good-looking woman in her early twenties, tried to throw herself into the grave, crying in a mixture of Hebrew and English that her life was over and it was only right she should be buried with her husband.

Guber, Borsky and Korditz stood together behind the relatives and close friends who ringed the grave. Guber had driven his two friends from the funeral home to the cemetery. He had purposely chosen to be the last car in the long cortege. The drive from Brooklyn to the cemetery in Farmingdale, Long Island, had seemed to take a long time.

When the casket was finally in the grave, each of the male mourners placed a shovelful of earth into the grave. Slowly the people returned to their cars.

Korditz sat in the rear. Driving out, Korditz had been in the front and Borsky in the back.

Guber waited until they were on the parkway before he said, "We have to begin again. A new shipment of diamonds and a new courier."

"How many times do you think you'll be able to get diamonds?" Korditz asked.

"If we get them now, I'll be satisfied. . . . I can't worry about what will happen later."

"I keep telling you," Korditz said, "that the Russians are playing with us. They've been taking on this end, but not delivering."

"How could it be the Russians?" Borsky asked. "They'd have to bring in gunmen and—"

"They're here already," Korditz said, leaning forward. "I'm telling you that sooner or later, the police will find out that the Russians have been doing the killing. They don't even have to have their own people do the killing. There are plenty of crazy people around who'd be willing to do the killing for them."

Guber swung out of a lane to pass a car. "Killings or not, we still have to send our goods to our contacts and bring Urishensky out. Afterward we'll worry about the others. But now Urishensky is in danger. If we don't get him out soon—well, he'll wind up in a mental institution or a prison in Siberia. We've got to bring him out."

Borsky clapped his hands and rubbed them together. "You're right, Max. But who are we going to send? Who will be crazy enough to want to go, now that Levitas has been shot?"

"So far the shooting has been played down by the newspapers. No one knows that Levitas had stones on him, thanks to Dalis."

"Not for sure they don't. But it won't take much for them to put two and two together. But answer me—who are we going to send?"

Guber eased into the left lane and stayed there.

"No one will go," Korditz said, lighting a cigar.

"Heckowitz's son," Guber said. "Julian will go."

"You're crazy," Borsky said. "He's not even a fit *kaddish* and you're going to send him to make a delivery. He'll piss in his pants the minute you mention it to him. Listen, he doesn't care about Jews."

"He's right," Korditz added. "Julian is a troublemaker. He's been asking questions in the exchange about Sam's diamonds. He's just no good. Tell him what's going on and he'll do something crazy with it—maybe put it on TV. All he is interested in is diamonds that don't exist."

"That's why he'll go," Guber said. "I thought the whole thing out. Julian is looking for Sam's diamonds."

"But Sam didn't leave any," Borsky commented.

"You know that. I know it. Korditz knows it. But Julian doesn't, or he doesn't want to believe it. Listen, we send him to one of our contacts abroad to find the diamonds. He'll carry a letter from us. Yes, only a letter. The diamonds will come later. We'll mail them to our people there. One contact will send him to another. Julian will still be looking for his father's diamonds. Somewhere along the line, the letter will become a packet, and he'll make the final delivery of the packet to the right party."

Korditz puffed on his cigar. "But that's good for only one shipment."

"One is better than none," Guber answered.

"I'm against it," Borsky said. "I don't care for Julian. I don't care for him at all. He's still wet behind the ears."

"He was in Vietnam with the marines," Guber replied. "From what Sam could read between the lines of the letters Julian sent, he saw some heavy fighting. He'll be able to take care of himself. I'm sure of it."

"And just how do you think you're going to convince him to go?" Borsky asked.

"I won't convince him of anything. He'll go because he's Sam's son and he mistakenly believes the diamonds will make up for the father he didn't have. He will go," Guber said with emotion, "because he understands hardly anything about his father and he's foolish enough to think he knows everything about him."

Neither Borsky nor Korditz said anything.

Guber guided the car on to the Belt Parkway. He looked down at his speedometer and slowed from sixty-five to fifty-five. A 747 flew low over the highway and came in for a landing at Kennedy. The roar of its jet engines seemed to engulf the car.

"And what if Julian should get killed?" Korditz asked when the sound lessened.

"Then we'll send another. We'll have to find someone else," Guber answered harshly. He was annoyed at the stupidity of the questions. Julian was their best bet, and they couldn't see it. "Is it agreed that Julian goes?" he asked.

Reluctantly, Borsky and Korditz assented.

"After this business is over," Guber said, "I'm going on vacation. Maybe down to Florida."

"Good idea," Borsky told him.

"I was thinking the same thing myself," Korditz said. "But I'd go to Spain, or maybe southern France."

Borsky and Korditz became involved in a discussion about the merits of visiting Spain or France. Guber looked out to his left at Jamaica Bay. The water was a grayish blue, and there was just enough wind to raise small waves that glistened in the sun. He moved his right hand over his chin and said, "Julian ran into one of Sam's friends from Paris. He's a dealer, Saul Kass. Did Sam ever mention Kass to either of you?"

"Something isn't kosher," Korditz responded. "Sam didn't deal with anyone in Paris for the last few years."

"Then why would Kass say that he had?" Borsky questioned.

"Because someone or some group wants to know what Sam was doing," Guber replied sharply.

"And someone or some group already knows enough about what we're doing to kill several of our friends and take the diamonds from them," Korditz said.

Guber shrugged but didn't answer; Korditz was right.

15

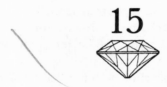

FOURNIER SAT AT A TABLE in a small café off the Place de l'Alma. Through the window, he could see the steps leading to the Métro station. He had arranged to meet an American by the name of Peter Childs, a representative of several American literary agents who also had connections with the CIA.

Childs had been with the OSS during World War II and had been parachuted into France a year prior to the invasion of June 6, 1944. He had spent that year working with the Maquis, and he had never left French soil since.

While he waited, Fournier took a sip of white wine. He knew what he was about to do would be considered highly irregular by his superiors, but so would his relationship to Shulamith. The momentary thought of her sent a surge of warmth through his groin. He was falling in love with her, though he was fully aware of the problems that most certainly would arise. He hoped when that time came, his organization and hers would understand the situation and allow them to make their own decisions, allow them to live their own lives. . . .

A number of people were emerging from the Métro. Several stopped at the news kiosk and bought a late edition of *Le Monde,* but most hurried away, buttoning their coats against the cold.

Fournier over the past years had had several reasons to meet with Childs. All the meetings had been authorized by his superiors at the Service de Documentation Extérieure et de Contre Espionnage. Because of these contacts, a mutual respect had grown up between them. Every few weeks, they'd meet for dinner or manage to go to the theater together. Since both were bachelors, the arrangements for an evening together were usually made on the spur of the moment. Though Childs was almost sixty, Fournier never considered him old, and where women were concerned Childs acted like a much younger man.

Fournier saw Childs the moment he came up from the Métro. Knowing his friend liked apple brandy, Fournier summoned the waiter and ordered a glass. He had asked Childs to meet him without specifying the reason.

Childs entered the café. He saw Fournier and immediately went to the table. A heavyset man with bright brown eyes, graying hair and a somewhat boyish face, he shook hands with Fournier and said, "The Métro was terribly crowded." He took off his coat and hung it on the coat hanger near the table. Then he sat down, picked up his glass of brandy, smiled and toasted Fournier's health. "I really didn't expect to hear from you so soon. We went out to dinner about three weeks ago, or was it longer? I've been so busy these past few weeks that I've lost track of time."

"It was three weeks ago," Fournier said with a smile.

"Well, it's always a pleasure to see you."

Fournier nodded.

"Why did you tell me to come by Métro when I could have taken a cab here and spared myself the crush of—"

"There would be less chance of your being followed on the Métro."

Childs raised his eyebrows. "You didn't tell me this was business."

"Nothing official."

"But nonetheless business?"

Fournier nodded. "Do you recall meeting Sam Heckowitz?"

"The Jewish diamond dealer?"

"Yes," Fournier answered. He hesitated for a few moments, using the time to weigh carefully what he was going to say. Then he said, "I need the help of some of your friends on a personal matter. I'm here without the authority of the SDECE."

Childs drank his brandy and ordered another.

"Sam Heckowitz was my father. Please don't ask me to go into details. The story is too long and too involved. I called him in New York and was told he had died of a heart attack."

"And you don't believe it?" Childs asked.

"That's right," Fournier answered. "Sam didn't have a history of heart trouble."

"But you can get the doctor's report without my help," Childs said, sipping at the new glass of brandy. "Besides, a man of his years might have no history of heart trouble and then—well, it happens."

"That's a possibility."

"What makes you think it didn't happen that way?"

Fournier ran the forefinger of his right hand over the checkered tablecloth. "Sam was involved in the exchange of Jews for diamonds."

Childs put his glass of brandy down and shifted his position.

"The KGB was onto him. . . . Word was passed to them from a source in Israel. So far, this source can't be traced."

Childs leaned forward, resting his elbows on the table. "You think one of their people might have been responsible for Sam's—I mean your father's—death?"

"Heart attacks can be induced," Fournier said.

"Do you want to give me any details about the exchange operation?"

Fournier slowly shook his head. "I can't."

"And I suppose you don't want me to reveal your connection to it?"

"It would be better if you didn't," Fournier replied.

"I'll pass the word along," Childs said. "But you know it would be better, Paul, if I had something concrete to place in the conduit."

Fournier picked up his wine. "The KGB agent heading the investigation is named Sergei Dimetrov. He is presently in New York."

"That should do it," Childs said. "That should send them running all over New York." He extended his hand across the table and took hold of Fournier's. "Someday I might come to you with something personal."

"If I could help, you know I would."

"Yes, I know that," Childs answered. "I know you're a man of honor."

16

"YOU MIGHT AS WELL call me Saul," Kass said. " 'Kass' sounds so formal."

Julian nodded and raised his martini glass. "All right, Saul it'll be." He looked around and said, "During Prohibition, this was a speakeasy."

"And now it's the Slate," Kass said, reading the name of the restaurant from the menu. "Tell me what you would recommend here."

"The roast beef used to be very good. I always ordered

an end cut. And the steaks are supposed to be excellent."

"I'll try the roast beef," Kass said, taking a swallow of scotch. He asked whether the bas reliefs on the wall had any particular significance.

"None that I can think of," Julian answered.

"It's a comfortable place," Kass said. "I much prefer to have the dining area separated from the bar."

Each had another drink, and then Julian ordered for the two of them, starting with fresh clams on the half-shell for an appetizer. French onion soup and roast beef. After each dish, he glanced at Kass to see if he approved.

"I would like my roast beef slightly rare," Kass interjected. "And I think a bottle of red wine would go well with the main course. A red Bordeaux would be fine."

Julian nodded and when the waitress left, he said, "I still can't get myself to eat meat any way but well done. Part of what I call the Jewish cooking syndrome. It was either fried or well done, just this side of being burnt."

"I don't understand."

"Neither do I," Julian said. "I think it must have had something to do with ideas of cleanliness, because it sure as hell couldn't have anything to do with the way the food tasted. Didn't your parents, or rather your mother, prepare food that way?"

Kass suddenly realized he could very easily find himself in great difficulty. The KGB didn't include Jewish cooking in their training. Stalling for more time to think, he took another drink of scotch, followed by water. Then he said, "As a Frenchman, I managed to escape what you refer to as the Jewish cooking syndrome."

"I was seventeen before I could get myself to eat ham without thinking God would strike me dead on the spot."

"My upbringing wasn't quite as rigid as all that." He searched for a beginning to another subject. The longer they continued to speak about Jewish cooking, the greater his danger.

But Julian unknowingly came to his rescue. "Did you manage to buy any stones?" he asked.

Kass smiled broadly. "Several excellent ones. I think I will be able to make a good profit on them."

"That's what it's all about, I guess," Julian answered wearily.

"A note of sarcasm? You don't approve of making money?"

"Only if—I'm sorry," Julian said. "Money was my father's god. That's all he was really interested in." Again, Julian apologized. "You knew him in a business way. I'm sure he was different in the house and out of it. The men who knew him in the Diamond Exchange have nothing but praise for him. And Guber, Borsky and Korditz probably think he was a saint. He wasn't. He was an isolated man, perhaps a lonely man. But who could get close enough to know? And he was most certainly not in love with my mother. Would you believe that I still can't remember them carrying on a conversation? I mean a real one. They spoke, but only about the essentials. The truth is, though she died of cancer, she would have withered away anyway if she had continued to live with him."

Kass was embarrassed. He had not expected Julian to be so frank. His own relationship with his father was so completely different that he was having difficulty understanding Julian's resentment. Kass loved his father not because he was his father, but because he realized he was a very special man. Once a scholar, a professor of philosophy at the Moscow University; then a soldier in the lines defending Moscow, later, an officer, he became a general by the end of the war. And through it all, he had never lost his sense of humanity, his love for his wife and son.

"Even in dying," Julian complained, "Sam couldn't make it easy. Look at this." He took out the note that had been put in his jacket pocket. "Now you tell me if he didn't leave diamonds."

Kass read the note, and as he passed it back to Julian, the waitress came with the two orders of clams.

"It would seem from the note," Kass told him, "that someone was trying to discourage you from—"

"They made a mistake," Julian said angrily. "They made a fucking mistake. I might have given it up after another day or two. But now I'm absolutely certain that someone has my father's goods, and I'm going to get them."

Kass finished his clams before responding. "Even if you find out who had them, he might not be willing to give them up without a fight. It could be ugly, and it could be dangerous."

"I'm already being followed."

"It is not inconceivable that someone might try to kill you. Another jeweler was shot down on Friday."

"Different situation," Julian said, wiping his mouth with the napkin. "I was there. . . . Well, not on the same floor. I was with Max Guber two floors below when we heard the shots. Levitas was dead when we got there. He took three rounds."

"The men in the exchange are reluctant to speak about the killings. They're frightened."

"Can't blame them," Julian commented. "They know it's the work of professionals."

"What makes you say that?"

"None of the men who were killed had stones on them. They were murdered and robbed, or to put it another way, they were murdered in order to be robbed."

"The Mafia?"

"Maybe. But whoever it is, it's someone who knows which men to hit, when to hit them and where."

The waitress poured a small amount of wine into a stem glass and handed it to Kass. He tasted it and nodded approvingly.

"Could the person who has your father's goods have some connection with the Mafia?" Kass asked when the waitress left the table.

"Possibly, but not probably."

Kass accepted the answer without comment. There was a glaring similarity between the men who had been murdered and the sudden death of Julian's father. None of them had been found with diamonds on their persons, and they should have had a few stones on them. Suddenly the possibility that Sam Heckowitz hadn't died of a heart attack occurred to him. If he hadn't—if he too had been murdered—why was it being covered up? Those questions would eventually have to be answered if Julian hoped to find his father's diamonds. But at this point, Julian appeared to be totally ignorant.

They were halfway through the main course when Julian said, "I know it must sound as if I'm crying over spilled milk, so to speak, when I talk about Sam, but I wanted you to know why I want his diamonds. I don't need the money they'd bring. But if I recover them, I'm going to sell the lot and have myself one helluva good time, though I'll give half of it away to some charity or other in my father's name. But I want to do what he never did—enjoy it!"

"I think I can understand that," Kass lied politely. He liked Julian and he felt sorry for him. Though Julian was a man, he was still a boy in regard to Sam. He was making a mistake if he thought the diamonds would really be a substitute for the kind of father he had so desperately wanted but had never had. Clearly his greed stemmed from a profound confusion.

"I'll tell you one more thing about Sam," Julian said, pointing a fork at Kass. "I was in Nam, with the First Marine Division. We fought against the North Vietnamese Regulars. My battalion took on the North Vietnamese Sixty-fifth Infantry, which had Russian advisors. But even without them, they would have been good. We slugged it out for the better part of a half-year in the highlands. Two of my best buddies were blown away in front of me. Well, my time was up, and I came home. One night I got the shakes. I mean, I thought I was going to fall apart. I got up and dressed. I had to get out of the house. Sam heard me. He came out of his room just as I reached the door. He wanted to know where I was going. I told him I had to get out. I said I had the shakes and needed to walk. He told me to go back to sleep. He said I was making a mountain out of a molehill. I told him he didn't know what the fuck he was talking about. I told him that some part of me had died out there in Nam, some part of what it meant to be a human being no longer existed. I told him I had seen my friends killed. And all he could tell me was to go back to bed. He said I was making too much of it, much too much. I lost my temper and told him he was a stupid son-of-a-bitch who couldn't see that his son was on the verge of a crack-up. And I left. I went on a two-day drunk. Sam couldn't admit that anyone who was not in the camps could suffer; Sam just didn't understand. He didn't want to understand."

"Perhaps," Kass suggested after a pause of several minutes, "he couldn't let himself be moved or he would lose control of his emotions. Your pain might have increased his, and he couldn't help you in any other way than he had. Sometimes it's like that."

Julian shrugged. "In his head, Sam never got out of Auschwitz, or maybe he was guilty for having gotten out. I've seen men like that after a firefight."

"Were you one?" Kass asked.

"No," Julian answered quietly. "I wanted to live. I was glad to be alive even after my friends were killed."

Kass sighed and took a long drink of wine. It was hard to believe that several years before, ten thousand miles away from where they now were, they had been enemies locked in a life-and-death struggle for one of the hills overlooking a place called the Ashow Valley. . . .

The waitress cleared the table and asked if they wanted dessert. Neither did, but they asked for coffee.

"I should think," Kass said after a few moments of silence, "that your father's friends—what are their names again?"

"Max Guber, Chiam Borsky and Marek Korditz. Max was in Auschwitz with Sam; they came from the same town—Bialystok."

"They should be able to help you find your father's diamonds," Kass said.

Julian shrugged. "So far they haven't even tried. But maybe that'll change when I show them the note."

"Perhaps I can help," Kass offered. "After all, I did business with your father, though I didn't know him very well."

"Thanks. Anything you might do will be appreciated. And thanks for listening to me sound off about my father. The note and the fact that I'm being followed got to me more than I realized. And all of it could have been avoided if Sam had put down in writing what he had and with whom he had left it. But that was not like Sam. Everything with him had to be a secret."

17

At 11:30 P.M., Dimetrov signed into the Soviet mission on East Sixty-seventh Street and went straight to the communications room. His meeting with Julian had provided him with the names of the men who had been closest to Samuel Heckowitz. Now he needed whatever information was available on each of them. From Julian, he had already learned that Guber and Heckowitz had not only come from the same town, Bialystok, but that the two had been in Auschwitz together. The relationship between Sam, Borsky and Korditz apparently had come about more recently.

Before reaching the communications room, he passed through several different doors, showed his ID card to a guard at each of them and before he actually entered the classified area, he signed another register, noting the time, his general ID number and then his specific number that gave him access to areas considered by the KGB to be under maximum security. Before the steel door was finally opened, he was frisked and relieved of the snub-nose .38 he wore strapped to his right leg.

The sealed communications room was manned twenty-four hours a day in three-hour shifts by a team of six: two radio operators, two code clerks and two high-speed teletype operators. To protect the electronic equipment, the room was climatically controlled to maintain a temperature of 20 degrees Centigrade, with a humidity factor of 36 degrees.

Dimetrov picked up a message form and filled it out.

First Chief Detective, Information Center, HQ., 2 Dzerzhinsky Square, Moscow. Code 24. Return information for sender only.

      Subject: Invest. under sender's jurisdiction.

    Request: Dossier on Max Guber. Former inmate of Auschwitz. Cross-check with file on Samuel Heckowitz.

          Dossier on Chiam Borsky. Background unavailable. Dossier on Marek Korditz. Background unavailable. All specifics.

                    Maj. Sergei Dimetrov

"Send this immediately," he said to the code clerk, a young woman with a round face and lovely green eyes. "I will be back sometime tomorrow for the answer."

"Yes, major," she answered. "If the computers in Moscow are on the line, the information could be back here within an hour."

"Tomorrow will do," Dimetrov answered.

She went to her desk, and using an electronic coding device, immediately began to transcribe the message into code.

Dimetrov left the communications center, retrieved his weapon and passed through the various doors that eventually led to the main corridors. He was tired and somewhat depressed, though there wasn't any reason for him to feel that way. He should have felt some slight satisfaction now that he had the names of Heckowitz's closest friends, and no doubt his associates, in the trading of Jews for diamonds.

The questions that had posed themselves to Dimetrov

while he was with Julian nettled him. That Heckowitz might have been murdered could mean that someone else had become aware of the KGB's interest in the operation and wanted to silence him—the single most important source of information about the illicit trade. It could just as easily have no connection to his investigation. Heckowitz could have been murdered for his diamonds. Murder and diamonds always went hand in hand.

Dimetrov entered the visitors' area of the mission and was about to leave the building when he saw Marrosov coming toward him. He had wanted to have a few words with Marrosov and had been too busy during the day to go to the mission. They shook hands.

Marrosov told him he was on his way to the compound at Lake Success where he and his family lived. "I would have been home hours ago," he explained, "but the day after tomorrow several of our doctors are coming to address the symposium here in the city on new surgical techniques. We had to arrange for their security."

"I will not waste words, comrade," Dimetrov said curtly. "I neither need nor enjoy the security you've given me. I do not want to see either that black Cadillac again or anyone from your staff unless I specifically request that individual."

Marrosov flushed.

"Even in New York traffic, your car was not difficult to spot."

"Believe me, I did it for your benefit. New York is a dangerous—"

Dimetrov shook his head. "Don't do it again," he said tersely.

Marrosov was about to answer, but Dimetrov waved him silent. He turned and hurriedly left the building, knowing he had not endeared himself to the area chief. He was certain by this time that Marrosov must have a very good idea of why he was there. If he didn't, he soon would.

Dimetrov sighed. His breath steamed in the cold December air. When he reached Fifth Avenue, he turned south toward the Plaza.

18

ON WEDNESDAY MORNING under a gray sky, Fournier and Shulamith drove toward Chartres from Paris on highway N-36. A light snow had fallen the previous evening. The highway was wet and slippery, but the fields on either side looked as if they had been dusted with fine sugar.

"I asked my American friends to check into Sam's death," Fournier said, glancing at Shulamith.

She shifted slightly.

"Sam didn't have heart trouble," he said. "He may have been killed."

"That doesn't mean he couldn't have a heart attack."

Fournier nodded. "I want to be sure. Better let your people know what I did. I don't want it to come as a surprise when they find out, as no doubt they will."

"I'll tell them," she answered.

Fournier changed lanes to pass a tandem truck and then swung back into the right lane. "I called my mother and told her you were coming with me."

"Did she mind?"

Fournier reached over and squeezed Shulamith's knee. "Only that I didn't bring you out sooner."

"But I didn't even know you until—" She stopped and began to laugh. "Your mother really didn't say that, did she?"

"Not really. But she did say it was about time I brought my woman to meet her."

"Am I your woman?" she asked, placing her hand over his.

He nodded. "I'd like to think so."

"Paul, my people know about us. Do yours?"

"Not yet," he answered. "Are you in trouble?"

"No," she answered, shaking her head. "I was simply told by Avigeor—he was the young man at the wheel of the car the other night—that he knows we're lovers." She leaned against him. "I think it will be all right for the time being."

Fournier agreed. He was concerned about the reaction his own people would have when they discovered he was having an affair with an Israeli agent. He doubted if his chief would be as noncommittal.

For the better part of a half-hour, neither spoke. Then suddenly they came in sight of the massive rock outcropping on which the town and cathedral of Chartres stood. "The snow makes it seem unreal," Shulamith said, breaking the silence between them.

"No matter when you see it," Fournier responded, "it seems that way. In the summer, it seems to burst out of the green of the trees."

The closer they came to the large hill on which the cathedral stood, the more defined its twin Romanesque towers became. The smaller one, Fournier remarked, was considered to be an example of perfect architecture. "One of the few in the world," he concluded.

"I'm impressed," she said. Then after a few moments of silence, she asked, "Does your mother know about Sam?"

"I think she senses something is wrong," Fournier answered. "I seldom visit on a weekday."

"We could have come here on the weekend."

"No," he said. "I thought she should know."

"Poor woman," Shulamith commented softly.

Fournier turned up a winding road that brought them to the square in front of the cathedral. Many tourists waited on the steps for the guide to lead them inside. Several were in the middle of the square, photographing the huge portal doors and the towers.

Fournier guided the car down a narrow, cobblestone street and came to a halt in front of a small house with a weather-beaten fence around it. The door to the house opened, framing a slight woman with beautiful gray hair. Fournier led Shulamith through the gate.

"Hurry, hurry," his mother called, "or I will freeze to death."

Fournier released Shulamith's hand and went to his mother, embracing her warmly; then, stepping back, he said, "This is my mother, Shulamith."

"And that is your Shulamith," Mme. Fournier laughed, reaching out for Shulamith's hands. "You must call me Francine." She kissed the young woman on both cheeks. "Come inside and have some coffee."

The three of them moved into a small living room, where a good fire was blazing in an old stone hearth. Fournier took Shulamith's coat and said, "Make yourself comfortable." His mother went into the kitchen and returned a short while later with a tray of cookies. "I baked them this morning," she said. "Paul, come and help me with the coffee."

"I'll help," Shulamith volunteered.

The two women disappeared into the kitchen, leaving Fournier alone. He stood in front of the fireplace and watched the flames chew into what was left of the center portion of a log. Within moments, it was gone, and the two remaining pieces crashed to the floor of the hearth, sending up a shower of sparks.

Shulamith came from the kitchen, carrying a tray with cups and saucers on it. She set it down on a small, highly polished coffee table. Mme. Fournier brought a carafe of coffee and placed it on an old brass trivet, which she took from the mantle above the fireplace. Fournier poured the coffee.

"You said," Mme. Fournier said, looking at her son, "that you had something to tell me . . . I'm waiting to be told."

Fournier glanced at Shulamith.

"Are the two of you married?" Mme. Fournier asked.

"No, mother," Fournier answered. "Perhaps that will come."

Shulamith felt the color rise in her cheeks.

"I would like that, Paul," Mme. Fournier said. "Yes, I think I would like that, Shulamith."

"Thank you," Shulamith replied. "I think I would like it too."

"Well, now that that's almost settled," she laughed, "what else is there?"

Fournier set his saucer and cup down on the tray. During the last few days, he had tested many ways of telling her about Sam. But now that the moment arrived, he said, "My father is dead." It was simple and direct and to the point.

Mme. Fournier uttered a small gasp and for a few moments seemed unable to decide what to do with the cup and saucer she was holding. Then she put them down on the tray and said, "I had the feeling that something had happened to him."

"He died of a heart attack in New York," Fournier said.

Mme. Fournier turned to Shulamith. "Did you know him?" she asked. There were tears in her eyes and a halting quality in her speech.

"Only by reputation."

Mme. Fournier nodded and, looking at her son, she said, "We did not marry for all sorts of reasons. Some were his and others were mine. Years later, when he was already married and the father of another son, we realized we had stupidly contrived to cheat ourselves of the happiness we should have had. Sam couldn't forget he was a Jew, and I didn't want to remember I was once a Catholic or become what he was. I didn't want, and still don't, either God or religion in any form. But Sam couldn't get away from either. He fought God, but loved Him. He himself didn't follow the religion, but he married a woman who did and made sure the son he had with her followed it until the boy revolted." She nodded, as if she had warned Sam before the difficulty with his son had started. "He loved you, Paul, and he loved his other son, Julian. From you he expected nothing but got everything. From Julian he expected everything and got nothing. He often said God made it happen that way just to be able to laugh at him. But he never forgot us. He supported two families. He was a very good man."

"He was a good father," Fournier said, standing beside his mother and putting his hand on her shoulder.

"I suppose I should have told you he was your father, but—"

"I think I've always known. But now that I do know, I'm glad it was him, very glad."

Mme. Fournier took hold of her son's hand and kissed the back of it. "For me, there was never any other man," she said softly. "I shall miss him very much, very much." She pressed her face against his arm and wept quietly.

With his free hand, Fournier stroked his mother's head. "If it would please you," he said, "I'll take his name."

She shrugged. "I don't think he would have expected you to do that. But you do whatever pleases you."

Fournier turned to Shulamith, who moved slightly forward and offered to pour hot coffee into Francine's cup.

"No, thank you," she said, drawing her shawl more tightly around her narrow shoulders. She stood up and, dabbing at her eyes with a handkerchief, she told Fournier, "I have something to show you. Sam gave it to me the last time he was here. I'll bring it down." Then to Shulamith she said, "Please excuse me."

"There's nothing to excuse."

Mme. Fournier left the living room and climbed the steps leading to the upper story of the house.

"She's a wonderful woman," Shulamith said in a low voice.

"Yes," Fournier agreed with pride, "she certainly is."

"Do you think Sam loved her as much as she loved Sam?"

"As much, if love can be measured. He was happy when he was with her, which counted for something, don't you think?"

"Yes."

Mme. Fournier returned, carrying a small, black metal box, which she handed to Paul. "Here's the key. He told me to open it if anything should happen to him, and to keep what I found."

"Sam never told you what was in it?" he asked. He placed the metal box on the mantel and unlocked it.

She shook her head.

Fournier opened the box. He took a deep breath. "I don't believe this," he said quietly.

"Well, what's in it?" Mme. Fournier asked.

"Look for yourself," he answered, bringing the box down to her eye level.

"Diamonds!" she exclaimed.

He tilted the box toward Shulamith.

"My God," she exclaimed, "there must be a small fortune there!"

"He never said a word about them. He told me to open the box if anything should happen to him and to keep whatever I found," Mme. Fournier repeated. "I always thought it was money, and maybe some stocks and bonds. But I never thought he'd leave diamonds."

It was several minutes before any of them spoke.

"Have you any scotch in the house?" Fournier asked, ending the silence.

"There's a bottle of cognac in the sideboard against the wall." She pointed across the room.

"Do either of you want a drink?" he asked, but the two women declined.

Fournier poured himself a whiskey glassful and bolted it down.

"We'll have to contact Julian," Mme. Fournier said. "He must have his share of this. I am certain Sam expected—"

"Julian has no idea we exist," Fournier cut in. "Sam said Julian wouldn't have been able to understand his father's double life. Besides, I am sure Sam left as much, if not more, to Julian."

"Can you find out?" she asked, looking up at him.

Fournier nodded. She seldom asked him to do anything for her, especially if it meant his using the unique privileges of his office. She knew of his connections to intelligence groups and preferred not to discuss them.

"If Sam has left something to Julian," Mme. Fournier

said, "I will not give him anything. But if he wasn't left anything, then half of what is in the box is his. Do you agree?"

"Yes, mother."

"Well, now I think I could use another cup of hot coffee," Mme. Fournier said.

"I'll pour it," Shulamith offered.

"Paul," Mme. Fournier said, "don't wait too long to marry this woman. I like her very much."

Shulamith blushed again.

19

DETECTIVE ANTHONY DALIS sat alongside Guber's desk, wearing a loose-fitting raincoat. He was a swarthy looking man with very black eyes and beetle brows. His black hair was starting to recede on his forehead, giving him the beginning of a widow's peak. A heavy smoker, two fingers of his right hand were stained yellow by the nicotine. "How well did you know Levitas?" he asked, letting smoke rush out of his nostrils.

"He wasn't what you'd call a personal friend," Guber said, "though we sometimes ate lunch together."

"Did you do much business with him?"

"Some."

"Was he a good businessman?"

Guber leaned forward. Dalis's question bothered him. "He knew what he was doing."

Dalis reached over the desk and stubbed out his cigarette in the ashtray. "Monday afternoon, about four thirty, I received a call at headquarters from some guy with a heavy European accent. Maybe he was German, maybe Polish, I couldn't tell which. Anyway, he says the police might learn something if they picked up two Mafia soldiers from the Spinelli family and asked them about Levitas."

"Gangsters?"

Dalis nodded. "I had them picked up. They told me that Levitas was a fence for them."

Guber leaned back; he was surprised. Levitas didn't seem the kind of man who played with fire.

"Now get this—Sam Heckowitz also had business dealings with the Mafia. He fenced some stuff for them, but concentrated mainly on smuggling diamonds into the country. How does that grab you?"

Guber heaved a deep sigh. "Nothing Sam ever did would surprise me. A man like Sam was capable of anything."

"And Levitas, was he too capable of anything?" Dalis asked, taking another cigarette from a soft pack and lighting it.

Guber shook his head. "Levitas should have known better than to become involved with gangsters."

Dalis let the cigarette dangle from the side of his mouth. Drawing his beetle brows together in a frown, he said, "There's a possibility Levitas was shot by people from the mob. He might have given one or two of them a bad deal, and they decided to cut their losses."

"How could the Mafia be responsible for the killings in Paris, London and East Germany?"

"Anything is possible with the kind of organization and money they have."

"I just don't know," Guber said with a shrug.

Dalis removed the cigarette from the side of his mouth and held it between his stained fingers. "Heckowitz was a friend of yours, wasn't he?"

"Yes. We knew each other from the time we were boys. We lived in the same town and later spent several years in Auschwitz together."

"How much do you know about his business connections?"

Guber placed his elbows on the desk and looked straight at Dalis. "I never asked Sam who he did business with, and he never asked me."

"The mob may have taken Sam out too," Dalis said. "Heart attacks can be induced."

The phone on Guber's desk rang. He answered it, listened for a moment and then said, "Send him in." He put the phone down. "Sam's son is here."

A moment later the door opened and Julian entered. Dalis made a half-turn toward the door. Julian stopped and looked questioningly at Guber, who motioned him in, explaining, "It's all right. Detective Dalis and I were having a friendly discussion."

"I was telling Mr. Guber about some interesting connections," Dalis said.

Julian dropped his coat on the couch. He sat down warily in the easy chair diagonally across from Guber, remembering that his meeting with Dalis after Levitas's murder had ended with a sarcastic exchange.

"I hear you've been asking questions in the exchange about your father's diamonds," Dalis commented, swiveling his body partially toward Julian. "I can tell you now, you're not going to get any information from the dealers."

Julian's heart suddenly began to thump in anger.

"I was just talking to Mr. Guber about your father. Did he ever speak to you about his business?"

"There wasn't much communication between us," Julian answered, suddenly sweating.

Dalis nodded, took a deep drag on his cigarette and blew a great deal of smoke out of his nose before he said, "Your father had many friends. He knew men from all walks of life, including a couple of junior Mafiosi."

"So what?" Julian commented. "I don't know why you think my father's friends are strange, even if they are Italian."

Dalis smiled. "You stuck that one in fast, didn't you?" Julian nodded.

"Suppose I tell you," Dalis said, "that your father was a fence for the Mafia and did some smuggling for them."

Julian started to stand, then abruptly changed his mind. He looked at Guber. "Was he?" he asked.

"Sam was a very strange man. I never asked him questions about what he did."

Dalis stood up. "I don't know yet if the mob was responsible for the killings, but it sure as hell looks that way from where I sit. If anything else comes up, I'll let you know." He reached across the desk and shook hands with Guber. He walked past Julian, but when he reached the door, he said, "I'll like to know if you find your father's stones."

"Sure," Julian answered. "But don't wait for my call."

Dalis shrugged, opened the door and left the office.

"If I had known he was here," Julian told Guber, as soon as the door closed behind Dalis, "I wouldn't have come. He bothers the shit out of me."

"So I've noticed."

Julian moved into the chair occupied by Dalis. "Sam just couldn't play it straight," he commented angrily. "He had to get involved with—"

"Sam did what he had to do," Guber said sharply, "without making excuses to anyone. He was a *mentsh*—a man who looked to no one and expected nothing from anyone."

"Goddamn it, you're always apologizing for him. I'm being followed, and I want you to look at this. If Sam hadn't been such a damn secretive bastard, this wouldn't have happened." He reached into his pocket and pulled out the note. "That's as much Sam's doing as the man who sent it."

Guber read the note, shook his head, but said nothing.

"Some of his gangster friends have his stones and want to keep me away from them."

Guber sat back and took time to unwrap and light a cigar. He wanted to tease Julian a bit, put the advantage on his side.

"I tell you," Julian railed, "Sam just didn't know how to do anything straight and simple. It always had to be circuitous. Always—"

"I didn't ask you here to discuss Sam," Guber said, cutting Julian short. "I have something to tell you."

"I'm listening," Julian answered, breathing hard. He was full of anger.

"There is a man—Saul Lublin—in Amsterdam, who might have what you're looking for."

"Sam's goods?"

"Possibly."

"Why didn't you tell me this before?" Julian asked, leaning forward.

"Because," Guber answered, "I didn't want to."

"I don't understand."

"I didn't think you were worthy of anything Sam might have left you. You're not much of a *kaddish.*" Guber puffed on his cigar.

Julian remained silent for several moments He didn't want to vent his anger at Guber and lose the only chance he might have to claim his father's diamonds. "What made you change your mind?"

"I thought about it and decided that maybe Sam wasn't much of a father."

"So you figured I deserved something by way of compensation, eh?"

"That's it," Guber lied.

"I appreciate it. You give me this Lublin's address, and I'll write to him."

"He won't answer you," Guber said. "You will have to go there, meet him and prove you're Sam's son."

"You write and tell him who I am."

Guber shook his head. "It must be face to face between you and Lublin. He might want a fee."

"What for?" Julian asked, afraid that Lublin might demand a percentage.

"How do I know? Either you want to go, or you don't. It's not a very complicated question."

"I have a script to do. I've got to get back to the Coast."

"That's your problem," Guber said. "I'm giving you the one lead I have. You can act on it or not. If you want what you think you want, you'll go. If not, forget it."

"I'll think about it."

"You do that."

Julian got to his feet, walked over to the couch and picked up his coat. Though he knew he would go to Amsterdam, he didn't want to give Guber the satisfaction of telling him. "I'll let you know what I decide to do," he said.

Guber waved.

Julian left the office, said good-bye to Rose and went out to the elevator. When he got back to the hotel, he'd have to call his agent and tell him that he was going to Amsterdam for a few days.

20

SNOW BEGAN TO FALL. The flakes were very large and melted as soon as they touched any surface. The streets were crowded. Julian walked up Sixth Avenue toward Central Park, disturbed by what Dalis had told him. That his father had been involved with the Mafia gave him a peculiar feeling of shame, as if in some mysterious way, he had taken part in the illicit dealings. It was guilt by consanguinity. Some of Sam's filth had rubbed off on him.

Julian's anger increased. At Fifty-sixth Street, he turned east and went as far as Third Avenue, where he found a small bar. Though it was crowded with lunchtime drinkers, he managed to find a place for himself off to one side. He ordered a double shot of Chivas. Oblivious to the hubbub around him, he continued to smolder.

Halfway through his drink, it occurred to Julian that Sam just might have left his goods with someone in the Mafia or connected to it. There must be other dealers in the exchange who did business with the mob.

Paying and leaving a tip, he went out into the street again. The snow was still falling, and it was colder. Here and there patches of white were beginning to gather on the tops of signs, grillwork and even along the sidewalk close to the sides of the buildings.

He walked south along Third Avenue. He wanted to find out who in the Mafia his father had dealt with. There was just the chance that the individual would tell him he had Sam's goods and there was no chance of getting it. At least if he knew that, he wouldn't have to go running off to Amsterdam. Julian returned to his hotel room and phoned Sal Calluchie's father at the Calluchie Private Car Service in Brooklyn. The man was pleased to hear from Julian; the snapshot of him and his son in their army fatigues sat on his desk.

After the greetings and the small talk, Julian said, "Sal once told me you and your brother have very interesting friends." Calluchie was silent.

Julian could hear the man breathing. "I have a problem your friends might be able to help me solve," he said, choosing his words very carefully. "Sal said if I ever need help, I should ask you."

"Is someone trying to hurt you?" Calluchie asked, his voice suddenly going hard. "If it's that—"

"It's not exactly that," Julian said, dropping down on the bed and lying back against the headboard.

"You've got to tell me more," Calluchie said.

Julian took a deep breath and then explained the events of the last few days. "My father must have left some diamonds with one of his friends," Julian said, suddenly realizing he must sound like a shit to Calluchie. He added, "I only want what is rightfully mine."

"I understand."

"When Detective Dalis told me about my father's business dealings," Julian said, "I thought you might be able to help me."

"You want me to find out who did business with your father?"

"Yes. And I want you to set up a meeting," Julian answered. "I want to know more about my father's dealings."

"Give me your number." Julian read it off the telephone. "You stay right there for a few minutes," Calluchie said. "I'll be back to you."

"Thanks."

"You were Sal's buddy," Calluchie answered in a tight voice. "That's good enough for me."

Julian put the phone down and stood up. He went to the window. It was still snowing and much more of it was beginning to stick. He walked to the desk and picked up a paperback edition of *Barracuda*. It was by the author of *High Terror*. He read the cover copy and looked toward the phone; then at his watch. Less than five minutes had elapsed since he had spoken to Calluchie.

Julian put the book down and returned to the window. He found himself recalling an incident that had occurred when he had been perhaps nine or ten years old. He had gone into Manhattan with his father. It had been either a holiday or a Sunday. His father had taken him on the subway to the area near the Manhattan Bridge where the Diamond Exchange had been located before it moved uptown to Forty-seventh Street. There were still many diamond dealers in the same place on the Bowery, off Canal Street. . . .

The day was cold. His father held him by the hand when they crossed the street. The people spoke a strange language. He wasn't frightened because his father was with him.

They went into a warm, dimly lit, sour-smelling place that had sawdust on the floor. There was a long, dark wood counter on one side of the room, a mirror behind it and a bottle in front of it. A man with a white apron was busy wiping glasses.

"Take off your coat and sit here," his father said, putting him in a chair at the table. "I have to talk to the men over there."

"Over there" was at another table in the rear, where three men in black suits were seated, all smoking cigars.

"Giorgio," his father called to the man behind the bar, "give my son a lemonade."

"Sure, Sam," the man answered.

His father walked to the table, said something, and the three of them nodded. Then his father sat down. Julian couldn't hear what his father or the other men were saying.

But he watched them. The man at the counter brought him a lemonade and said, "So, you're Sam's boy. Well, you got yourself one helluva father."

At the table, the men continued to talk. After a while, his father took out a small purse from his pocket. Julian knew that his father was showing them diamonds. Then the talk was over. All of them shook hands with Julian's father. When they left the place, Julian's father said, "Don't tell your mama about where we went. Keep it a secret between us."

"Yes, papa," Julian said, feeling very grown-up that he and his father shared a secret. . . .

Julian moved his hand over his chin. He hadn't thought about that incident in years. He moved away from the window and wondered how many other places Sam had taken him that he no longer remembered.

The phone rang. He picked it up. "Julian Heck," he said.

"You go to number sixteen Emerson Drive in Staten Island and speak to my friend Paul Spinelli."

"When should I go?"

"I told him you'd be there later this afternoon," Calluchie said.

"Thanks again. I'll call around Christmastime."

"Take care," Calluchie said and hung up.

Julian dropped the phone onto its cradle. He took his coat and left the room. Within minutes he was on a subway going to South Ferry, at the tip of Manhattan, where he'd board the ferry for Staten Island.

The ferry-boat ride took thirty minutes. Julian spent the entire time inside on the upper deck. Because of the snow, visibility was very poor, and shortly after the ferry left the slip, it was enveloped by grayness. The melancholy wail of foghorns came from every direction. From time to time, the ferry added its sad voice to those coming out of the fog.

Just outside the ferry terminal on Staten Island, Julian found a cab. Emerson Drive was twenty minutes away. Spinelli's large ranch-type house was surrounded by spacious lawns which were covered with a light blanket of snow. Julian was admitted by a servant, taken through a large foyer with several good paintings on the wall and brought to a den, where he was greeted by Spinelli, who was a man of middling height with iron gray hair, very white teeth, a naturally dark complexion, a broken nose and pale blue eyes. He might have been sixty-five or older.

Spinelli shook Julian's hand and offered him a drink. A picture window overlooked the Verrazano Bridge and the bay on either side of it. The walls were lined with books. There was a huge fireplace in one wall with a good fire in it. Soft music came from hidden speakers.

When they were comfortably seated with drinks, Spinelli said, "I watched some of your shows. You write good stuff."

Julian thanked him.

"Sam told me about you," Spinelli said. "He was one of my favorites. We go back a lot of years."

Julian drank part of his scotch. "This was put in my pocket the other day," he said, passing the note to Spinelli. "I'm trying to locate the diamonds my father left."

Spinelli read the note and frowned. "You think one of my people wrote this?"

"Maybe."

"Give me a few minutes," he said, setting his drink down on a small table and picking up the phone. He dialed a number and became involved in a rapid-fire conversation in Italian.

Julian went to the window. The nearest tower of the bridge was just visible through the falling snow. He turned. Spinelli was still on the phone. The man looked like a corporate executive. It was hard to believe he was a kingpin in the underworld.

A model of a full-rigged ship on one of the shelves attracted Julian's attention. He crossed the room to look at it and discovered that the hull, mast and spars were made of ivory.

Spinelli put the phone down. Julian turned to him.

"None of my people know about or have anything to do with the note," Spinelli said. Julian returned to his seat.

"What makes you so sure your father left any stones?" Spinelli asked.

"Does it make sense that he didn't?"

"As far as I know, he didn't."

Julian finished his drink and set the shot glass down on a nearby end table. "Why did you do business with my father? I mean, aside from the fact that he was willing to smuggle stones, why did you trust him?"

"He was an honest man."

"Honest men don't fence, and they don't smuggle gems for the mob."

Spinelli stood up and poured himself and Julian another drink. "Sam did both and he was an honest man. I knew him a long time. Whatever favors he asked were never for himself. The money he made was only part of it. I think the danger was also part of it. But he never kept much of the money."

"I don't understand."

"In the last ten years, practically all the money he made, he converted into lire. I know that because I also deal in money, and I helped him send those lire to the transit camps in Italy. Yes, he sent practically all of what he got to help the Jews coming out of Russia. Sam was a good, kind man. He worked for me for many, many years. He trusted me, and I trusted him. But I don't know about any diamonds he might have left for you."

They spoke briefly about Hollywood, and Spinelli told him he had connections there, too. Then he took out a business card and wrote a name on it. "You go see this man. He'll give you a gun. Something small, like a twenty-five-caliber automatic. He won't charge you anything, because he's a friend of mine."

"Why would I need a gun?" Julian asked.

"To off the guy who might try to off you," Spinelli said matter-of-factly. "Someone wants you out of the picture. Take the card and think about it."

"I had enough of guns in Nam."

"That was different," Spinelli said. "That was just dumb."

Julian took the card and put it into his pocket.

"I'll have one of my men drive you back to the city," Spinelli said.

"Just to the ferry will be fine."

A short while later, Julian settled into the rear seat of a Mercedes sedan. He was totally confused by his father's actions. He did not understand his business association with the Mafia or his generosity to the Jews in the Italian transit camps. Ordinarily, a man involved in one would exclude the other. Yet Sam had managed to connect one to the other, through Spinelli. Julian could not understand how Sam could have done it without having engaged in some kind of double-think, or perhaps having been a completely schizoid personality. He wondered if his mother had known.

21

AT FOUR IN THE AFTERNOON, Dimetrov entered the guarded area of the communications center in the mission and asked the clerk on duty if there was a message for him.

"Yes," the young woman answered. "But as you requested, it has not yet been decoded."

"Is a code clerk free?" he asked.

She summoned another young woman from the other side of the room. "Major Dimetrov would like this message decoded."

"How long will it take?"

"A few minutes," she answered. "Do you want the usual copies made?"

"No copies. Decode it and return the original to me. I'll wait here." He slipped out of his coat and sat down on the hard wood bench against the wall.

"Would you like a cup of coffee, major?" the duty clerk asked.

"Thank you, yes. I take it black, no sugar."

She smiled at him and walked behind a partition.

Dimetrov watched the movement of her buttocks. He was still a bachelor and enjoyed the company of many different women in Moscow or wherever he happened to be. But he had not made any effort to find a woman in New York.

The young woman returned. "Black, no sugar," she said with a smile.

Dimetrov nodded, stood up and took the plastic container from her hand. Her black eyes were filled with laughter, her hair piled high on her head in a bun. She had the characteristically high cheekbones of a Russian with Tartar blood. His guess was that she came from the Uzbek region.

Still looking at her over the rim of the container, Dimetrov sipped at the coffee. He was about to ask her to join him for dinner when he saw the code clerk approach. He set the container down on the counter.

"Your message," the code clerk said. Dimetrov took the paper.

"I'll need your signature on this disposition form."

Dimetrov signed and picked up the message:

From: First Chief Directorate, Information Center, HQ., 2 Dzerzhinsky Square, Moscow
To: Maj. Sergei Dimetrov
Sub: Req. info Max Guber, former inmate of Auschwitz; req. info Chiam Borsky and Marek Korditz

Guber, Max, Auschwitz # A3457689. Cap. age 25. Came from Bialystok. Slated killed by gassing. Life saved by Samuel Heckowitz, sub. your invest. According to sources available this Hq., Heckowitz bribed guards with diamonds. No info on source of diamonds. Borsky, Chiam, Auschwitz #A4562378. Cap. age 22. Came from Krakow. Not known if sub. knew either Guber or Heckowitz. Korditz, Marek. No rec avail.

Maj. P. D. Lyudin
Information Cent.
Hq., Moscow

Dimetrov folded the message. "Please shred these now," he said to the duty clerk.

She fed the papers into the machine. "Aren't you going to finish your coffee?" she asked.

"It's probably cold," he said, putting on a coat.

"I can warm it for you."

"Thank you, but I must go." He turned and left the communications center. He could understand why Guber, Heckowitz and Borsky were close; they had shared a common experience. But Korditz's relationship to the other three men puzzled him.

Dimetrov stepped into the street. It was still snowing, and it was colder. He walked up to Fifth Avenue and turned south. Traffic was backed up.

Dimetrov had to know more about Guber, Borsky and Korditz. He was sure the best way of accomplishing that was through Sam's son, Julian. By the time he reached the Plaza, he decided to phone Julian and invite him for cocktails.

Dimetrov made the call from the hotel lobby. Julian wasn't in. Dimetrov left a message, asking Julian to return his call; then he went up to his room and watched TV, becoming engrossed in what the Americans called a soap opera.

The phone rang. Dimetrov switched off the TV and picked up the phone just as it rang for a second time. "Hello," he said.

"This is Julian Heck."

"Thank you for returning my call. I thought we might get together for drinks."

The conversation went on for two minutes more before they agreed to meet in the cocktail lounge of the Pierre at six o'clock.

22

THEY SAT AT A SMALL ROUND TABLE at the far end of the long, narrow room of the Hotel Pierre's cocktail lounge. It was crowded and smoky, and the hum of conversation, often punctuated with laughter, rose above the sound of the piano.

Julian munched on a pretzel. Looking around him, he said, "I wish I could enjoy it the way some of the people seem to."

"It's hard to relax when things don't go right," Kass responded. From the moment they had met at the bar, Julian appeared to be even more upset than he had been during their previous meeting. But rather than ask him what was wrong, Kass preferred to wait and let the martinis do the work. Sooner or later he would tell him of his own accord; of that, Kass was certain.

Julian took another sip of his drink. "To paraphrase Shakespeare, 'It's a wise son who knows his own father.' "

"There's truth in that. Father and son must rely on the truthfulness of the mother."

"The mother comes into play only in relation to the legitimacy of the offspring, Kass. But there are most certainly other kinds of knowing."

Kass turned his head toward the piano player, who suddenly began to sing Gershwin's "Summertime." "Good voice," he said, referring to the pianist. "But I wonder how she manages with an audience that seems so indifferent?"

Julian shrugged, too involved with questions of his own to consider that one. "I saw one of my father's friends today," he said.

"One of the three you mentioned?"

"No," Julian answered, shaking his head. "He was some-one I had never met before." He took another sip of his mar-tini. "This man was part of my father's secret life. I guess you didn't know him well enough to know he had a secret life."

"I only started to do business with him in the last few years, but every man has some sort of secret life."

"That's probably true," Julian agreed. "But now you tell me—how many of them are involved with the Mafia?"

Kass raised his eyebrows.

"He fenced for them and now and then did some smug-gling," Julian said, purposefully keeping a light tone in his voice. "You see, he was a man of many, many talents."

Kass was taken aback. He couldn't think of an adequate answer. There really didn't seem to be one.

"You're surprised, aren't you? Well, I am, too. I knew my father—no, that's wrong, too. I obviously knew him less than even I thought. I'll rephrase it. I realized my father was not like other men about the time I reached my fifteenth year, maybe earlier. But when I reached fifteen, I was able to admit to myself that he was different. Only then I didn't realize how different."

"And you found this out today?"

"I found a lot of things out today," Julian said acid-ulously. He motioned to the waiter. "Another round of drinks and a plate of hot hors d'oeuvres." Then he continued speak-ing to Kass. "First, I was told by Max—Max Guber—that if I wanted the diamonds my father left, I would have to go to Amsterdam for—"

"Amsterdam?"

Julian held up his hand. "Listen to me."

"I apologize. I didn't mean to interrupt."

"Max called me early this morning and asked me to come to his office. He said he had something important to tell me. Well, when I arrived there, I found Detective Dalis already there. Now, I met Dalis on Friday when Levitas was killed. I think Dalis is an ass. Dalis tells me that Levitas was involved with the mob. I won't go into the details of how he discovered that. But in the process of finding out about Levitas, he also found out about Sam Heckowitz, my esteemed father."

The waiter brought their drinks and a plate of hors d'oeuvres consisting of cocktail frankfurters, meatballs and steak tidbits.

Julian picked up a frankfurter. "Again, I'll pass over the details, but later in the afternoon, I had a meeting with the man who did business with my father."

"From the Mafia?"

Julian nodded. "This man knew my father for many years. He said that Sam was a very honest man. That's his opinion, not mine. Now this is really where it becomes absurd. My father sent practically all the money he made to the transit camps in Italy for—"

"Jews coming out of Russia," Kass said.

"Right. One hundred percent right. Did he ever mention that to you?"

Kass shook his head. "I just guessed at it. Considering his experience, it wasn't a hard guess."

Julian sipped at his martini.

Kass said nothing. What Julian found difficult to understand was perfectly intelligible to him. Sam was providing his people with sustenance. Kass couldn't help but admire him. It took a very brave man to run those risks. And his son seemed blinded. Kass wondered how long it would take him to learn, and be affected by, the truth.

"My father may not have been much," Julian said. "But he was still my father. For all his shortcomings, I would not have wanted to think of him as—"

"What did his friend Guber say when the detective told you about his involvement with the Mafia?"

"I quote: 'Sam did what he had to do. He did it without making excuses to anyone. He was a *mentsh*, a man who looked to no one and expected nothing from anyone.' "

Kass picked up a meatball. Now that he had read the report on Guber, he could understand his loyalty to Sam.

"I think if Max found out my father committed some terrible crime, he would still defend him."

"Their friendship—"

"Max wasn't altogether blind to his faults. He said that one of the reasons he was sending me to Lublin was that he thought that Sam did owe me something."

"Lublin is in Amsterdam?"

"Right."

"He's a diamond dealer, too?"

"Yes. Saul Lublin and my father did business. I'll be leaving for Amsterdam in a day or two." Kass helped himself to one of the small pieces of steak, sure of Lublin's complicity in Sam's business dealings.

"It's just possible," Julian commented, "that I'll discover more of my father's secret life. Perhaps he has a son or a daughter there, or somewhere else in Europe. I told Guber I wished he had."

"I don't understand."

"A son and a wife who understood and loved him."

"But you love him. If you didn't you wouldn't care about his dealings with the Mafia."

Julian said nothing. He reached over to the candle and ran his forefinger through the cool part of the flame.

"I remember hearing Lublin's name," Kass lied. "But it wasn't from your father. He never spoke about the dealers he did business with."

"For obvious reasons," Julian commented sarcastically. "Well, I'll give you a call before I leave."

Kass nodded. "I won't be here too much longer myself. I think my business in New York will be over very soon."

"I think," Julian said, "I think I'm slightly sloshed."

"You well might be," Kass replied. He called for the waiter and asked for the check. "I'll take you back to your hotel."

"No need to," Julian said. "Just put me in a cab and I'll get there."

23

JULIAN LEFT THE ELEVATOR and walked through the carpeted hallway. He was drunk, but only enough to make him slow of speech and movement. He looked forward to tumbling into bed and sleeping for a few hours. Later, he decided, he'd walk up to the Brasserie on Fifty-third Street and have an herb omelet. He also came to the conclusion that he liked Kass. Not only was the man a good listener, but he was also understanding of a situation which was doubtless foreign to him.

Julian reached the door of his room, fished for the key in his pocket and finally inserted it into the lock. He opened the door and stepped into the room.

The lights lit up two men in black ski masks.

Julian tried to retreat into the hallway, but one of them leaped behind him and pushed the door shut. The other said, "You should've paid attention to the note. You should've gone back to California. Now we're going to teach you a lesson." He drove his fist into Julian's face.

The blow knocked Julian to the floor. Blood flowed out of his nose and mouth. One of the men picked him up. He was struck again, this time in the stomach. He vomited. He took a blow on the head and felt himself suddenly drop into a swirling black vortex.

When he regained consciousness, his body was filled with pain. He opened his eyes and found himself looking up at the ceiling. He forced himself to stand. There was a mixture of dried blood and vomit all over him.

He staggered into the bedroom. Everything he owned had been dumped on the floor. They had torn up his rough notes for the script he was going to write.

"They didn't have to do that," Julian said. "They didn't have to do that!" He went into the bathroom, stripped and showered. When he was dressed, he dialed 911, told the woman on the other end what had happened and asked her to contact Detective Anthony Dalis of the Homicide Squad.

Within minutes, the police arrived. Just as Julian was about to give his statement to the sergeant, the phone rang.

Dalis was on the other end. He told the detective what had happened.

"It's the mob," Dalis said.

"The hell it is!"

"Listen, they're giving you a message. They don't want you poking around."

"Listen to me. I tell you it's not the mob. I want those fuckers caught."

Dalis hung up.

"The bastard!" Julian swore, slamming down the phone. "The bastard hung up on me." He turned to the sergeant. "How the hell do you communicate with a man who has a one-track mind? I bet he sees the mob in his dreams."

"I must have your statement," the sergeant said.

"Just a minute, I want to make another call."

"Can't it wait?"

Julian ignored the question and dialed Guber's number. The phone rang three times before Guber picked it up.

"This is Julian."

"So?"

"When I entered my hotel room, there were two men in

black ski masks waiting for me. They went through everything, tore up my notes for the TV script and then beat the shit out of me."

Guber uttered a deep sigh. "I think you should change your hotel room," he said. "Yes, that's what I think you should do."

Julian pulled the phone away from his ear and looked at it. He frowned. Then, with an abrupt movement, he brought the phone back. "That's a brilliant answer. You tell me to change my hotel and Dalis tells me I'm looking at a message. I wonder what kind of comment I'd get from Kass. I mean, someone I know must have something to say other than it's a message or change your hotel."

"Who is Kass?" Guber asked.

"I told you about him. He's the dealer from Paris who knew Sam."

For several moments, Guber said nothing.

"Are you still there?" Julian asked, moving toward the window. The police sergeant motioned to him. "In a few minutes," he told the man.

"Who's there with you?" Max asked.

"The police."

"This Kass," Guber said, "I'd like to meet him. Bring him around; maybe we could do business together."

"Is that all you ever think about?" Julian asked. He was exasperated by his suggestion that he change hotels.

"No," Guber said quietly. "I often think about other things—like when are you going to Amsterdam?"

"I said I'd let you know."

"We can't play the game by your rules, *boychical.* I must have a yes or no, now."

"Can't it wait—"

"Yes or no?"

"I'll go," Julian said. "I'll go as soon as I can get a flight out." He walked away from the window and sat down on the bed.

"You have one the day after tomorrow," Guber said.

"You're damn sure of yourself."

"Where money is concerned," Guber answered, "it's part of my business to be damn sure of myself."

"It's not your money, it's mine."

"Money is money, and it should always be treated seriously."

"I won't have a chance to bring Kass around," Julian said, changing the subject.

"Tomorrow afternoon will be fine," Guber told him. "About three o'clock. I'll have Borsky and Korditz there. Maybe the three of us will do business with him. Good night."

"Good night," Julian said, putting the phone back on its cradle.

"Now will you give me your statement?" the sergeant asked.

Julian nodded.

24

JULIAN INTRODUCED KASS to the three men. He shook hands with each one of them and sat down on the couch next to Julian. Borsky sat in a chair near the wall, and Korditz was alongside the desk.

Guber took out paper cups and a bottle of scotch. They drank to health and good luck.

"Julian tells me you knew his father Sam, may he rest in peace," Guber said.

"We did some business together."

"And you're here to buy goods?" Korditz asked.

Kass nodded. "This is actually a stopover before I return home. I was on the West Coast for business reasons and decided to stop off and buy some stones. Of course their quality and price would have to be right."

"And did you?" Korditz asked.

Kass told them what he had bought and from whom. "When Julian phoned me this morning, he said that you might have some stones for me."

Guber spread out a square of black velvet on top of his desk, went to his safe and removed several paper packets. "Most of these stones are in the two-carat range," he explained, coming back to the desk. He opened each and spread the diamonds out in clusters so that each one was close to the envelope from which it came. "Please look at them," Guber said.

Kass took his loupe out of his pocket and stepped up to the desk. He knew he was being tested but wasn't in the least bit nervous. Quickly he examined the stones. Then he studied several of them. Finally he selected two and looked at them in the natural light coming through the window. "If the price is right," he told Guber, "I'll take these." He held the stones in the palm of his hand.

Guber took the stones, fitted his own loupe to his eye and examined the two diamonds.

"When did you see Sam last?" Borsky asked.

Kass remembered what he had told Julian. "Two weeks before he died. He was in Paris, and we had dinner together."

"Did he mention anything about his health?"

"Not a word," Kass said. "But he seldom spoke about himself." Borsky nodded.

"You picked two beauties," Guber said.

"If the price is right, I'll take them off your hands."

Guber looked at the packet and checked its number against a corresponding number in a ledger. He was about to weigh the stones when Borsky suddenly said, "If you gentlemen will excuse me, I am not feeling well."

"You look pale," Guber said with concern.

"I think I have a touch of the flu," Borsky responded. "Please excuse me. I'm glad I met you." He shook Kass's hand. "Don't worry, I'll be fine." He slipped into his coat and left the office.

"Should I weigh the stones?" Guber asked.

"Yes," Kass answered.

"Maybe you should follow him," Guber suggested, looking at Korditz. "He didn't look good to me."

"If I go after him," Korditz replied, "he'll only become angry. You know how stubborn he can be."

Guber agreed with a silent nod. He removed a small balance-beam scale from the bottom of the safe, placed the instrument on the desk and proceeded to weigh each of the stones separately.

25

IT WAS A SPECIAL ROOM used only for overseas phone calls. It had cork walls and was windowless. There was a desk, a swivel chair and a phone, and on the desk a lamp, a pad and a sharpened pencil.

Dimetrov leaned back in the swivel chair, wedging the phone between his shoulder and his ear. Soon after he had left Guber's office, he had called the communications center and had them arrange a telephone conversation with Paul Fournier, an agent with the French counterespionage organization. Through an elaborate system of scramble phones and other complicated electronic techniques, he would be able to speak with Fournier, who was in a safe house somewhere in Paris.

He'd never met Fournier, but he had spoken to him on one other occasion. Then their conversation had to do with the fall of Saigon. Fournier had been able to supply certain details of the American evacuation plan that Dimetrov had passed along to the North Vietnamese.

Dimetrov could never understand why any man would want to be a double agent. It was, in his opinion, tantamount to committing suicide. Over the years, he had learned that none of the double agents gave much thought to the possible consequences. They were involved with two opposite groups, for the money or the danger. Often these considerations outweighed all others. But before he left Moscow, he had been ordered to contact Fournier should he require assistance that could not be given by anyone inside the KGB. An order was an order.

"Stand by," a male voice said.

Dimetrov eased his position in the chair. The light from the lamp on the far right-hand corner of the table reflected a small yellow circle on the ceiling and a wider, more diffuse one on the desk.

"Fournier here."

"I need some information from Interpol," Dimetrov said. "Do you think you will be able to get it for me?"

"Yes."

"It would be simpler if we could go directly to Interpol, but as you know, we don't have any connection with them."

"I don't think it will be a problem," Fournier answered.

Dimetrov gave Fournier a complete description of Borsky and Korditz. "I want to know everything Interpol has on them," Dimetrov said. "No detail is to be omitted. You will be able to set up another phone call through the mission—or better still, I will phone you. Yes, that would be much better." Dimetrov realized he'd probably be in Amsterdam the next time he'd be speaking to Fournier, and the less Fournier knew about his movements, the better.

"By the way," Fournier asked, "did you send out feelers about the recent killings of diamond dealers?"

The question surprised Dimetrov. It was too close to his own work to please him. "Why?"

"We had some inquiries by way of Italy," Fournier answered.

"What made you think I wanted that kind of information?"

"I was curious about where the initial request might have originated."

"I assure you I did not send out any feelers."

"In any case," Fournier said, "we have information that at least two of the killings—the one in London and the one in Rome—might have been committed by members of East German neo-Nazi groups."

"And you say the information came from Italy?" Dimetrov asked, leaning forward and resting his elbows on the desk.

"No. The request for it came from Italy. The information, from what little we have to go on, seems to have originated from sources in Israel's intelligence organization. Perhaps the Sheruti Bethahar?"

"Yes, that's very interesting. I'll be in touch. Thank you for your help. Good-bye."

"Good-bye."

Dimetrov put the phone down and leaned back. He closed his eyes and, pressing his hands together, placed them at the tip of his nose.

That some of the killings might have been committed by an East German neo-Nazi group could become a source of trouble. Dimetrov knew the government permitted the groups to flourish because they were the most vocal about German reunification, its own goal. But there was also the possibility that the killings might be considered a necessary expedient by which a political entity was able to fund itself. They might also know the people who were trading Jews for diamonds. If East Germans were involved, he would have difficulty moving against them. He'd have to be very careful. The other possibility was that members of the Sheruti Bethahar would find them before he did. If that should happen, his problem would be eliminated and with it would go the opportunity of discovering whether there had been a connection between the killers and the people in Moscow, who were his main concern.

He did not like the way the situation was developing. With a weary sigh, he stood up and left the small office. On the way out, he stopped at Marrosov's office to tell him he would be leaving New York the following day. But Marrosov was out. Out of courtesy, Dimetrov wrote a note to inform Marrosov of his departure and to thank him for his hospitality, adding that he could be reached at the Hotel De l'Europe in Amsterdam.

26

MARROSOV FOUND THE Weathervane easily enough. It was on Twenty-ninth Street, between Park and Lexington. Its exterior was some designer's idea of a colonial-type inn, complete with a wooden sign hung from a black cast-iron bracket. Inside, the room was long, narrow and wood paneled, with the bar on the left side. Christmas decorations were already hung across the top of the mirror in back of the bar.

Marrosov handed his coat and hat to the hat-check girl and sat down at the corner of the bar near the door. He ordered a scotch and lit a cigarette. He was angry. He did not want to be there. But he had no choice. He didn't like dealing with Jews. But again, he hadn't any choice. He hadn't minded so much when he had met with Heckowitz, because Heckowitz hadn't been like most Jews: Heckowitz had been a man of the world.

Stubbing out his cigarette, he drained half his drink. His involvement with Jews had made him a wealthy man, with almost a quarter of a million dollars secure in a numbered

Swiss bank account. In recent weeks, he had given serious thought to defecting to the United States. The information he had on KGB operations in the United States and other countries could bring, in addition to political asylum, many more tens of thousands of dollars. But he had decided to wait until Dr. Urishensky had been brought out of Russia. Marrosov acknowledged that had been a mistake, perhaps the biggest mistake he would ever make.

Marrosov ordered another scotch and asked the bartender for pretzels. In his years in New York, he had developed decidedly Western tastes. His need to live well had made him an easy mark for the group known to him only as Blue-White. He had never met any of its members. His role as a small cog in a very elaborate operation was simply to clear each Jew through the KGB and secure the necessary travel papers.

He nibbled at the pretzels. Now he was in too deep to get out. That Dimetrov had suddenly shown up frightened him. He had used many of his overseas contacts to discover why, but he had received contradictory reports. He had been told by his sources in Italy that Dimetrov had been sent to investigate the killings of diamond dealers, which made him think that Dimetrov might be part of the Blue-White group. And then other sources had told him the killings might have been done by members of an East German group. If that happened to be so, he could do nothing. Any questions he might put to headquarters about them might arouse the suspicions of his superiors. If such a group was in operation, then it might have the unofficial sanction of the government. He did not know which, if any, of the reports to believe.

Marrosov shook his head, increasingly angry, and drank his scotch. He glanced at his watch; it was six o'clock. Marrosov took another pretzel, uncomfortable at being alone in an unfamiliar place. Though he was armed, he felt very insecure. Suddenly in the mirror he saw Borsky enter, stop and give his coat and hat to the hat-check girl. He made no effort to attract Borsky's attention.

Each pretended surprise. Borsky ordered a vodka on the

rocks with a twist of lime. "There was a man in Guber's office this afternoon who claimed he did business with Sam in the past two weeks. He said he saw him in Paris two weeks ago."

Marrosov nodded. "Before you continue, let me tell you I've received word that East Germans might be responsible for the killings."

"This man in Guber's office goes by the name of Kass," Borsky said. "He's tall, thin, has well-defined features and green eyes."

Marrosov's hand began to tremble. "He's a KGB agent. His name is Sergei Dimetrov." The vodka Borsky was sipping went down his trachea instead of his throat. He immediately started to gag, and couldn't stop. Everyone at the bar stopped to look at him. His eyes began to tear, and he tried to regain his composure.

Marrosov slapped him on the back several times. "Take a deep breath and hold it." Borsky nodded. After three or four minutes, the coughing subsided. He leaned close to Marrosov and asked, "Can he be bribed?"

Marrosov shook his head. "His father was a hero in the war. He himself volunteered for service in Vietnam. He's too ideologically committed to take a bribe."

"Something must be done. We've already arranged to send another man to Amsterdam."

"When?"

"Tomorrow. Sam's son, Julian, is going. He brought your Dimetrov to Guber's office."

Marrosov nodded and said, "Let's take a walk. I can't think in here."

Borsky paid both checks. Outside, they turned north. "Do you think Dimetrov will follow Julian?" Borsky asked.

"There's no reason to think he won't."

"He must be stopped. He mustn't be allowed to interfere, even if he must be killed." For an instant, Marrosov stopped and glared at him.

"Give me an alternative." Borsky said.

"There isn't any," Marrosov answered. "But let me figure out how it must be done."

They reached Thirty-fourth Street and continued to

walk together for another two blocks. Then Borsky lagged behind until it appeared that they had nothing to do with each other. By Thirty-ninth Street, Marrosov turned west to Fifth Avenue, and Borsky continued on.

When Borsky reached Grand Central Station, he went inside and found a telephone booth. Dialing Guber's home number, he waited impatiently for his friend to answer. As soon as Guber picked up the phone, he said, "I spoke to our Russian friend. Kass belongs to his group."

Guber heaved a deep sigh. "What is our friend's suggestion?" he asked.

"His friend must be eliminated."

"And who is going to do that?"

"He will take care of it. He knows none of us can do it."

"Better come to my office first thing tomorrow morning," Guber said. "I'll call Korditz and have him there, too."

Without saying anything more, Borsky hung up. His heart was beating very fast and his brow was wet.

Marrosov walked up Fifth Avenue. As he approached the Plaza, he thought about paying Dimetrov a visit. Perhaps he could buy him off, and if that failed, he would kill him. But neither idea had deep roots. He passed the Plaza and continued to walk to the mission. When he arrived back in his office, he immediately found Dimetrov's note.

He read it twice before he took off his coat and hat and finally sat down. If he had had any doubts about eliminating Dimetrov, they vanished the instant he finished reading his note. He sat back in his chair and lit a cigarette. Dimetrov was not only a threat to the continuing operation of Blue-White, but he was a personal threat as well. So far Dimetrov had not connected him and Blue-White, but the moment it happened, Marrosov had no doubt about what Dimetrov would do. Given a reversal of their places, he would do the same.

Marrosov took a long drag on the cigarette and as he let the smoke rush out of his nose, he decided to have Dimetrov killed in Amsterdam.

27

THE CLUB NEGEV was a disco with an Israeli flavor a short distance from Sheridan Square in Greenwich Village. Every night, seven nights a week, the club featured disco dancing that started at nine o'clock and continued until four the following morning. It attracted a great many celebrities.

Korditz often went there, both to see the action, and to be seen. He enjoyed dancing. It gave him the opportunity to meet a number of young women, one of whom he usually took home with him. But this visit to the Club Negev was promoted by the phone call he had received from Guber. He sat at a small table with the club's owner, Hershel Begin.

"The combination of the note planted on him in Grand Central and the visit they paid Julian worked. He is more determined than ever to go after his father's diamonds. And Max is just as determined to use him as a courier," Korditz said.

Begin nodded appreciatively. He was a heavyset man with porcine eyes and a small, petulant mouth. He smoked long, pungent cigars. "Then what's the problem? You said there was a problem. You weren't supposed to contact me until Julian—"

"We have a problem," Korditz said, dropping his voice below the blare of the music in order to be heard. "Kass, Julian's friend, turns out to be KGB." He lifted his beer and drank some of it. "Julian doesn't know that."

"And you think Kass—"

"His real name is Sergei Dimetrov."

"Do you think he'll go to Amsterdam?"

"He already knows about Lublin through Julian. When Dimetrov was up in Guber's office, he said that he had seen Sam just two weeks ago. Borsky was with Sam two weeks ago in Paris. Sam spent some time away from Borsky on personal business, as he always did whenever he went to Paris. But Borsky had the feeling that Dimetrov was lying. He met with Marrosov, and from him, he discovered who and what Dimetrov really is."

Begin rubbed his chin. "We can't have him getting in the way."

Korditz agreed, though he was distracted by a long-legged, braless blond who was going through some delightfully erotic movements. He imagined her naked and was just about to leave the table and dance with her when Begin said, "Then our people will have to take him out."

Korditz turned toward him.

"It shouldn't be that difficult," Begin commented.

Korditz moved his eyes back to the blond. She was wearing white, very tight slacks. He could see the separation between the lips of her vagina.

"What about our friendly KGB agent here?" Begin asked.

"Worried. He may not be so friendly in the future." He was still staring at the young woman. He was sure she'd be wild in bed. But sometimes the wild-looking ones weren't any damn good. There wasn't any real way of knowing.

"It won't matter," Begin said. "I don't think you'll be doing business with anyone after we take the goods from Julian. I have already arranged to have my men trail him the moment he lands in Amsterdam. You'd better give me a full description of Dimetrov. By the way, through some of our contacts in Tel Aviv, we passed word to a few people in Europe that the East Germans are responsible for the killings in London and Rome and might have some connection with the murders in New York and San Juan. It makes sense for neo-Nazis to go after Jews." Korditz agreed and gave Begin a complete description of Dimetrov.

"How much will Julian be carrying?"

"A half-million."

"That would make it three and a half million. Not bad for a dozen men who know what they want and go after it. What are you going to do with your cut?"

"Go back to Israel and live a quiet life."

"I'm going to expand this place," Begin said, "and let my broker do my thinking for me."

Korditz smiled. "I just want to enjoy myself," he said, looking toward the blond.

"She's here a lot," Begin said.

Korditz stood up and went toward the young woman. He put his hands out toward her and began snapping his fingers to the music.

She smiled at him, lifting her hands to meet his.

"Hi," he said.

"You were staring at me."

"You've got a lot to stare at, honey," he answered, looking down her body.

She laughed and intertwined her fingers with his.

He drew her to him. She was soft and very warm. He glanced back at the table. Begin was gone. "I know we're going to have a good time," he said. She rubbed against him.

28

IT WAS A COLD, gray day with a wind from the north. Fournier and Childs met on the rue Saint Honore just before they entered the place du Franc. Childs had called Fournier in the morning and suggested they meet at four in the afternoon. They agreed it was unusually cold and that snow was probably in the offing. Then Childs said, "You know, I sometimes think all of our lives in some way or another are governed by coincidences. I mean, they play an enormous role in the things that happen to us."

"Yes, you're probably right," Fournier answered, wondering what Childs was leading up to.

"You asked me to check Sam out with my people; well, I did."

"Thank you," Fournier said, waiting for a traffic signal to turn green.

"Now this is what I mean by coincidence. His son, Julian Heck, just happens to believe his father left him a fortune in diamonds and pays a visit to my Italian friend to ask about the diamonds. You know the people I mean, don't you?"

The mention of Sam leaving Julian diamonds made Fournier's heart race, but he said nothing.

"My friend knew Sam a good many years. They often did business together. But my friend has no idea that you exist, nor that Sam had any dealings with you."

"I wouldn't think that Sam spoke much about it," Fournier said.

"At any rate," Childs continued, "it seems that Julian has been spending a great deal of time trying to find those diamonds. But my friend told me that Sam left Julian over a hundred thousand in stocks and bonds."

"Really!" Fournier exclaimed. He suppressed a smile; he had guessed correctly. Sam had meant him and his mother to have the diamonds and had given Julian the cash and the negotiable securities.

"Did you know any of Sam's friends—those from New York, I mean?" Fournier shook his head.

"Your friend Sam," Childs said, "turns out to be very interesting. Our FBI has been watching him on and off for several years. They seem to think he was involved with a smuggling operation."

"He might have been," Fournier answered, knowing that Sam probably had been smuggling gems into the United States for various people if the price had been worth the risk. "But what did you find out about his death?"

"After Julian asked my friend about Sam's goods, my friend became interested. After all, he had known him for a very long time."

Fournier nodded.

"Sam died of a heart attack, but from what my friend

could find out in a limited amount of time, no autopsy was performed. The police weren't called, even though he died alone in his apartment."

"How does your friend know that?"

"He must have sent someone to see the building superintendent. In any case, a man by the name of Max Guber took care of all the funeral arrangements. Do you recognize Guber's name?"

"Sam mentioned him now and then. They were in the same concentration camp."

"My friend suggests Sam might have taken his own life."

Fournier stopped. "Why would he have done something like that?" Then quickly he added, "Sam wasn't the suicidal type. He was—if he was anything—a survivor, a fighter."

"I'm only telling you what I was told."

Fournier resumed walking. That Sam had looked very tired the last time he saw him he could not deny. But Sam hadn't said a word about being despondent, other than to comment that he was getting old.

"I could check further," Childs offered.

"No, thanks," Fournier said, "you've done enough."

The two men continued to walk until Childs suggested they stop at a café. "I'm cold and I have to piss so badly I think it'll come out of my eyes if I don't get to a urinal soon."

They turned down a side street and entered a café with a zinc bar, sawdust on the floor and a very fat bartender, who smiled when they came in. "Order a calvados for me," Childs said as he rushed toward the men's room.

Fournier ordered two.

Childs rejoined him and asked, "What are you going to do about Sam's son?"

"Nothing, at least for the time being."

"That's probably the best course," Childs said, licking his lips. "Oh, by the way, my friend says that Julian is going to Amsterdam. Guber told him he might locate the diamonds there."

"Interesting," Fournier said. "Very interesting." He

drank his calvados slower than he ordinarily would. Something about Julian going to Amsterdam didn't sit right with him. The more he tested, the less right it seemed. Someone was setting Julian up, and there wasn't much he could do about it.

29

JULIAN WAS EDGY. He couldn't sleep, and the prospect of flying to Amsterdam added to his unrest. Since Nam, where he had been flown into combat aboard 'copters, he hadn't enjoyed flying. It was something that he had to do now and then, but the less often the better.

He had called Kass earlier in the evening and was surprised to be told he had checked out. No message. But he realized there was no real reason he should have expected Kass to do anything.

Julian walked to the window. Other than one corner on the top floor of the building across the street, all the offices were dark. He wondered if there were people still working in the corner office, or if someone had simply neglected to switch off the light.

The patch of sky he could see was clear, though the light from the city made it impossible to see any stars. He hoped for good weather during his flight. He had had flights during which the plane had bounced all over the sky, and others where the clouds had been so dense he could scarcely make out the navigation light on the tip of the wing.

He switched on one of the lamps on the dresser and looked at the TV program with the hope of finding something he could watch for a while. But at 3 A.M. there was nothing. He put the program down, switched off the light and went back to bed.

He realized he had only been in New York ten days, though it seemed much longer. He found himself wondering if his trip to Amsterdam would be worth the effort; if his search for the diamonds was worth the effort. After all, he had been left a sizable sum of money.

Julian removed his hands from behind his head and folded them over his chest. He uttered a loud sigh. The diamonds didn't really mean anything to him, either, at least not in terms of money. He had enough of his own. It wasn't even for any principle that he wanted them, though there wasn't any reason a stranger should have them.

Julian turned on his side, facing the window. There was more to it than just preventing that. Sam owed him for so many things, he couldn't begin to remember them all. And the diamonds would be a payment of sorts, a way to own something of Sam's, a part of the man.

"Goddamn it!" Julian exclaimed. He threw himself into the chair next to the window. He was suddenly filled with the kind of ache he hadn't felt in years. "Goddamn it, Sam, you always managed to get to me, even now." He cleared his throat, surprised by the feelings for his father which remained. He thought they had been played out, had dried up and withered in the aridity of their relationship years ago.

"There was a time," Julian said, "when I loved you more than I ever loved anyone." He stood up and walked to the window. The light in the corner office was out now, and the building dark and silent. He used his hand to brace himself against the window sash. He could see his reflection in the gray pane. Suddenly he remembered something that had happened a long time ago. Perhaps he had been nine or ten years old when the police had come for his father.

Julian shook his head. He hadn't thought about that incident for years. And now it was all there in front of him, suspended between his hotel window and the dark building across the street. . . .

His mother was in the kitchen sobbing. He could hear her from his bedroom. And then Sam said, "These things happen. I knew the risk."

"But where will you go?"

Sam didn't answer, or if he did, Julian couldn't hear it.

"How will we live?" she wept.

"There's enough money to last for a while."

"Then what?"

Again Julian couldn't hear the answer. He got out of bed and went into the kitchen. His mother was seated at the table. Sam was standing at the sink. He had his coat and hat on. In his hand, he held his valise. When he saw Julian, he said, "I've got to go away. You take care of her."

Julian ran to his father and threw his arms around him.

"No need to cry," Sam said, lifting Julian's face up. "I'll be back soon."

"I don't want you to go."

"I must," he answered, looking toward his wife. He stooped and kissed Julian; then he was gone.

Hours later the detectives came. They searched the house—every drawer, every closet. They even looked in the can that held the flour. There were four of them. They kept calling him Sonny and asked him over and over again if he knew where his father had gone.

He answered with a shake of his head.

"Your husband," one of the detectives told his mother, "is in a lot of trouble. You tell him when he calls you that he'd be better off giving himself up."

"I don't know what you're talking about," she cried.

"Handling stolen goods, fencing diamonds is a crime, a serious crime," the detective answered.

That only made her weep more.

When the detectives left, Julian stood at his mother's side and said, "Don't worry, papa will be all right. You'll see. He'll be all right."

She took him in her arms and hugged him fiercely. . . .

"God," Julian said aloud, "I was frightened, so very frightened that something would happen to him." He dropped his hand from the sash to his side. The next few weeks had been terrible. He had spent a lot of time at the Gubers'. And when he was home, he'd stay in his room and listen to his mother cry. At the yeshiva, when the other boys played, he sat off to the side and prayed to God to bring his father home safely. Then on Friday night, just after his mother had *benchen lecht,* Sam opened the door and walked into the kitchen as if nothing had happened. Julian leapt into his arms and covered his face with kisses.

None of them ever mentioned the incident. It was as if it had never happened or had been a bad dream.

Julian clenched his fist and ran his knuckles across his teeth. He had loved Sam once, a long time ago. He dropped back on the bed.

"I tell you, Sam," he whispered, "I don't know how it changed between us." But Julian knew that wasn't true. He did know how it had changed; he even knew what had caused the change. And he said, "I was here in this country and you were still in Europe, still in Auschwitz. I was an American, and you never ceased being European. You wanted me to feel your pain and I couldn't. I couldn't do it. Then when I had my own pain, you couldn't believe it was real—or maybe, as Kass said, you couldn't stand the idea that I was in pain, and therefore refused to acknowledge it."

Julian suddenly realized tears were coming out his eyes and streaming down his cheeks. "I'm sorry we never had the chance to talk about it. I'm really sorry, Sam, that it's too late to talk about it." He felt foolish. His weeping wouldn't change anything.

He turned toward the window. It was already graying with the light of a new day. He closed his eyes, but the tears continued to come.

30

GUBER DIDN'T SLEEP after Borsky's phone call. He prowled around his apartment. He was worried, very worried. Not only was the operation to bring Jews out of Russia in danger of being stopped by murderers and thieves, but now the KGB had suddenly swooped down on them; brought dangerously close by the very man who would carry the diamonds to the exchange point. If Julian wasn't so damned innocent about what his father had been doing during the past ten years, Guber would at least have been able to take pleasure in venting some of his anger at him.

Though Guber was in Manhattan early, he didn't go to his office. He walked up to Central Park, then down to Forty-second Street and finally back to the Diamond Exchange. By that time, the streets were crowded and the traffic heavy.

Guber stopped at a luncheonette for his breakfast before going to his office. He took his time with two poached eggs, a toasted bagel with cream cheese and two cups of coffee. By nine thirty he was on the elevator, and when he opened the door to his office, Rose announced that Korditz and Borsky were waiting for him.

"I don't want any phone calls," Guber said. Crossing the outer room and going into his office, he closed the door behind him. He took a few minutes to remove his hat and coat and sat down at his desk.

Korditz was on the chair against the wall and Borsky was on the couch. "It isn't as big a problem as it seems," Guber said, biting off the end of a cigar. "It's big, but not that big."

"But the KGB is involved," Borsky said.

"You look like you didn't get much sleep," Guber commented.

"Sleep . . . Who can sleep now?"

Guber lit his cigar. He was forcing himself to remain calm. He understood Borsky's fears because they were his own. But he couldn't afford to let either of his friends see that he too was afraid. If Sam were here, he would know exactly how to handle all of them, what to say to make them do what had to be done in spite of their fears. But Sam wasn't here. He would have to do the best he could. "Our problem isn't Kass or Dimetrov—whatever his name is—he just might provide the protection none of our people ever had before."

"Since when does the KGB protect Jews?" Korditz asked.

"Since it makes sense for him to protect at least one of them—Julian." Guber blew a large cloud of bluish white smoke across the desk. "He doesn't want Julian, he wants to put an end to *his* people's involvement. And because he thinks Julian will go to them, he will protect Julian as much as he can."

"Isn't Marrosov going to eliminate him?" Korditz asked.

"That's what he said," Borsky answered. "But who knows if he'll do it?"

"If he does," Guber said, "that'll be fine. He'll have the problem of protecting himself and lose the opportunity of paying too much attention to Julian. No matter what happens, he's not our problem."

Borsky was on his feet. "According to you, Max, we don't have a problem, and if we don't have a problem, why are we all here worrying?"

"We have the same problem we had before Dimetrov came on the scene. Our problem," Guber said, pointing his cigar at him, "is the people who'll try to kill Julian before he makes the delivery of the goods."

"And where will that be?" Korditz asked.

"London."

"Why there?"

"Because that's where Julian will be the safest." Guber moved his eyes to Borsky. "Can you arrange it to take place in London?"

"Probably." He sat down again.

Guber nodded and took several more puffs on his cigar. "The plan is to get Julian to Amsterdam; then to Paris and finally to London. He will be given the diamonds in Paris. They will be waiting for him."

"Why doesn't he go straight to Paris?" Korditz asked.

"He must continue to think that he's looking for Sam's goods." This was what he had thought about for most of the night and morning. He watched his two friends, looking questioningly at each other.

Korditz spoke first. "Then you have no intention of telling him what he's doing?"

"None," Guber answered with a shake of his head. "The less he knows, the better."

"What if he should be killed?" Borsky questioned.

Max shrugged. "I don't have an answer to that. Should it happen, then I will have to answer for it. But Urishensky must be gotten out. Time is running short."

"Will the men Julian sees tell him anything about Sam?" Borsky asked. "They should, if he's not to become suspicious."

"Each of them knew Sam in Auschwitz. They will certainly tell him things, and when he comes back here, I'll tell him the rest."

"Including the fact that his father committed suicide?"

"Yes, that too. I'll even show him the letter Sam left," Guber answered. "It will be the only reward he'll receive for having risked his life. And besides, it will be the only chance he'll probably ever have to know what kind of man his father really was."

Neither Borsky nor Korditz made any comment.

Guber leaned back into the chair and puffed on his cigar. "The success of Julian's mission depends on his remaining innocent of what he is doing."

"He is not a fool," Korditz said. "He knows people are already following him."

"Yes. But he has the reason all wrong," Guber answered. "Those people who are following him, who broke into his room, are the same people who'll try to kill him. He wasn't killed because he didn't have any stones. Had he been carrying diamonds, they'd have killed him."

Korditz agreed.

Feeling the situation to be resolved, Guber told his friends he had work to do before Julian came to the office that afternoon.

"Are you telling us to leave?" Borsky asked.

"I'm hinting."

"I'd rather be told," Borsky said.

"Then leave," Guber laughed. "Leave and let me do my work." He accompanied his friends to the door of the outer room, shook their hands and returned to his office, telling Rose that she could now put phone calls through to him.

Alone in the office, Guber stood by the window and finished his cigar. Christmas was twelve days away and the pace of business in the Diamond Exchange was becoming more and more frenzied. When he finally stubbed out what remained of the cigar, he opened the window to clear the air and sat down to read the *Times*. Later in the morning, he sold several good-quality stones to a dealer from Boston.

By three o'clock, he started to become anxious about Julian and began to pace. But as soon as his phone rang, he knew Julian had come to say good-bye. He picked up the phone and told Rose to send him in. Then he settled behind his desk with another cigar. "I'll be with you in a minute or two," he told Julian as the door opened, pretending to be engrossed in one of the many ledgers on his desk. Finally he looked up and smiled. "So, are you ready for your trip?"

"I'm all packed and checked out of the hotel."

Guber nodded. "I have a letter here to Lublin," he said, reaching into the top drawer of his desk. "You could do me a big favor and give it to him. I was going to mail it, but since you're going to see him, it would be quicker to give it to you. Besides, it would save me postage."

Julian shook his head, but he reached out and took the letter. "Listen," Guber explained, "I have to cut overhead wherever I can."

"I think it's down to the bone now," Julian said, looking around at the shabby office. "If you cut it anymore, you'll be collecting charity."

Guber laughed, stood up and offered him his hand. "Good luck."

"I'll let you know what happens," Julian said.

"Go, *gezunterhait,*" Guber answered, lapsing into Yiddish.

Julian nodded and let go of his hand. "See you." He turned and left the office.

Guber dropped down into the swivel chair. He felt very tired and very sad. He picked up his cigar and smoked it, though the pleasure had gone.

31

KLM's FLIGHT 101 left JFK at 8:20 P.M.. It was on time and, according to its captain, the ETA at Schiphol was nine A.M., GMT, adjusted by adding one hour for the winter season.

Julian had a window seat just aft of the port wing in the no-smoking section. Once the plane was airborne and made its regulation 180-degree turn, the lights of New York came into view. Cliché though it was, the city looked to him be-jeweled, a fantasy of dark structures and dots of glittering light.

The view of the city lasted only two or three minutes at the most; then the plane changed course even as it continued to climb toward its cruising altitude, which the senior flight stewardess had announced would be thirty-five thousand feet. Julian settled back. He took the paperback edition of *High*

Terror out of his attaché case and a yellow, legal-size pad. He began to reconstruct the notes for the TV script that had been destroyed by the men who had worked him over.

But the environment of the plane wasn't at all conducive to work. After a few minutes, he gave up, and when the stewardess asked him what he wanted to drink, he ordered a double scotch. When the man sitting next to him asked for a double scotch, too, Julian took note of him for the first time. With a smile, the man said, "One little bottle can never do anything for me."

Julian agreed with a nod.

"My name is Carlo Fuentes," the man said, extending his hand.

"Julian Heck." He shook hands with a slight, dapper-looking man with a dark complexion, high cheekbones and a small, well-groomed mustache. He used a light cologne and his nails were manicured.

"To tell the truth," Fuentes said, "I don't like flying much. I get the feeling I'm up here and there's nothing down there."

"I know what you mean." Julian laughed.

The stewardess brought them their drinks and Fuentes toasted, "To a safe landing."

Julian discovered that Fuentes was going to Amsterdam for business reasons, and that he traveled widely. After dinner, Fuentes watched the movie, while Julian listened to stereo music for a while; then he removed the earphones, propped up a pillow between the window and the upright portion of the seat and rested his head on it. He realized that Guber had been right when he had said, "Other memories of your father will come back. That's the way it always is."

Plagued by bits and pieces of the past, he now found himself realizing how much time he had spent with his father . . . . On Saturdays and Sundays, especially during the summer, they'd spend both days, if the weather was good, in Coney Island, where his father rented a locker with some other men for the season in the Giant Racers Bath House.

They'd stay all day in the sun, spending hours on the

beach or in the open-air solarium, where all the men were nude. Then before they'd go home, they'd shower and go into the steam room. Julian couldn't take the heat at the top tier. He'd sat down below and talked to his father through the steam.

On some Sundays one of the men, whose name was either Kahn or Hann, would bring steaks for everyone. These would be broiled in the fire of the furnace used to make the steam. Other men would bring potatoes and they would be put into the fire, too. And some brought the beer, which came in large, amber-colored bottles that were kept in ice-filled ash cans. . . . Julian could remember eating a chunk of well-done steak and looking up at the nearby roller coaster.

He shifted his position and faced out. The blue flame in the rear section of the jet engine was clearly visible. Beyond it on the tip of the wing, the red portside navigation light glowed, and beyond the light, far beyond, going down the curve of the sky, were a staggering number of stars.

Julian glanced at Fuentes, who was still engrossed in the film. He closed his eyes and went back to his own world of memories. . . . Even the way his father had taught him to swim had been uniquely different. . . .

One afternoon Sam took him far out on the wooden jetty that, in combination with a breakwater made of huge rocks and the brown sand beach, formed an enclosure in the shape of a U lying on its side. The tide was in, and a wind brought big waves smashing against the rocks and jetty. The two of them had walked out to the tip of the jetty, where the water was rough. There was a lot of spray in the air and spume was coming off the whitecaps.

Sam said to him, "It's time you knew how to swim." Without another word, he picked him up and threw him into the water. "Swim," he shouted. "Swim for the beach."

Julian sank, came up and started to scream for help.

"Swim," Sam shouted back, making vigorous movements with his arms to show him how to move. "That's right. Now kick . . . kick . . . you're swimming!"

Julian fought his way to the beach. Several times he sank

and swallowed enough to make him gag. But he continued to fight his way to the shore. He was too blinded to see where Sam was, but soon he realized his father was standing knee deep in the water, urging him on. He staggered onto the beach, gasping for breath. Sam led him up to the warm, dry sand and gently slapped his back.

"I could have drowned," Julian screamed, between fits of coughing.

"But you didn't," Sam answered. "You swam."

They went back to the bathhouse and Sam told all his friends that Julian had learned how to swim. Then he gave Julian a small paper cup and poured some beer into it. That was the first time Julian drank beer. He didn't like the taste but he drank it. Later, as they were dressing to go home, Sam said, "I learned how to swim the same way: my father, may he rest in peace, threw me into the river."

"But a river isn't the ocean," Julian replied.

"Now a river will be easy for you to swim across," Sam said, "very easy. . . ."

Julian opened his eyes. In front of the wing, the sky was pink and yellow. They were flying into the dawn.

32

THE TELEPHONE woke Fournier. He reached for it and pushed himself up into a half-sitting position before giving his name.

"I am Dimetrov, Sergei Dimetrov. We have mutual friends."

"Yes, we have," Fournier answered, totally awake now.

"Can you recommend a place for lunch?" Dimetrov asked.

Fournier frowned and looked down at Shulamith, who was awake. "Yes, there's the Deux Frères, on the corner of rue Vaugirard and the boulevard Pasteur. It's best to arrive there at one thirty."

"I am sorry. I must be there earlier."

"Then eleven-thirty would be best."

"That will be fine."

Fournier put the phone down. He glanced at the clock on the nearby end table. It was only eight. "That was Dimetrov," he said.

"Why should he be here in Paris?" Shulamith asked, sitting up. Her breasts were bare, nipples hardening in the cold air.

"Because Julian is on his way to Amsterdam, and Dimetrov wants the information I have." He slipped his arm around her naked shoulder and brought her close. "Better contact your friends. Tell them where we'll be; they might want to photograph him."

She nodded, touching his cheek with the tips of her fingers. "You're worried about your brother, aren't you?"

"He doesn't know what's happening."

"Someone has to make the delivery," she said softly.

Fournier agreed. "Unless he's very lucky, he doesn't have much chance of making it. We still don't know who the killers are. What we know, your people know, and I'll soon tell Dimetrov."

"Do your people know about us yet?"

"Yes, my chief has made some remarks that led me to believe they know." He kissed her passionately. "Marry me and—"

"Would you give up your position with the SDECE?"

"Sooner or later," he said, "I know I'm going to have to make some sort of choice, and once I do, I cease to be of any use to an intelligence operation—yours, mine or the KGB."

"I will marry you," she said, "as soon as this business is over."

His hand moved over her breasts and down between her thighs.

"Yes," she whispered. "Make love to me again!"

The café was empty except for two men at a table at the far side.

Fournier arrived early and sat down near a window. Outside it was raw and blustery, inside pleasantly warm and scented with aromas from the kitchen at the rear of the establishment. At exactly eleven thirty, Dimetrov entered. He glanced around, saw Fournier, waited for him to nod, then went directly to the table. They shook hands and ordered a large carafe of the house red wine.

"What have you got for me?" Dimetrov asked.

"Borsky is clean, but Korditz is a different matter," Fournier told him.

"How different?"

"To begin with, he has had several different aliases, but Korditz is his right name. He has been in prison twice, once in France for eighteen months and once in Israel for six. Both crimes had to do with diamonds. In France, it was a swindle, where paste was substituted for the real stones. In Israel, he was a fence. Before he left Israel, he traveled with some very rough people."

"Anything on him since he's been in the United States?"

"Wait, listen to this. There is no certainty he was ever in a concentration camp."

The waiter interrupted their conversation. He placed two long-stem glasses and the carafe of wine on the table. "Today's special," he said, "is broiled sweetbreads."

"Just some Brie, please, and crackers," Dimetrov told him.

"There is a minimum—"

"It is all right," Fournier said. "Just bring the cheese and crackers."

When they were alone again, Dimetrov poured wine into both glasses. "Our records show he was in Auschwitz," he told Fournier.

"They could be wrong. According to what I was able to find out, he was born February 22, 1935, in Mexico City."

"But the number on his arm—how could that have gotten there?"

"He put it there," Fournier answered. "It must have helped him in his line of work. He dealt with people who survived the camps. He had to be as much like them as possible."

"Are you sure of your information?"

The waiter returned to the table with the cheese and crackers.

"Yes, I'm sure," Fournier said. "He must be the leak."

Dimetrov helped himself to some Brie and a cracker. "There's one more bit that may interest you, though I'm not sure it's connected to Korditz in any way."

Dimetrov nodded and drank some wine.

"Remember I asked if you knew who put out feelers about the recent killings of diamond dealers?"

"Yes."

"We were able to trace them back to the source. They came from your mission in New York."

"I already told you I didn't put them out."

Fournier took a bit of wine. "Someone did. Second bit of information: the rumor about the East Germans having a hand in the killings didn't come from the Sheruti Bethahar. It came from an outside source claiming to be part of the Sheruti Bethahar. I understand several of its high-ranking members are very angry; so angry, in fact, that they've assigned a few of their people to find out who was responsible."

Dimetrov accepted the information without comment. He had a bit more cheese and another cracker before suggesting they leave.

"You go ahead," Fournier said. "I'm not in a hurry."

Dimetrov started to reach into his pocket.

"I'll pay," Fournier told him.

"I might be back this way very soon," Dimetrov said as he stood up.

"Then we might have the opportunity to meet again."

"Yes, we might." Dimetrov shook Fournier's hand and hurried out of the café. In a matter of minutes, he had turned down another street.

Fournier called for the check, paid it and left the café. He crossed the street and continued to walk along the boulevard Pasteur. It took less than five minutes for Avigeor to catch up to him.

"Did he say anything interesting?" the Israeli agent asked.

"No. I did most of the talking. I gave him the information you gave me. He was more surprised by what I told him about the source of the feelers than he wanted to show."

"So would I have been," Avigeor answered with a smile. "No one on the inside wants to deal with one of their own apples."

"Do you know?"

Avigeor nodded. "Sooner or later, he must be compromised to protect the others who really run the exchange operation. The KGB will be unhappy that one of their area chiefs is involved, but it will divert them from looking in other places at people whose help we must have."

"Then getting Urishensky out will not be the last exchange?"

"The last for awhile," Avigeor said. "But there are a great many Jews in Russia whose talents could be better used here in the West."

Though Fournier agreed, he said nothing.

Dimetrov walked quickly, taking a circuitous route to 79 rue de Grenelle, the Soviet Embassy. The streets were rapidly becoming crowded with people out for lunch. The bells of the churches and cathedrals tolled noon.

He appreciated the information given to him by Fournier, yet his impression of the Frenchman was mixed. He neither trusted nor distrusted him. His own total commitment to his country and its ideology made it difficult to accept someone like Fournier, who no doubt did what he did for money.

Dimetrov looked forward to a few hours of sleep in Amsterdam. Even as he walked, he reviewed his conversation with Fournier. He couldn't understand how the feelers had come out of New York. There wasn't anyone there who'd be interested in the killings of the diamond couriers. Even he wasn't concerned with that particular aspect of the situation. Then suddenly it occurred to him. He quickened his pace but was forced to stop for a red light. Why would Marrosov want the information? Marrosov might have been concerned about his sudden appearance in New York. He didn't want to think that Marrosov was involved in trading Jews for diamonds, but the possibility strongly suggested itself. There was no other explanation for the feelers.

There weren't too many things he could do to Marrosov at the present time. If he alerted his chief in Moscow, Marrosov would be suspect and perhaps flown back to Moscow for intense interrogation. But that approach would temporarily put an end to the illicit operation and ruin his chances for meeting the man or men he was hoping Julian would eventually contact. He decided to first see where Julian would lead him.

The more Dimetrov thought about the situation with Julian, Guber and the rest of them, the more he was convinced that Julian was being sent on a fool's errand. Somewhere along the line, Julian was going to be turned into a courier, most probably without his knowing it. He would be given the names of one, possibly two other men and told that they might have his father's stones. And then one of the men would give him a small package to deliver to still another man. From that point on, Julian's life would be in danger. If Korditz were the informer, then his people would probably try to kill Julian.

Dimetrov was astonished by these conclusions, and even more so at the number of different groups attempting to use

Julian for their own purposes. It was remarkable that Julian remained innocent, yet on second thought, that wasn't true. Blinded by his quest for his father's diamonds, he couldn't possibly see anything else, or, if he did, recognize it for what it was.

For all Julian's ingenuity in concocting plots for his TV suspense dramas, he was totally innocent when it came to something that might very well cost him his life. Perhaps he'd guess that he was being used when he was asked to deliver the package. If so, he would have to decide then what to do.

That was the moment Dimetrov was waiting for. If Julian decided to make the delivery, Dimetrov would have a chance to come face to face with the men who were betraying their country. And Korditz would place his men in position to kill Julian and take the diamonds from him, as they had done to the other couriers.

He turned another corner and the Eiffel Tower came into view. He was close to the Soviet embassy. That he had developed a liking for Julian was something of a surprise to him. They were totally different, had even fought against one another in Vietnam. But he appreciated Julian's tenacity in the face of open violence. And in some strange way, he understood Julian's love-hate relationship with Sam Heckowitz. Now there was a man he would have liked to have met!

Dimetrov realized he couldn't help Julian without compromising his own position. But for the first time in his career, he was sorely tempted to put his personal likes first. He couldn't violate his loyalty to his country, though; that took precedence over anything else.

Then suddenly it occurred to him that he could do something that would help Julian and at the same time play Marrosov.

Quickening his pace, he entered the embassy and immediately made arrangements to speak with Marrosov. Within minutes, he was in a small room much the same as the one he had used in New York when he had called Fournier. But this time, he was waiting for the call to be put through to Marrosov's home in Lake Success, Long Island. Though it was past noon in Paris, it was only 6 A.M. in New York.

Dimetrov drummed on the table with the fingers of his right hand. He glanced at the electric clock on the wall, checking the time shown by it with his watch. They were within five seconds of each other. His watch was slower.

Marrosov's private phone did not have an electronic scrambler, but other less elaborate devices protected it from possible bugging.

"Stand by," a woman said.

Dimetrov leaned forward. Marrosov answered the phone. His voice was full of sleep.

"This is Dimetrov."

Marrosov repeated Dimetrov's name and asked where he was.

"Paris. I stopped here to obtain some information. Now listen carefully. I want you to place Marek Korditz under close surveillance. Have you a pencil and paper?"

After a moment's hesitation, he answered, "Yes."

"Korditz lives at 134 East Eighty-eighth Street, apartment eleven C."

Marrosov repeated the information he had written down.

"I want him followed twenty-four hours a day. I'll be in close touch with you."

"May I know—"

"He is suspected of being involved in the murder of several people—Jews." Except for Marrosov's hard breathing, Dimetrov heard no other sound. He waited a few moments, then he said, "You are to consider that information top secret."

"Is there anything else, comrade?" Marrosov finally asked.

"No, nothing."

"You can be assured of my full cooperation," Marrosov said.

"Thank you."

Dimetrov put the phone down and walked slowly out of the room. He was anxious to reach Amsterdam.

33

Julian checked into the Jan Luyken, a small hotel with a vestibule of blue, white and yellow tiles. He was shown to a room overlooking a small garden, which must have been a delight during the summer. But now, with winter just days away, it was barren except for the two pine trees in each of the far corners.

Kicking off his shoes, he opened his collar and loosened his tie before picking up the phone and dialing Lublin's number. The switchboard operator answered and he asked to be connected to Mr. Lublin.

"Miss Koss," another woman answered. "May I help you?" She spoke with a decided English accent.

"Is Mr. Lublin in? I'm Julian Heck."

"Mr. Lublin asked me to give you his apologies. He has been called away for two days. He hopes that this does not inconvenience you. He asked me to tell you that you may make full use of the company's car. It is chauffeured and is available to you any time of the day or night."

Julian scowled, but he kept his voice pleasant. "Thanks," he told her. "I'll call back in two days." He was about to hang up when Miss Koss said, "I was very sorry to hear that your father died."

"Thanks," he said again, cocking his head to one side.

"He was a very kind man. Whenever he came to the office, he always stopped at my desk and chatted."

Julian found himself at a loss for words.

"Mr. Lublin thought very highly of him. He once told me your father was the bravest man he ever knew."

"You have me at a disadvantage," Julian said. "Perhaps if we had dinner together tonight, I would be able to—"

"There's no need for you to do that. . . . I genuinely liked your father."

"All the more reason for you to accept my invitation. Sam would approve." She laughed and agreed.

"Have the company car pick me up at about seven, and then we'll come for you. Tell the driver where you live and how to get there."

"He knows," she answered.

"By the way, what's your full name?"

"Cynthia Koss."

"All right, Cynthia, at some time after seven, then."

They said good-bye.

He set the phone down and stretched out on the bed. It was very strange to hear a young woman speak so well of Sam. Julian shook his head and closed his eyes. He was tired from the flight and sleep came rapidly, though not before he recalled one more detail of the day he had learned to swim. . . .

He and Sam were in the subway going home. Only it wasn't a subway; in that part of Brooklyn, the train traveled on a trestle. It was very crowded and noisy.

Julian held onto a white pole and Sam stood next to him.

"I'd have gone after you," Sam said, "if I didn't think you'd be able to do it."

Julian looked up at him.

"You swim in the ocean, or in life; it's the same. The main thing is to swim or you sink."

"Yes, papa," Julian answered.

Sam put his hand on Julian's shoulder and let it rest there until they got off the train at the Prospect Park Station. . . .

Julian smiled at the memory of that strong hand resting so firmly on his shoulder so many years ago.

Julian and Cynthia sat at a small table against a stone wall curving above them to become part of a vaulted ceiling. A candle was stuck in an empty wine bottle whose neck and sides were covered with wax drippings. The flame cast a soft yellow light over Cynthia's face, which was spotted with freckles, and the white tops of her breasts.

He had been pleasantly surprised. Cynthia turned out to be a very attractive woman with a lovely svelte figure, an upturned nose, light green eyes and long hair the color of dark honey that swept around her shoulders whenever she moved. She had suggested they go to Die Port Van Cleve because it was very old and served excellent steaks and potatoes. During dinner they had spoken about the weather, life in the United States and the coming holidays, during which she intended to return to Bristol, where she had been born.

Julian had asked how she had managed to come to Holland to work. She had replied to an advertisement in the Sunday newspaper. Asked about his work, he had explained that he had begun to write a new script based on the novel *High Terror*.

And now over coffee, Cynthia said, "Your father never failed to mention how well you were doing. Sometimes he'd even show me your name in a newspaper clipping." Julian nodded. Throughout dinner, his father's presence had been almost palpable; yet until a moment ago, neither one of them had mentioned him.

"I think he was a very sad man," Cynthia said, raising the coffee cup to her lips.

Julian uttered a deep sigh. "He was, I guess."

She raised her eyebrows questioningly.

"A classic case of noncommunication," he answered with a forced laugh. "Generation gap, it's now called. Do you communicate with your parents?"

"My God," she laughed, "when we're together, we do nothing but talk and talk. My brothers and sisters do the same. We have a regular debating society going whenever we sit down at the table. I think I learned more about history and politics from those sessions than I did at Oxford. But I'd have to say that at the university, it was more organized."

"How many Kosses are there?"

"I'm next to the oldest and that's Nathan; Richard

comes after me; then Nina and Paul. Have you any brothers or sisters?"

Julian shook his head. "But I've always wanted a brother," he said.

"Older or younger?"

"Older, someone I would be able to talk to," he answered.

She nodded sympathetically. "Nathan was very good that way."

The turn of the conversation suddenly depressed Julian, and he said as much. "I'm sorry," she said apologetically. "I imagine it must be very difficult for you to adjust to your father's death."

"The real difficulty," he said, with a hint of a smile, "is adjusting to his life. But that's my problem, not yours. . . . I have an idea. Suppose we go to a disco. I imagine there must be one here."

"There most certainly is."

"Good. We'll go."

A short while later, they were in the Voom-Voom. The music was loud and the singing even louder, but they did enjoy themselves. Cynthia turned out to be a good dancer and Julian found her movements surprisingly erotic. The longer they danced, the more exciting she became. He had not had a woman since he had left the Coast eleven or twelve days before. A long stretch by his standards.

When they finally left the Voom-Voom, they were pleasantly tired. A light snow was falling.

"I don't live far from here," Cynthia said. "We can easily walk it."

"That's okay with me."

"I'll tell the driver to go," she said. "He must be tired. I know I am." While he waited, Julian pulled up the collar of his coat. His breath steamed in the cold night air.

"Poor man was asleep when I came up to the car," Cynthia said, as they started to walk. "I think I startled him."

Julian slipped his arm around her waist. He was pleased she did not remove it; nor did she resist his effort to hold her closer. They turned down a street that bordered on Prinsengracht, one of the four canals in the city. Light streaming out of the windows in the high, gabled houses on either side of the waterway made it seem unreal, especially with the snow beginning to settle on the cobblestone walkways and the stoops of the houses.

Julian suddenly stopped. Impulsively turning Cynthia to him, he kissed her passionately on the lips. She stood motionless, letting him kiss her.

After a few moments, Julian moved away. They continued to talk. "You expected that, didn't you?" he asked.

"Yes," she answered.

He was going to ask her why she was angry, but changed his mind, deciding she was being coy. They reached her building. There was a street lamp across the street, alongside the canal, and at the side of the stoop a small, lovely gas lamp that gave off a fan of soft yellow light. Earlier in the evening, she had just come out of the door when he had arrived in the company car.

Julian put his arms around her and kissed her again. "I want you," he told her.

"I know that," she answered, looking up at him.

He pressed her to him.

Cynthia shook her head. "It's not that I don't want to, also," she said, "but I'm not the kind of a woman who does something at night and the next morning hates herself for what she's done." She eased herself out of his arms. "Good night and thank you for a lovely time."

"And that's it?" he asked, filled with a sudden surge of angry frustration.

"I'm sorry."

"Hell, if you're sorry, can you imagine how I feel? Look, there's nothing wrong—"

"It would be wrong for me. . . . I'm not good at one-night stands."

Without another word, Julian turned and hurried away without looking back. He had no idea of the direction of his hotel, but he was lucky enough to find an empty cab.

A short while later, he paced the width of the room, angry with himself for wanting her. And he was furious with her for denying him. He went to the window. The snow had stopped but the sky was still overcast.

"The truth is," he said aloud, "that you made a fool of yourself. Just because you take a woman to dinner and go dancing, that's no reason to expect her to jump into bed with you."

He turned and looked at the phone. With a shrug, he walked over to it and asked the night operator to dial Cynthia's number.

After two rings, she answered.

"Look, I'm sorry," Julian said.

"It's good of you to call," she told him. "I know you were angry, but—"

"Forget it!"

"Yes, that's the best way. But I did have a wonderful time."

"I'm glad you did."

"I tell you what," she said, "if you come around to the office tomorrow morning, or more precisely later this morning, I'll take you on a tour through the plant. Maybe you'll be able to use some of the information about diamonds in one of your scripts."

"Will you have lunch with me?"

"I really have a great deal of work."

"Lunch, or you don't get to take me on a tour."

"All right. But it must not be a long one. I have tons of work. . . . Good night."

"Good night," he said. He put the phone down, feeling better than he had in a long time.

34

FUENTES SAT IN THE LOBBY of the Hotel de l'Europe, unaware of the opulence surrounding him. His eyes were riveted to the large swinging door tended by a man in white livery.

He slowly smoked a Cuban cigar. His fee for killing Dimetrov was ten thousand dollars, to be deposited in his checking account at Branch Six of the Chemical Bank, on Park Avenue and Forty-eighth Street in New York, when the job was done. It was his standard fee for taking someone out, unless he happened to be short of cash; then he'd work for as little as five hundred dollars a hit.

But he had been lucky in recent months, and with the ten grand he'd earn for this job, he'd have seventy-five thousand in the bank. With satisfaction, Fuentes told himself it was more than enough to take a long vacation. If all went well, he'd be on his way back to the States on the first plane out of London the day after tomorrow.

He planned to leave Amsterdam by auto as soon as the job was done. He'd drive to Paris, then fly to London. He had reserved rooms in both cities to provide cover, and a very good friend of his was already waiting for him in the hotel in Paris.

Despite Fuentes's musings, his black eyes never left the door. For a second, he scrutinized the face of every man who entered the hotel. Marrosov had given him a photograph of the man he wanted him to kill and had said, "In all probability, the man would use the name Kass to register in the hotel." Fuentes hadn't asked Marrosov any questions about Kass. It wasn't his style.

Earlier in the afternoon, he had called Marrosov to inform him that Kass had not yet checked into the hotel. And Marrosov had been in a temper. Kass had made an unscheduled stop in Paris, and Marrosov had been in a rage over it. . . .

"I want it done," the Russian shouted. "I want it done as soon as possible."

"Cool it, man. You're going to have a fit." Then Fuentes hung up. . . .

A cab pulled up to the front of the hotel. Fuentes watched the door open and saw a tall man ease himself out. Snow was falling, making it difficult for him to see the man's face clearly. The man waited until the doorman opened the door. His luggage, one large leather valise, was already in the hands of a bellboy. Fuentes moved his eyes over the man's face. It matched the one in the photograph.

Fuentes waited until the man had finished registering and stepped into an elevator before getting up. He went up to the desk clerk and in excellent French asked the clerk if the man who had just registered was Mr. Kass.

"Why, yes. He just came in."

Fuentes thanked him and went to the bar, where he ordered a Genever, *graf koud,* cold as the grave. The bartender smiled at his use of the Dutch expression, and told him, "That's the only way to have it."

Fuentes agreed and asked, "Is there a house phone in the bar?"

"You can use the phone at the end of the bar."

Fuentes thanked him, went to the phone and asked to be connected to Mr. Kass's room. It was his way of making sure that when the time came for him to kill, he would not kill the wrong man. Once he had had the misfortune to do that, and the people who had hired him for the job had beaten him so badly that he had been hospitalized for three months.

The phone rang three times.

Fuentes shifted from one leg to another. He would not have been pleased if Kass had just dropped his bag and left the hotel.

"Yes," the man in the room answered.

"Mr. Grasso?" Fuentes asked.

"No. You have the wrong number."

155

"Your room number is eight-oh-six. That is Mr. Grasso's room."

"This is six-oh-eight, and my name is Kass."

"I'm so sorry," Fuentes answered.

Fuentes put the phone down and walked back to his place at the bar. The tone of Kass's voice was that of a tired man. Fuentes guessed he had caught him in the shower and that probably now Kass would sleep for a few hours.

Fuentes picked up his Genever and drank it slowly. He could afford to relax for an hour or two before taking up his vigil in the lobby opposite the bank of elevators. He had already decided to kill Kass in his hotel room sometime that night. He would make it appear as if the motive for the killing was robbery.

Marrosov had told him that Kass was involved in the diamond business and would probably be carrying some gems with him. Since Marrosov had not said anything more about the diamonds, Fuentes figured he would take them as a bonus.

He drank another Genever, *koud,* lit up a fresh cigar, paid for his two drinks and left the bartender a generous tip before he walked back into the lobby. He stopped at the combination newsstand and bookstore to buy the day's edition of the international edition of the *Tribune.* Then he found a comfortable club chair facing the bank of elevators and ensconced himself in it. Sooner or later, Kass would come down. Probably when he became sufficiently hungry . . .

It was seven o'clock in the evening when Fuentes finally saw Kass step out of an elevator. Kass went to the desk, left his key there and walked toward the door of the lobby. Fuentes followed as far as the door.

Kass ordered a cab.

Fuentes turned, dropped his newspaper on an empty chair and took the elevator up to the sixth floor. Using a simple metal rod, he quickly opened the lock to Kass's room, entered it, closed the door behind him and switched on the light.

Kass's valise was neatly set on a luggage rack. There were a few things on the dresser: a razor, aftershave lotion and cologne. Fuentes went through the dresser drawers; they were empty. He placed the valise on the bed and dumped its contents out. The usual clothes and a passport case. He picked it up and opened it. There were two passports, one French for Kass, and a second, a special Russian passport with a picture of Kass on it. Fuentes could not read Russian, but intuition and experience combined to make him aware that Dimetrov, alias Kass, was worth more than ten thousand dollars.

But the only way to get more was to make Marrosov aware of what he knew. He couldn't wait to take Dimetrov out; he needed a new agreement with Marrosov now. Though there was a certain amount of risk involved, he decided to do some fast renegotiating.

He picked up the phone and, using Kass's name, put through a call to Marrosov at his home on Long Island.

"I'm sorry," the overseas operator said, "but the transatlantic lines are busy. I will have to ring you back."

Fuentes canceled the call. He was sure that Marrosov was acting on his own, and just knowing that should be worth another ten thousand dollars. Even men like Marrosov, with a great deal of power, were not at liberty to kill without orders from Moscow. . . . Fuentes would have been willing to bet that no such order existed.

He slipped the passport into his breast pocket and switched off the light. Crossing the room, he sat down in a chair next to the window, but facing the door. He fitted a silencer to his .38 and lit another cigar. He would fire the moment Kass closed the door behind him. One shot at the head would certainly kill him. But Fuentes planned to fire twice; once at the face between the eyes, and then at the left side of the chest. After it was over, he'd take a few minutes to search Kass's pockets. He was sure he would find the diamonds in one of them.

After a while, he leaned over and eased open the window to let the smoke out. It was snowing, and the street below was already covered white. He leaned back and thought about which of his friends read Russian. . . .

Dimetrov went to the Bali for dinner. Not only was the *rijsttafels* there one of the best in the city, but the waiters with their orange turbans and the lovely Indonesian paintings on the walls combined to produce an exotic ambiance that appealed to Dimetrov. He particularly enjoyed the jasmine tea and the small rice cakes he ate for dessert.

By the time Dimetrov left the restaurant, the snow had stopped, but the weather had turned sharply colder. It was still early enough for him to walk along the streets before going back to the hotel. Practically all the shops were decorated for the coming holiday season. Though he was a confirmed atheist, he secretly responded to the pageantry of Christmas, especially the idea of gift giving.

Dimetrov arrived back at his hotel at eleven thirty and decided to stop at the bar for a nightcap. The last thirty-six hours had, as the Americans would say, made him very uptight. One or two glasses of Genever would sufficiently take the edge off his anxiety.

The bar was doing a thriving business. Several of the men and women were wearing evening clothes. Many were Americans. He found a place near a lovely Indonesian woman who wore her black hair braided and piled into a bun on the top of her head. She smoked a cigarette through an amber-colored holder, and though she glanced at him when he settled into the space next to her, she seemed oblivious to his presence. Dimetrov ordered a very cold Genever, very much aware of her floral perfume. The woman made a slight turn toward him and smiled. Her teeth were very white and her eyes very black.

"May I buy you a drink?" Dimetrov asked. He knew she was a professional. The woman nodded.

He summoned the waiter and told him to give the lady whatever she wanted.

"Scotch on the rocks," she said. "The same as before."

"My name is Saul Kass," Dimetrov said.

"Luana," she said.

Dimetrov shook her hand, suddenly realizing how delicate she was. Since his arrival in New York, he hadn't even thought about a woman, but now there was one alongside him he wanted. As easily as snapping his fingers, his passion, or lust, had ignited. Their drinks were put down in front of them and Dimetrov toasted to luck.

"Yes," she told him in English, "luck even includes health and wealth. A person cannot have either health or wealth without having luck."

Dimetrov agreed with her.

When they finished their drinks, Dimetrov ordered another round. He considered asking her to come to his room, but decided not to. He paid for the drinks and bid her good night.

She raised her eyebrows questioningly.

"I'm just too tired," he explained.

"I know ways to ease that feeling," she answered.

"I wouldn't be much good," he said, leaving money on the bar for her to buy another drink. He went directly to the elevator. On the way up, he told himself that as soon as he could, after the mission was over, he'd take a vacation. He needed one. Perhaps he'd go to Yalta on the Black Sea for a few weeks.

The elevator stopped and the door slipped open. The door to his room was no more than a dozen meters from the elevator.

He stopped. He had the peculiar feeling that he was being watched. He turned and looked at the doors to the rooms behind him. They were shut. He remembered having the same feeling in the jungles of South Vietnam. Prickles raced down his spine.

Dimetrov took several deep breaths before he slipped his automatic from its holster and eased it into his coat pocket. He hoped no one would come into the hallway from any of the rooms or from the elevator. He moved quietly to the door of his room and listened.

There was the sound of some movement inside.

Dimetrov nodded. He reasoned that the person behind the door was either a common thief or had been sent from the intelligence organization of another government; or, lastly, the person in the room had come from the people under investigation, if his own activities had become known to them. Any one of the three possibilities could cost him his life.

Suddenly the phone in the room began to ring. It rang several times.

"But I told the operator to cancel the call," he heard a man say. A moment of silence followed. Then the man said, "All right. I'll speak with him." Another long moment of silence.

The man spoke again. "You didn't tell me who he was. . . . It does make a difference. My fee is twenty thousand. . . . No, I'm not fooling. . . . Listen, Marrosov, you are not in any bargaining position."

The phone was slammed down.

Dimetrov was sweating profusely. He eased himself away from the door, went directly to the service stairs and hurried to the lobby. He walked swiftly back into the bar. He saw Luana and went directly up to her.

"We'll be closing in ten minutes," the bartender told him.

Dimetrov nodded. Then to Luana, he said, "I've changed my mind. I decided to have another drink or two."

"And that's all?" Luana laughed.

"Perhaps not. Is there any other place we might go?"

"Yes. There's a small brown café not far from here."

"Let's go," he said, slipping Luana's coat onto her narrow shoulders. He led her out of the hotel lobby.

"It's only on the next street," she said.

He took her by the arm and walked swiftly toward the café. It was a small, charming place with old, dark wood beams and the strong scent of beer. They found a table off to one side.

Dimetrov ordered two beers. He drank slowly, without talking to Luana. That Marrosov was trying to have him killed confirmed his suspicions about the man. In some way,

Marrosov was connected to the exchange of Jews for diamonds. But his immediate problem was the man in his room. He must either frighten him off or kill him. If he frightened him, it would only provide a temporary respite. Dimetrov realized he had only one choice.

He looked across the table.

Luana was listening to the music, a song sung in English about love.

"Luana," he called, to have her complete attention. "I have something to tell you."

She looked directly at him. "My place is not far from here."

"There's a man in my room who is trying to kill me," Dimetrov said.

Her eyes went wide; then almost closed as she began to laugh. "That's the best line I've heard in a long time."

"It's the truth. And I need your help."

"You can stay at my place."

Dimetrov shook his head. "He will continue to try."

"But what can I do to help?"

"Call him," Dimetrov said. "Tell him I'm drunk . . . Tell him I'm somewhere . . . a place where I might have a chance. . . . Bring him to me."

She drew back. In a low voice, she asked, "Do you want to kill him?"

"I already told you, he wants to kill me."

"You're serious, aren't you?" she asked with a frown.

"Absolutely."

"I don't want to get mixed up in—"

"A thousand American dollars to make the phone call," Dimetrov offered, taking out his wallet. He removed ten hundred-dollar bills from it. "Then you go your way and I go mine. . . . It's a fair amount of money just to make a phone call."

The tip of Luana's tongue swirled around her lips. "A thousand just to make the phone call?"

Dimetrov nodded.

"It's worth more."

"How much more?"

"Another thousand."

Dimetrov looked into his wallet. "Five hundred more."

"Seven hundred and fifty."

"Five hundred," he repeated, adding five more hundred-dollar bills to those already on the table.

Luana stared at the bills and slowly reached across the table for them.

Dimetrov pulled his hand back. "Make the phone call and it's all yours."

"How do you know I won't go to the police?"

"I don't. But if you do, you might find it difficult to convince them you were telling the truth. But should they believe you, my friends would be annoyed, and doubtlessly they'd pay you a visit."

"I think I understand."

"Yes, I think you do."

Luana pursed her lips. She used a lace handkerchief to wipe the beads of perspiration from her forehead. "I will make the phone call," she said in a low voice.

When the phone rang again, Fuentes was sure it was Marrosov. He was in no mood to bargain. His price was a firm twenty thousand. He picked up the phone but remained silent.

"Your friend is very drunk," a woman said.

"What? Who are you?"

"Is this room six-oh-eight?"

"Yes."

"I'm going to leave Mr. Kass outside of Vondel Park, across from the Lido," she said; then hung up.

Fuentes put the phone down. He had not expected the situation to take such an unexpected turn. Either he was being set up, or he was just lucky. He had no way of knowing which without going. Dimetrov would be a formidable enemy. Rather than risk a protracted hunt, Fuentes decided he had to take the chance. He slipped on his coat and left.

Luana turned to Dimetrov. "Do you know where the park is?"

"Yes," he said, handing her the fifteen hundred-dollar bills. "And thank you."

"Will I ever see you again?" Luana asked, putting the bills in her purse.

"No, I don't think so."

"Good luck," she said. Then with a lovely smile, she added, "I really could have made you feel good."

"I know," he replied with a nod. "I am sure you could have done it, if anyone could have."

"Good luck again," she said, and walked swiftly away from the telephone kiosk.

Dimetrov waited until she turned the corner before he hailed a cab and told the driver to take him to the Municipal Theater of the Leidseplein.

He walked from there to the entrance to Vondel Park and took a position across from it, behind several large pine trees. Though it was cold, Dimetrov was sweating; and from time to time he stamped his feet to keep them warm.

Some distance from the entrance to the park, a cab stopped and a man got out. The cab pulled away, and the man walked toward the park. Dimetrov watched the man. He came closer. Though Dimetrov couldn't see the gun, he knew by the way the man held his arm there was one in his right hand. The man moved into the park for several meters and looked around. Then suddenly he began to back out of the park. As soon as the man was out of the park, Dimetrov picked up a rock and threw it to the right of him.

The man whirled toward the right and fired. The shot made a pop-like noise, immediately followed by the distinctive ping of a ricocheting bullet. Another shot made a pop-like sound. The man continued to back out of the park.

Dimetrov was close enough to kill with his hands. He tossed another rock, this time to the left.

But the instant the man raised his hand to fire a third time, Dimetrov ran toward him. Within seconds, he was behind the man. Before the man could wheel around and fire, Dimetrov struck him in the back of the neck with a chop from his right hand. The bone crunched. The man's head suddenly flopped to the left side; he dropped to the ground, letting go of his gun.

Breathing hard, Dimetrov stood over him. The man tried to move, but he jerked around like a fish suddenly out of the water. He was dying slowly and no doubt painfully. He made low, wordless sounds. To end his suffering, Dimetrov reached down and picked up the .38. At point-blank range, he put a bullet into the man's heart. Then he bent over the body and went through the man's pockets. He recovered his own passport, and from a Master Charge card he discovered his would-be assassin was named Carlo Fuentes. Dimetrov remembered having heard the name.

To confuse the police, Dimetrov took Fuentes's watch and the money in his wallet. He threw Fuentes's credit cards into a nearby clump of bushes. On the way back to the hotel, he dropped the watch into the Single Gracht Canal. But he kept the revolver.

Early the following morning, Dimetrov went directly to the Soviet consulate, where one of the clerks made the necessary phone calls to the Amsterdam police to find out where Julian was staying. After he had that information, he put through a call to Detective Dalis in New York.

As soon as Dalis was on the line, Dimetrov said, "If you watch a Mr. Korditz, you'll discover some interesting connections between him and the men in the Diamond Exchange who were killed."

"Who the hell are you?"

"An interested party," Dimetrov answered calmly.

"Where are you calling from?"

"Amsterdam."

"Amsterdam, New York?"

"No, Holland," Dimetrov said; then he hung up. Later that morning he drove by the Jan Luyken Hotel in a cab. He was surprised to discover how close it was to the entrance of Vondel Park. Not more than fifteen minutes away.

When he returned to the hotel, Dimetrov called the consulate and arranged to have Julian followed.

"I want him to know he's being followed," Dimetrov told the agent on the other end. "That's absolutely essential." It was his way of alerting Julian to danger without compromising his mission.

In the afternoon, Dimetrov bought a newspaper. There was a picture of Fuentes on the front page. Though Dimetrov was unable to read much of the text, he could make out enough of the words to know the police thought the dead man had been the victim of a mugging. Dimetrov went back to his room with the newspaper, cut out the picture of Fuentes, placed it in an envelope and addressed it to Marrosov. He mailed it early that evening.

35

THE COMPANY CAR came for Julian at the hotel and drove him to Lublin Enterprises, Inc., on the Stahoudeskade. The building was a narrow, two-story gabled structure overlooking a canal. He went inside and told the receptionist who he was.

"Please sit down," she said, "Miss Koss will be with you shortly."

Julian thanked her, opened his coat and dropped into a comfortable-looking chair near a table loaded with magazines in various languages. On the walls around the room were photographs depicting various phases of working diamonds from raw stones to the finished product.

Cynthia came through a door behind the receptionist. She wore a lovely blue pants suit.

"I thought I'd have a longer wait," Julian said, getting to his feet, pleased to see her again. They greeted each other with a firm handshake.

"Mr. Lublin phoned. He will be here tomorrow," she said.

Julian nodded.

"Come, follow me," Cynthia told him. "You may leave your coat in my office."

"How did you sleep?" he asked, following her into the processing portion of the building.

"Excellently. And you?"

"Excellently," he repeated with a smile.

The tour through the plant took the entire morning. It began with the cleaving room, where the raw stones were shaped along their lines of cleavage. He met and spoke with the man whose responsibility it was to cut the diamonds, whose misplaced blow could shatter a stone.

Cynthia took him into the sawing room, where the cut diamond crystals were separated. The sawing was always done in two different directions. These were noncleaving.

"To use the crystallographer's terms," Cynthia explained, "one is in the cube direction and the other in the dodecahedral."

She continued to explain the process and led Julian into another room where diamonds were bruted: one diamond crystal was rubbed against another to remove the rough edges produced by the other two processes.

Then they moved into the grinding operation, where surfaces on the stones were made flat by grinding them on a wheel covered with diamond powder and special lubricants. Finally they entered the polishing room, where each diamond was given its final treatment before being graded.

Julian was not only impressed with what he saw but

with Cynthia's knowledge of the technical processes, and he said as much.

"After a while," she laughed, "if you're at all interested, you begin to pick it up, but I must admit I did a great deal of reading about diamonds. And," she added with a smile, "my father was in the business. Nothing like Mr. Lublin or your father. He owned a small jewelry store in Bristol."

Julian chuckled.

"Funny?" she asked.

"Amusing," Julian answered. "I spent so many years running away from diamonds and people who had anything to do with them. Now I'm here to take you to lunch and you obviously have a great deal to do with diamonds."

"Yes, I do," she answered. "If you want to break our lunch date—"

"Get your coat," he said. "We're going to lunch."

They returned to Cynthia's office before they left the building. Outside it was raw. The sky was very gray, and wind came off the sea.

"There's a delightful café on the next street," Cynthia told him. "They serve a thick vegetable-and-meat soup and excellent fried fish, and during the season, some of the best herring in Amsterdam."

"Soup would be fine on a day like this," Julian replied, taking hold of her gloved hand.

The café had an unpronounceable Dutch name, and it was delightfully pleasant inside. A huge open fireplace kept the stone-walled room warm. The beamed ceiling and wooden tables and chairs gave it a unique atmosphere.

"Your father liked this place," Cynthia said as they settled down at a table for two close to the fireplace. "He especially liked the herring, when he could get it."

Julian looked around, nodded, but made no comment. From the very beginning of the tour, Sam had been very much in his thoughts.

The waiter came. Each of them ordered vegetable soup and fried sole with fried potatoes and dark Amstel beer. "I can't imagine my father enjoying this place," Julian said, buttering a piece of dark bread. "It's not like anything I'd imagine he'd like."

"How did he get into the diamond business?" she asked.

"I don't really know. He never told me. And I never heard any stories about it when I was a child. If I had, I'm sure I'd have remembered them."

The waiter brought their soup to the table. It came in large, tan stoneware bowls with covers on top. "There's enough for two in one bowl!" Julian exclaimed.

"The Dutch have healthy appetites," she said and laughed.

Julian felt comfortable with Cynthia. Though unpretentious, she was nonetheless self-confident.

"Tell me how you decided to become a writer," she asked.

"After Vietnam," he answered, finishing the last spoonful of soup in the bowl, "there really wasn't anything else for me . . . Nothing else made sense."

"I don't understand. You might have become a doctor or a lawyer."

"My father would have loved that . . . But neither was in the cards. I guess I lost the impulse to make an honest living." He spoke with a straight face, waiting for her to react.

Her head cocked to one side, and her eyes began to twinkle with laughter. "You just slipped that one in there," she said, making a waving motion with her hand.

"To see if you were really paying attention," he answered. "But the truth was that if Nam taught me anything besides how to kill a man, it taught me that all any man really ever had was his own dreams and aspirations, and to ignore them was a crime as heinous as the war itself. I wanted to be me, and me—well, me was a man who wanted to write. I went to Hollywood to get away from Sam. I began to write for TV because it was the medium available to me."

The waiter replaced their empty bowls with large platters of fried fish and potatoes. He made another trip for two steins of beer.

"Had I stayed in New York," Julian said, "I might have gone into something else, perhaps the novel or the Broadway stage. But since staying in New York was out of the question, I directed my writing to the available market for it."

"Have you ever thought of writing a novel?"

Julian shook his head. "No, I don't think so. I like TV, and I'm in a position to do the kind of scripts that have substance."

"Then you like what you're doing?"

"Absolutely," he said without hesitation.

They finished eating and took a few minutes for coffee before they left the café. On the way back to the office, Julian asked Cynthia if she would have dinner with him.

"Yes," she answered. "I'd rather like that. I'll send the car around for you at seven."

"Good," Julian answered. "I think I'll spend the afternoon enjoying Amsterdam. It's my first visit here."

"Then by all means, enjoy it."

When they reached the front of the building, Julian stopped, took her in his arms and kissed her. She put her arms around his neck and kissed him back. Then, moving away, she said, "See you at seven." She turned and went inside.

Julian spent a delightful three hours in Vincent Van Gogh Museum, enjoying not only the paintings and drawings of the artist but also his letters, which were on display. Though they were written in Dutch, there were translations into English, French and Italian that made it possible for Julian to recognize Van Gogh's literary gift as well.

He left the museum at four. It was sufficiently dark for the street lamps to be on. The company car was waiting for him, but Julian told the driver he'd prefer to walk. The hotel was close by and Julian was looking forward to being with Cynthia again.

He passed a newspaper vendor and glanced down at the stack of papers. He took another step forward, stopped and returned to the vendor. On the front page there was a picture of Carlo Fuentes, the man who had sat next to him on the plane. Since almost everyone in Holland spoke English, Julian asked the newspaper man if he could tell him why the man's picture was in the paper.

"Mugged," the man said, "and murdered, just outside of Vondel Park. The police are asking for those who knew him to come to the central police station."

Julian thanked him, bought a newspaper and, tucking it under his arm, hurried back to the hotel. He was shocked that someone like Fuentes, who was so full of life, should have his own taken from him by a mugger. There were times, and this was one of them, that Julian felt the true rulers of the world's cities were the hoodlums of the streets who preyed on others and on themselves. They were the destructive stratum of society, taking and killing, more often than not for pleasure.

When he reached his room, Julian called Cynthia at the office. Upset, he wanted to be comforted. But she had already left, and rather than phone her at home he decided to wait until he saw her. He was undecided about going to the police. He didn't want to become involved in something that might conceivably prevent him from leaving the country.

The phone rang. Julian answered it, hoping it would be Cynthia. There was a momentary pause; then came the familiar click of someone on the other end hanging up.

Julian called the hotel operator and asked if he had just received a call. "Yes," the operator answered. "A man distinctly asked for you, Mr. Heck; then he hung up. I thought the conversation was brief."

"There wasn't any conversation," Julian said. He thanked the operator and put the phone down. A sudden chill passed over him, making him tremble; the call upset him, though he didn't know why.

Julian decided he had overreacted to the phone call. The person who called had made an honest mistake. For him to think otherwise would require him to admit that the same people who had worked him over in New York had followed him to Amsterdam. He could not accept that, unless he had grossly undervalued the worth of Sam's goods. Besides, only Guber and his friends knew he was in Amsterdam. Kass also knew, but he—

Julian suddenly stopped thinking. He picked up the phone. "Would it be possible for you to obtain a phone number in Paris for me?" he asked the hotel operator. "The name is Saul Kass. I don't have his address. But he might be listed under jewelers or diamond dealers, if there is such a listing."

"I'll call you back in fifteen or twenty minutes," the operator said. Julian put down the phone. He showered, brushed his teeth and combed his hair before the phone rang. He answered it before it rang a second time.

"There are two Kasses listed in the Paris directory," the hotel operator said, "but neither of them with the first name of Saul."

"Thank you," Julian said. He put down the phone and rubbed his hand over his chin. He found himself worrying about Kass. The diamond dealer from Paris suddenly became a question; more specifically, several questions.

"Well," Julian told himself, "he knows I'm here and there's nothing I can do about that." But it wasn't easy to dismiss Kass from his thoughts. The fact that Kass turned up at Sam's apartment so soon after his death suddenly changed from having been a coincidence to something suspicious.

That Sam might have left his goods with Kass—Julian was allowing his imagination to run away and that was the very worst thing he could do. There was probably a very good reason that Kass's number wasn't in the Paris directory. His number might be unlisted; he might live in an outlying district of the city that was not included in the directory . . . Kass was a friend, and there wasn't any reason for him to think he was something else.

Julian shook his head. It was too easy for a person to become paranoid: the reason could be real or imagined—and then the human mind with its enormous capacity for invention did the rest. Satisfied that he had reasoned himself out of a foolish state of mind, he began to think of the evening with

Cynthia. He decided to obtain tickets for the evening concert at the Concertgebouw. He was sure the concierge would be able to get them for him.

They were in front of the building where Cynthia lived. Once again it was snowing; very small powderlike flakes were falling. Julian was hard put to remember a better evening. He had not mentioned anything about Fuentes to Cynthia and was pleased that he hadn't. Nothing had come between them and their enjoyment.

"Better tell the chauffeur not to wait," Cynthia said.

Julian nodded, went back to the limousine and told the driver to call for him at the hotel at about ten the following morning.

The man nodded and winked.

Julian felt the color rise in his cheeks, but he said nothing. A few minutes later he was in Cynthia's apartment. It was small; one large room served as kitchen, dining room and living room. There was a small bedroom and a bathroom. Two windows in the large room overlooked the canal. The bedroom window faced the brick wall of the building on the next street. A garden separated the two buildings.

"Would you like a drink?" she asked, standing against the table.

Julian shook his head.

"I had this all planned out," she told him. "But now—"

"Come here," he said, moving toward her.

She went to him. He put his arms around her. "I want you," he said softly, speaking close to her ear. "I think you want me."

"Yes," she answered. "I did last night, too."

He led her into the bedroom, and a short while later they lay naked in each other's arms. Her body was exquisite. He kissed her passionately on the lips; then moved his tongue over the pink nipple of each breast. They hardly spoke.

He noticed the small blue veins on the outside of each of her breasts and traced them with his finger, then with his lips. He kissed the small hollow of her stomach and then the lips of

172

her sex. She moaned with pleasure, repeating his name over and over again. Then she changed her position, taking his penis in her mouth.

When they finally moved together, they faced each other on their sides. One of her thighs was over his and the other beneath him. He kissed her again and again, as they thrust against each other.

"I can feel it," she gasped. Her body tensed. "Oh, I can feel it." She flung herself against him, raking his back with her nails.

An instant later, he climaxed, making a low, throaty sound of pleasure.

"Would you come to the States with me?" Julian asked, after a long silence. He had weighed the question before posing it and realized that he more than liked her. She was one of the few women he knew who was more impressed with the fact that he wrote than with the money he made by doing it.

"You didn't have to ask me that," she answered.

He caressed the back of her head. "Yes, I did; otherwise how would I know?"

She put her hand on his chest. "I know it's a dumb thing to say, particularly at this moment. But the truth is we don't know each other. There's a huge difference between love and lust."

"And love without lust can never be," he responded. "Will you come back with me?"

"Let me think about it," she said after a few moments of silence.

"Is it a possibility?"

"Yes, but I still want to think about it."

"Think about it," he answered, moving his hand over her breasts. "But remember I wouldn't have asked if I didn't really want you with me."

"Thank you," she said and kissed him gently on the lips.

36

"THE SHELTER, on Seventy-seventh and Broadway; that's where I told Marrosov we'd meet him," Borsky said to Guber and Korditz, who were in the cab with him.

"Why up there?" Korditz asked.

"Why up there—okay, you tell me a better place. I don't know why up there. I read about it recently. Writers and publishing people go there. There's a group of them that meets on Wednesday afternoons."

"What do you say, Max?"

"I say you should stop asking dumb questions," Guber answered, without taking his eyes from the window. Outside, the sidewalks were wet from an early rain and clouds still covered the sky. His answer silenced the other two until the cab stopped in front of the restaurant, and Korditz said he would pay the fare.

Marrosov was already there. He was sitting in the back, off to one side, hunched over his drink. Guber led the others to the table. Without a word, he sat down opposite the Russian. Borsky and Korditz flanked Guber: Borsky on his right, Korditz on his left.

A waitress came to the table and asked if they wanted anything to drink. Guber ordered a vodka. Borsky and Korditz asked for scotch on the rocks. Marrosov said nothing, focusing his attention on Guber.

Borsky made the opening gambit by saying, "Our friend has had another unforeseen difficulty?"

Still looking at Guber, Marrosov said, "The man I sent to Kass found out he really is Dimetrov and wants another ten thousand for—"

The waitress approached the table with the tray of drinks.

"If the money isn't paid," Marrosov said, when they

were alone again, "he has enough to go to my people." He stopped and took a sip of his drink. "Have you any idea what they'll do to me?"

"What did you tell your friend?" Guber asked.

"Nothing. He didn't give me a chance. He told me to deposit the additional money in his account."

"You don't have much of a choice, do you?" Guber commented with a shrug.

"It's not I who haven't much of a choice," Marrosov said. "It's you people."

"You said you would take care of the matter," Borsky reminded him.

"That was for one sum of money. Now it's double."

"Suppose your man decided to increase it again, and again after that?" Korditz asked.

Marrosov glared at him. Looking down at his drink, he said, "There are ways of putting an end to that kind of thing."

"Then why not use them?" Guber asked.

Marrosov shook his head. "Someone might make the connection between the two. The man I sent to do the job is known for the kind of work he does. If he should suddenly be killed, it would look too suspicious, especially to the people who sent Dimetrov here."

Guber lifted his vodka and drank most of it. "What would you do if we refused to pay?" he asked.

"But you're not going to refuse, are you?"

"Obviously not," Guber answered. "But what would you do?"

"I'd have no choice but to turn myself over to the CIA," Marrosov said. "That, of course, would put an end to your hope of getting Urishensky out or, for that matter, anyone else, until the network could be completely rebuilt—and that's not likely until you find someone to replace Heckowitz. The CIA would like to know about your operation, if for no other reason than to model one of their own after it."

"We will give you the additional money," Guber said. "But you must give us a few day."

"How long is a few days?"

"Three," Guber said, looking at Borsky for confirmation.

"Three is all right," Borsky responded.

"What about you, Marek?" Guber asked, turning his head toward Korditz, who agreed with a wordless nod.

"Borsky," Marrosov said, "I'll meet you at the Weather-vane on Wednesday night at seven."

"I'll be there."

"A word of advice," Guber said in a normal tone. "Don't be a fool and go to the CIA." And before Marrosov could respond, he added, "You're into us as much as we're into you. Don't ever be so stupid as to forget that."

"Are you threatening me?" Marrosov asked, his voice edged with anger and his eyes narrowed to slits.

"Only reminding you of your obligations," Guber said, and summoning the waitress, he asked for the check.

Marrosov flushed. "Jews," he muttered, "goddamn stink-ing Jews."

Guber nodded, stood up and left the table. Borsky and Korditz followed him. Outside, Guber turned downtown. He walked quickly, followed by Borsky and Korditz. He was in a rage. Forced to stop for a traffic light, he turned to the other two and said, "Someone like Marrosov makes me wonder if some of us were made in an image other than God's. That one back there looks like a man, talks like a man and does every-thing a man does; but is he a man?"

The light changed and they crossed the street. "I'm going back to my office," Guber told them. "But I have to walk, or I'll explode."

"I'll walk with Max for a while," Borsky said.

They stopped and shook hands. Guber and Borsky con-tinued down Broadway.

As soon as Korditz reached his apartment, he phoned Begin and told him he'd be at the Club Negev by seven. Then he napped for almost an hour, showered and dressed. He remembered the blond he had danced with the last time he had been at the club. Her name was Alice Hicks. He had wound up in the sack with her, and she had even more talent there than she had displayed on the dance floor.

When he left his lobby Korditz discovered it was drizzling. He paused for a few moments to decide whether he should go back for an umbrella. He chose to continue without it, and started to walk again. He became vaguely aware of a man coming out of the building and walking in the same direction.

At the corner, Korditz hailed a cab, and twenty minutes later he entered the club. Begin was waiting for him at a table close to the door. Korditz scanned the dancers for Alice, with no luck. He checked his coat and hat before he joined Begin and sat facing him.

"Our Russian friend has just asked for another ten thousand," Korditz said.

"For what?"

"Blackmail."

Begin leaned forward. "What the hell are you talking about?"

"The guy he sent to take out his comrade found out who his comrade really is and wants to be paid accordingly, or—now get this—he'll go to the CIA."

Begin rolled the cigar in his mouth from the left to the right side. "You think he meant it?"

"I don't think we can risk finding out," Korditz said.

"This time we have more trouble than we had on all the other hits put together."

"It's hard to be lucky all the time," Korditz answered. "Sometimes you have to work a little to make luck turn your way."

Begin took the cigar out of his mouth and sipped at the drink that was in front of him. "Tell me what you think about our Russian friend's threat."

"He'll make good on it."

"But you said it would happen only if you and your people didn't come across with ten big ones."

"For now," Korditz answered. "This guy he got to do the job has him by the balls, and he'll squeeze him whenever it suits his purpose."

"Then you think it's only a matter of time before he goes over?"

Korditz nodded.

"Before or after the diamonds are delivered?"

"Can you figure what a Russian will do?"

Begin put the cigar back in his mouth, rolled it to the left side and said, "I'll have a couple of guys up here from Florida. It'll cost us five Gs, but the job will be professional. We'll make a call to the *Times* after it's done and tell 'em it's the work of the Polish Liberation Front."

"Is there such a group?"

"Who the hell knows?" Begin said with a shrug. "If there's not one, there should be."

Korditz smiled. "When are you going to have your visitors come up?"

"I'll make the call while you're out there dancing. Did you score with that blond?"

"Yes. I didn't see her when I came in."

"She usually shows up later."

"I was thinking of going to Paris," Korditz said. "That way I could follow things along until the stones reach London."

"As long as you don't get in the way," Begin answered. "Now there's a guy who knows how to move. He came in a few minutes after you, and already he latched onto a chick."

Korditz turned around to watch a man in a gray vested business suit dance with a petite woman with long black hair.

LUBLIN WAS A CRICKETLIKE MAN with a pair of white metal-rimmed glasses perched on the tip of his nose. He sat behind a large mahogany desk and smiled graciously at Julian as he apologized for being away. "Sometimes there is a burst of activity in this business, too," he explained. "But thank God not very often." He spoke English with a slight German accent.

Julian nodded understandingly and said, "I have a letter from Max Guber. He asked me to give it to you."

"If you don't mind," Lublin said, reaching across the desk for the sealed envelope, "I'd like to read it now."

"Go ahead," Julian responded, using the time to look around the office. The walls were lined with bookshelves and from what he could make out, the books on them were written in many languages. Some were enclosed in glass cases. He guessed that Lublin must be a collector.

"Max with his little jokes," Lublin commented, setting the letter down. "Always little jokes."

"Now suppose you tell me why you're here," Lublin said, placing his hands on the desk as though his fingers were about to strike the keys of a piano.

"I thought Max might have said something about it in his letter," Julian said.

"No, it was all business," Lublin answered, tapping the letter with the forefinger of his right hand.

"I'll come right to the point," Julian said, moving slightly forward on his chair. "I want to know if my father left any of his goods with you before he died."

Lublin's eyebrows went up. "That's an odd question."

"I'm sure my father left—"

"Why would he leave anything with me?"

"You were his friend, weren't you?"

"Yes."

"Are you sure Max didn't write anything—"

"He mentioned you were curious about your father."

"I came here hoping my father left his goods with you," Julian said. He was finding it difficult to hide his exasperation. "I was almost sure his goods would be with you."

Lublin leaned back. "How much do you know about your father?" he asked.

"What has that got to do with my reason for coming here?"

"Nothing really," Lublin answered. "But since I don't happen to have his goods, I thought you might take something of less monetary value but nonetheless of some worth—though of exactly how much value, you'd have to be the judge."

"I suppose you're going to tell me what a wonderful man he was."

Lublin leaned back. The chair was actually much too big for him and he looked like an oversized child sitting in a grown-up's chair. This impression was made all the more intense by his wispy gray hair. Lublin pressed the balls of his fingers together and moved his hands just under his chin. "Sam not only managed to survive Auschwitz, but he saved the lives of many of his friends, including myself."

"Guber and Borsky."

"Yes, and others. But do you know how he did it?"

Julian shook his head.

"By becoming the lover of the wife of one of the SS officers and by trading in gold."

"He never spoke about what he did," Julian said, finding that the words stuck in his throat.

"Sam was a very handsome man. Not good-looking in the way American movie stars are, but the way someone is when he's a manly-looking man. He was that way in the camp."

"You mean he prostituted himself?"

Lublin dropped his hands down to the desk, rapping it sharply. "He did what he had to do to bring us food, to stop them from taking me to the gas chamber. He did what no man should ever be asked to do and still call himself a man."

"And the gold, did he get that from the woman?"

"Your father was in charge of taking the gold out of the teeth of those Jews who had been gassed. He always managed to take some of the fillings for himself to buy food, to buy lives, to buy anything that would keep some of us alive one day longer. Sam was a remarkable man. He made many friends and many enemies."

"All right," Julian said, "he was a remarkable man. But I didn't come here to hear that. I came here to claim what is rightfully mine. . . . I don't see anything to smile about. Everyone tells me how remarkable or how wonderful my father was. Okay, he was. But that's not why I came here."

"Yes, you're right. That was rude and I apologize for it. In your place, I don't think I'd appreciate anyone smiling at my situation. But I assure you I have nothing here that belonged to your father. But there is a man in Paris who might. He was a very good friend of your father's."

"So were you," Julian answered sarcastically.

"Whether you go or not," Lublin said with a shrug, "is up to you. I can only give you his name and address." He leaned forward, picked up a pen and wrote on a small piece of light brown note paper. When he was finished, he pushed the paper toward Julian. "Take it. If you decide to go, you'll have it. If not, you can tear it up."

Julian took the piece of paper and put it in his wallet. "This is a wild goose chase if there ever was one," he commented, getting to his feet.

Lublin walked him to the door and shook his hand. "It's not so wild as you might think," he said. "You might find something even more valuable."

"Like what?"

"If I could answer that, I would be much more than a diamond dealer—very much more." There was a hint of laughter behind the glasses that covered his eyes.

Julian opened the door and left the office. He was too annoyed to do anything more than mutter, "Thank you."

"Don't mention it!" Lublin called after him.

Julian stopped at Cynthia's desk. She looked up from her work and smiled at him. He tried to smile back.

"Is anything wrong?" she asked.

"I'll call you later," he answered, going to the small closet where he had left his coat. "I have a lot to think about."

The phone on her desk began to ring. She frowned.

"Go ahead and answer it," Julian said. "I'll phone later." Then he leaned over and kissed her on the forehead. "Don't worry about me. I just have some things to think about." He headed out the door, down the hallway and finally out of the building.

He hadn't any specific direction in mind and began walking. He was very angry with Max for allowing him to think Lublin might have Sam's goods. He pursed his lips and continued to walk until he came to the place across from the Lido where there was a boat that took tourists through the canals.

Julian bought a ticket, went aboard and found a seat under the glass roof near the stern. The boat was almost empty. By the time it left dockside, the weak sun gave way to clouds. But the inside of the boat was comfortably warm.

Julian was too wrapped up in his own thoughts to pay any attention to the lovely-looking young woman who described the various things they passed as they moved through the canals. What Lublin had told him about Sam took hold of him, or perhaps he took hold of it, trying to understand what had happened in Auschwitz. Suddenly he began to tremble. He felt cold without being in the cold. He wept without making a sound, without really knowing why.

Julian wiped his eyes and blew his nose several times before he realized a man was looking at him from across the aisle. "A cold," he explained, "a very bad cold."

The man's face was blank.

Julian gave a theatrical sneeze.

Smiling, the man nodded. Julian blew his nose and moved closer to the lecturer.

The boat was now in the large waterway called the Het Ij. The various freighters at the docks came from every part of the world. After a few minutes, the boat made its way back into the canals and eventually tied up at the dock across from the Lido, near the entrance to Vondel Park.

Julian was one of the last passengers to leave the boat. He decided to go to Paris the following day. Hailing a cab, he told the driver to take him to the KLM ticket office, where he bought a ticket for the eleven o'clock flight. Then he went into a nearby café and called Cynthia. Julian assured her he was all right and confirmed their dinner date; then he asked to speak with Lublin, and told him his plans.

"You have all the information you need on the slip of paper I gave you," Lublin said.

"I'm sorry if I was rude," Julian apologized.

"I have forgotten all about it," Lublin answered.

"When I finish in Paris, I'm coming back to Amsterdam. Perhaps we could have dinner together."

"It would be my pleasure," Lublin said. "Good luck and good-bye."

Julian thanked him again and put the phone down; then he went to the bar, ordered a beer and a *broodjeswinkel* of ham and cheese. He took the piece of paper that Lublin had written on out of his wallet. The man he would see in Paris was M. Saul Legris; his address was 22 rue Cygnet. Lublin had also written Legris's phone number.

Julian refolded the piece of paper and returned it to his wallet. He sat at the bar eating and drinking his beer. He was going to Paris, he told himself, because there might be a chance Legris had his father's goods. Since he was already in Europe, it would be stupid not to go. But if Legris didn't have them, that would be the end of it. He would have to accept that Sam either hadn't left any diamonds, or if he had, that they would remain in someone else's possession.

Julian shook his head. He still couldn't bring himself to believe Sam hadn't left some stones with one of his friends.

By the time Julian left the café, a drizzling rain was

falling. It was dark enough for the street lights to be on. Looking in vain for a cab, he started in the general direction of the hotel, which he knew from his previous day's visit to the museums. The KLM office was located nearby on the Museumplein. There was a rawness in the air that bothered him more than the rain did, and he turned his collar up.

Julian stopped for a traffic light and looked at the brightly illuminated store window. And he saw him. The same man that he had seen on the boat? He wasn't sure. The man was standing off to one side of the window.

The light changed. Julian dashed across the street, walking very fast. At the next corner, he looked over his shoulder. The man wasn't anywhere behind him. He turned the corner and made his way back to the hotel, stopping now and then to see if he was still being followed. He wasn't.

Julian reached the hotel and asked the concierge to have room service bring him a cup of hot tea. Warmed, he lay down for a nap. Sleep came quickly. He slid into a sepia landscape made up of photographs he once had seen of the concentration camps . . .

Naked bodies were stacked like cordwood. Their mouths were open, frozen in the last scream of agony before the gas stopped them from breathing. He went from mouth to mouth, smashing their teeth out. There were huge piles of white teeth and huge piles of stained teeth. He smashed the teeth, reached into them and scooped out gold. The gold ran through his fingers and turned into the blond hair of a woman, whom he mounted and brought to a shuddering, squealing climax even as she grabbed his genitals between the blood-red lips of her vagina. He screamed in pain, looked up and saw the sun-colored smoke rising from the chimneys above the crematorium. The smoke of people, his people; the smoke of burning Jews . . . God, this can't be happening, he shouted.

"This can't be happening," Julian moaned.

The phone rang.

Julian sat up, drenched with sweat.

The phone rang again.

As soon as he answered, the line went dead.

Julian held the phone for several moments before he slammed it down. "Fucker," he shouted, "Goddamn fucker!" He wiped the sweat from his forehead, got off the bed and began to pace. Someone was following him; he was sure of that now. And the only reason for anyone to do that had to be because he was still looking for Sam's goods. Whoever was following him wanted to frighten him off. "Well, it's not going to work," Julian said, looking at the phone. "It's not going to work!"

They sat in a small café, where the light from a flickering candle gave their faces a yellowish red glow and cast their shadows on the stone wall alongside the table. They held hands. Neither felt the need to talk.

Cynthia smiled and said, "I know you're with me because I have hold of your hand. But are you with me in your head?"

Julian let go of her hand, lifted his stein of beer and took several sips. "Mr. Lublin told me a few things about my father that I have not found easy to take." He put his hand over hers and squeezed it gently. "My father—"

He was forced to stop by the sudden constriction in his throat. After a few moments, he continued to tell her what his father had done to save the lives of several men, including Lublin. "I'm just having difficulty coming to terms with it. You see, we weren't very close. He was always a solitary man. I never really understood why."

"Perhaps he had to be that way in order to live."

"With his wife and son? We might have made life easier for him if he had let us. But he never said a word about what happened in Auschwitz. All I knew was that he was there and that he had terrible memories. I had no idea what those memories were."

"I don't know what to say," Cynthia answered. "But you must not shoulder all the blame. Certainly some of it was his as well as yours."

"Not blame," Julian responded. "But guilt—that's what I feel."

"But surely you can't be guilty if you didn't know?"

Julian shook his head. "Guilt doesn't function that way," he said, patting her hand. "He was my father . . . I owed and never paid. I agree there's a certain degree of irrationality about it, but no more than is involved in the belief of God. At least I could see and hear my father and knew—" He stopped. There was a man watching them. He was at a table diagonally across the room. "I think we should leave," he said, still looking at the man.

"What? I haven't finished my beer."

"We're being watched," he said. "This is not the first time. It started in New York."

"Do you recognize the man?"

Julian shook his head. "It was not the same man who was on the boat with me this afternoon."

"How can you be sure?"

"Believe me, I know what I'm talking about. By now, I'm an expert."

"But why would you be followed?"

"Because I'm getting close to my goal, and they—whoever they are—want to stop me."

Julian called the waiter, paid the check and left. He hailed a cab and told the driver to take them to the Jan Luyken Hotel.

"Now what are you going to do?" Cynthia asked.

He put his lips to her ear and whispered, "Make passionate love to you."

"Do be serious."

"I am," he answered, straightening up. "There's no need to worry. That man in the café isn't going to come looking for me. He knows where I'm staying, and when I leave the hotel again he or someone like him will be there to follow me."

"I think you just made the whole thing up to—"

"To get you back to the hotel and into bed as quickly as possible," he said with a lascivious laugh.

When Julian stopped at the hotel desk for the key to his room, the clerk handed him a message. "From Mr. Lublin," Julian said to Cynthia. "He wants me to phone him." He handed her the piece of pink paper.

"That's his home phone number," she commented.

Julian escorted her into the small elevator. When they were in his room, he put through a call to Lublin.

"I am sorry to disturb you," Lublin said. "But I have a parcel of stones for Legris. He called a few hours ago and asked for them. Ordinarily I would send them by mail or use one of my own men to deliver them. But since you're going to see him, I thought I'd ask you."

"I'll pick them up before I leave tomorrow," Julian said.

"Are you sure it's no trouble?"

"It's no trouble at all. After all, I'm going to see the man."

"He knows you're coming. And thank you. Good night."

"Good night," Julian responded, and as he put the phone down, he realized Cynthia was standing at the door. She was breathing rapidly. Her blue eyes were alive with anger.

"You might have at least told me you were leaving," she said. "Or were you going to casually mention it after we finished fucking?"

He moved close to her. "I intended to tell you in the café, but then I saw that man."

"I'm going," she said, opening the door.

Julian rushed forward and threw his weight against it, slamming it shut.

"What are you going to do, rape me?" Cynthia challenged.

Julian took a deep breath and exhaled slowly. He didn't want to lose his temper. "I have to go to Paris for a day, two days at the very most. I have business to take care of there."

"You might have said something."

"I told you I would have but—"

"You know I don't even know why you're in Amsterdam. I know you're not a diamond dealer. But I don't even know why you're here."

Julian nodded. Though he had spoken to her a great deal about Sam, he had never mentioned his reason for being in Amsterdam. "There's nothing mysterious about it," he said in a calm voice. "If you sit down, I'll tell you."

"I can listen standing up."

"Please sit down in the chair," he said. "Please?"

Cynthia walked away from the door and sat down in the chair near the window.

"My father left me a hundred thousand dollars in cash and bonds," Julian said. "But he did not leave me any diamonds."

She raised her eyebrows questioningly.

"You told me your father was a jeweler," he said.

"He is."

"All right, then, besides cash and perhaps bonds, what else would he leave you and the rest of the family when he dies?"

"Diamonds . . . He has more faith in their value than in the pound sterling."

"Exactly. My father felt the same way about diamonds, that much I knew about him. But he didn't leave me any diamonds, and I know he must have. He must have left them with one of his friends."

"So you came here thinking Mr. Lublin had your father's diamonds."

"Yes."

"And that's why you're going to see Mr. Legris?"

"Yes, again."

"But what makes you so sure that he left diamonds?"

"Because he believed in them and because people have been trying to frighten me off."

"By following you?"

"That and a beating in a New York hotel room," Julian said. "Now I'm in Europe and they're here, too. I must be close, very close."

"Then you think Mr. Legris has them?"

"Either that or he knows where they are."

"Suppose the people who have them really want to stop you and—"

"It's possible they might try to kill me."

"And you're not afraid?"

Julian shook his head. "I'm frightened out of my wits. But I want what was Sam's and what should now be mine.

It's not so venal as it sounds," he said after a momentary pause.

"You're a better judge of that than I. But even if you find the diamonds, you can't relive your life with your father. The diamonds, or the money you'll get from them, won't make up for the father you never had."

"You're right, absolutely right."

"Then why the frantic search?"

"Because they're mine." Julian walked to the other end of the room and faced her. "Maybe in the beginning I wanted them because I felt cheated by him, cheated by the kind of childhood I wanted and never had. Cheated of the friends I wanted and never had. Cheated in many, many different ways. But—but now I want them because Sam sweated for them; because he was my father and what he left belongs to me."

"Because you really loved him?"

"Yes," Julian answered softly. "Because I loved him."

"I think I understand."

Julian nodded. "Do you still want to leave?"

"No," she answered. "I'll stay."

Julian crossed the room and lifted her to her feet, hugging her fiercely to him. "I'm falling in love with you," he said.

"And I with you," she told him, raising her lips up to his.

38

A BRIGHT WINTER SUN cut a wide swath in Marrosov's office. He sat at his desk, transfixed by the newspaper photograph of Fuentes's body.

Marrosov had hoped for more time, but he could no longer afford to wait for the trade to be made for Urishensky. He would have to act, or his own people would swoop down on him. He had taken part in more than one operation like that . . . The man was usually drugged and placed aboard a Soviet transport in charge of other KGB people . . . Marrosov didn't want that to happen to him, and the only way to prevent it was to seek asylum in the United States.

He had already discussed the matter with his wife and had arranged a particular code. He picked up the phone, and within moments he was speaking to her.

"I want something special for dinner," he said, using the opening words of their code. He waited for her answer. He could hear her heavy breathing on the other end.

Finally she replied, "I will go to the supermarket and buy a turkey."

"Yes, that's a good American bird."

"What time will you be home?"

"I'm leaving the office soon," he said. "Meet me at the station. I'll be coming in by train." He was telling her that he was going to the FBI office in lower Manhattan, and he wanted her and the children to meet him there.

"Good-bye," she told him.

"Good-bye," he answered. As soon as he hung up, he shredded the photograph and the envelope in which it had come. Then he put on his coat. On the way out, he told his secretary that he needed some fresh air. "The smoke from my own cigars has given me a headache." She laughed heartily.

Outside it was colder than Marrosov had suspected. He pulled up his collar and turned toward Madison Avenue. There weren't too many people on the street. Suddenly there was the screech of a car's wheels on the surface of the gutter. He glanced over his shoulder. A black car sped toward Madison. Suddenly it swerved close to the curb. Marrosov saw the gun barrel of an automatic rifle jutting out from the rear side window. He started to run.

The car slowed.

The burst caught him in the back and knocked him down. Marrosov heard the sound of the shots as he fell. Blood filled his mouth. He tried to move but the pain crushed him. He knew he was dying.

Korditz was the last to be questioned by Detective Dalis. Guber and Borsky were outside waiting for Dalis to finish. Dalis had questioned them individually, and now it was his turn. For several minutes neither he nor the detective said anything.

Korditz was very calm. He looked around the grubby, windowless cell that Dalis called home for the better part of each day. The green paint was peeling near the ceiling and the desk looked as if it had been bought in a Salvation Army thrift store. He had been in similar rooms in the past, in various police stations, in different cities.

Dalis was a cigarette smoker, and the ashtray on the right side of his desk was filled with stubbed-out butts. He took time to light a fresh cigarette. The smoke swirled into his right eye and he moved his head back. Waving his hand in front of him to disperse the smoke, he said, "Your friend Begin has a rap sheet a mile long."

Korditz said nothing. He knew he had been tailed.

Dalis set his elbows down on the desk. "And you aren't exactly without some dirt in your past, now are you?"

"I suppose you're telling me, not asking," Korditz responded.

"What's your connection to Begin?"

"A friend."

"Not the kind of friend most men have."

"A friend," Korditz repeated. The Dalises of the world did not intimidate Korditz. He had come up against them many times in the past and had, more often than not, managed to walk away.

"You also have another friend," Dalis said, blowing smoke across the desk, "who told me to keep an eye on you."

"I'm not interested in police protection."

"Don't be a wise-ass, Korditz," Dalis said sharply. "Now tell me why you're going to Paris."

"You really have been protecting me!" Korditz exclaimed.

"Answer my question."

"I like the women there," Korditz replied. "Now if you don't intend to charge me, I will leave."

"You'll go when I tell you to," Dalis told him.

Korditz threw up his hands. "Whatever you say, lieutenant."

"The way I see it," Dalis said, "one of you is the finger man for the mob."

"You have three to choose from," Korditz replied. "Take your pick. But now we're down to basics. Unless you charge me, you can't hold me, so with or without your permission, lieutenant, I'm going to get up and walk out of here."

Dalis stubbed out his cigarette. "Something isn't kosher with you guys. You're into something, I don't know what. But as sure as God made little green apples, I'm going to find out."

"That's your job," Korditz said. He stood up. "No one is going to rub your face in the mud for doing your job."

Dalis got to his feet. "I'm going to keep my eye on you and your friends."

"You do that," Korditz said, walking to the door. "See you around, lieutenant." A moment later he was out of Dalis's office and in the waiting room.

Guber and Borsky saw him and stood up. The three of them left the police station. They walked two blocks before Guber said, "Dalis is on to us."

"I think so, too," Borsky said.

Korditz remained silent. All Dalis seemed to have was his connection to Begin. And if things went right for the next three days, that wouldn't matter. Not only would he be in Paris, but he'd be a very rich man.

They passed a newspaper stand. Borsky stopped to buy the final edition of the *Post.* "My God!" he exclaimed, calling the attention of the other two to himself. "Marrosov has been shot dead." He gave the newsman the quarter and taking the newspaper, he began to read the story: *"Igor Marrosov, senior cultural advisor to the United Nations from the Soviet Union, was shot to death early this afternoon on East Sixty-eighth Street, not far from the Russian mission's offices. The killing, the work of a Polish Liberation group, took place in front of two city policemen assigned to guard the mission . . ."* He continued to read until he finished the brief story.

"I can't believe it," Guber said, shaking his head. "I just can't believe it."

Borsky tucked the paper under his arm. "Nothing has gone right with this operation. Absolutely nothing." He was grim. "I think we should consider canceling the mission," he said as he walked on.

"Then Urishensky will never get out," Guber responded. "Have you any idea what will happen to him if we don't finish what we started? He must be gotten out."

"I agree with Max," Korditz told them.

"All right," Borsky said. "But we don't have much of a choice now. With Marrosov dead, the final exchange should be made in Paris and not in London—the longer we wait, the more dangerous it becomes. I don't think we should take anymore chances."

"Our contacts can call their friends in East Berlin from Paris as easily as they could from London," Korditz commented.

"Borsky," Guber said, "call Lublin and Legris tonight. Legris can make the arrangements. Lublin already has the stones."

"I think one of us should go there," Korditz told them.

"I can't," Guber said. "It's my best season."

Borsky shook his head. "I'm in the same boat as Max."

"I'll go," Korditz said.

"What about Dalis?" Guber asked. "What if he calls you again? How do we explain your absence?"

"I'll only be away for a few days . . . If he has any more questions, you tell him that I had important business to take care of in Paris. I'm sure he'll understand."

"All right," Guber replied. "You go. I'd like to see this one finished." The others agreed.

Then Korditz said, "I'll leave tomorrow and be back here by Sunday."

Guber nodded, as did Borsky. The three of them shook hands and separated.

Korditz smiled as he walked away.

39

It was Dimetrov's last night in Amsterdam. He sat in the office of the area KGB chief and thanked him for his cooperation. "Your men have done a good job keeping track of Heck," he said.

"He's not an American agent, is he?" the chief asked. He was a rotund man with pronounced Asiatic features.

"No," Dimetrov answered. "But please don't ask me any more questions about him."

The man nodded. "I understand."

Dimetrov stood up and leaned across the desk to shake the chief's hand.

"By the way, Marrosov was shot in New York," the chief said.

"Shot?"

"Apparently he was killed by a Polish Liberation group."

Dimetrov's eyes went wide, and then, shaking his head, he expressed the proper concern. "This is not the easiest or safest profession we follow. But the state would be in great danger if we did not guard it."

"Well put, comrade," the chief said as he walked his guest to the door. "I hope you conclude your mission successfully."

They shook hands again.

Dimetrov walked toward the center of the city. That Marrosov had been shot disturbed him only slightly. Dimetrov was quite certain that as soon as Marrosov had received the newspaper photograph of Fuentes's body, he had made up his mind to defect or even possibly end his connection with the people who had been trading diamonds for Jews. He was equally sure that Korditz and his friends could not permit either to happen and had shot Marrosov down. Anyone could call the newspapers or the police and give the name of a group who, because of their anti-Soviet politics, could be responsible for the killing.

When he reached the dam, Dimetrov slowed his pace. He decided to have dinner at the Tolde Binnenhofje, a restaurant he had been told about by a friend some months before. Then, afterward, he planned on going to a brown café, a late-hours place, and with any luck he'd meet a woman with whom he might enjoy himself for a few hours. It had been almost a month since he had been with a woman, and he felt the need keenly. He had even thought about the possibility of looking for Luana, but decided it would be too risky. She might demand more money or possibly cause difficulties that he wasn't prepared to deal with. There were enough single women around for him to be sure of meeting one. He smiled at the prospect and, hailing a cab, he told the driver where he wanted to go. Less than ten minutes later, he entered the small but charming courtyard where the restaurant was located.

Julian arrived at Lublin's office at ten thirty. Sunlight streamed through the window, giving the office a delightful warmth.

Lublin came around to the front of the desk to greet Julian. "As I told you yesterday," he said, shaking his hand, "I don't mean to trouble you."

"Please," Julian responded. "It's no trouble at all. After all, I'm going to meet the man."

Lublin returned to the desk, opened the top middle drawer and handed Julian the package of stones.

"How much is this worth?" Julian asked.

"Close to three hundred thousand dollars," Lublin answered. Julian examined the package. It was wrapped with plain brown paper and was about five inches long and three inches wide. The ends of the wrapping were taped down, and a piece of tape went over the edge of the paper.

"Thank you again," Lublin said, extending his hand across the table.

Closing the door behind him, Julian left the office. He went directly to Cynthia and said, "I should be back in two days, no more than three . . . Can you arrange to take a leave and come to the States with me?"

"When did you decide that?"

"At breakfast, when I watched you walk away from the table," he answered with a smile, knowing she'd remember she had worn nothing more than a pair of very sheer panties. "I enjoyed watching you so much, I decided I'd better take you back with me. Besides, there are a great many other things I like about you."

"Yes, I know," she answered, flushing deeply.

He leaned over and kissed her on the mouth. "I'm coming back for you," he said from the doorway. "I love you." Before she could answer him, he was on his way down the hallway.

At Schiphol, he queued up for the Paris flight. He was

surprised at the number of people going to Paris. It reminded him of the shuttle flights between Los Angeles and Las Vegas. At ten to eleven, the flight was announced over the loudspeaker and the passengers began to board. He was almost at the gate when he had the peculiar feeling that someone was looking at him. He stopped and turned around. The man behind him said, "Please make up your mind, either continue to walk or drop out of the line."

Julian saw no one he recognized. He boarded the plane and sat down in the aft section. He still had the feeling he was being observed. But no one was paying the slightest attention to him.

The stewardess asked him to fasten his safety belt. He nodded, fastened the belt and, closing his eyes, he leaned back waiting for the takeoff . . .

40

Julian registered at the desk of the Hotel Jean Goujon. The bearded clerk asked him how long he intended to stay.

"Not more than two nights," Julian said, looking off to the side where there was a small, well-furnished sitting area in the style of Louis Quatorze. A few minutes later, Julian was installed in a small room with a window overlooking the street and a bed that appeared to have been built into the wall. He tipped the bellboy. As soon as he removed his coat and jacket, he put through a call to Saul Legris. "This is Julian Heck," he said after Legris answered the phone.

"Yes . . . Yes . . . I have been expecting your call," Legris said in a nervous, high-pitched voice.

"Would it be possible to see you this afternoon?"

"Yes . . . Yes."

"I have something for you from—"

"Please, we will talk about it when I see you," Legris told him. "You know my address?"

"Yes."

"Three o'clock then," Legris said.

No good-byes. The line on the other end went dead.

Julian set the phone down. Legris was obviously very agitated and almost sounded as if the call had annoyed him. Julian shrugged; there wasn't a damn thing he could do about that.

He opened his collar, loosened his tie and went into the bathroom to wash his face and hands. After a flight, even a short one, he always felt grimy. The small hotel-size soap was scented and the towels were very large. He always appreciated large towels. Just as he finished drying his hands, the phone rang.

He hurried from the bathroom, picked up the phone and said, "Hello?"

The line went dead.

Julian flung the phone down. "Goddamn bastards!" he shouted. "Goddamn bastards!" He was sweating profusely now and was forced to wipe the sweat from his eyes. He picked up the phone and asked the operator if the person who had just called had asked for him by name.

"Yes, monsieur, he did," the operator said.

"Was it a man or a woman?"

"A man."

"Thank you," Julian said and hung up. He began to pace, stopping at the window for a few moments to see if there was anyone in the street who looked in the least bit suspicious. The street, as far as he could see in either direction, was empty.

He started to pace again and then stopped. He couldn't stay in the room; he had to get out and walk. With deliberate slowness, he closed his collar, pulled up his tie and looked at himself in the mirror before picking up his jacket and coat from the bed and leaving.

At the desk he asked the concierge, "Is there a place nearby where I'd be able to have lunch?" He spoke in halting French, but it was good enough to make himself understood.

"If you go right when you leave the hotel and walk straight up the street, you'll come to the Champs Élysées. There are many places along there."

Julian thanked him and left the hotel. He hadn't gone more than a block when he felt he was being followed. He turned. There was an old woman some distance behind him. He quickened his pace and within a few minutes, he reached the crowded Champs Élysées. He looked at his watch; one fifteen. He stopped for a moment to consider which way to go. This wasn't his first visit to Paris, and he remembered a café that was somewhere above the traffic circle. He turned right.

As in New York and Amsterdam, the shop windows were decorated for the holidays. Suddenly he realized it was already the twentieth, and Christmas just five days away.

He saw the café; it was on the corner of the rue Pre Charron. Though it was busy, he arrived just as a table for two became available. The table was alongside the window and gave him a good view of the street. He ordered sausages, potatoes and a carafe of the house red wine. Though still certain he was being watched, he was much calmer now than he had been in the hotel room. Nothing could happen to him in broad daylight in a café on the Champs Élysées.

He ate slowly, trying to enjoy the food and wine. But it was difficult for him not to think about his pursuers. He seemed to have moved from reality to a fiction that he might have created for TV. But the more he thought about it, the more he realized there could be only two reasons why someone would be tailing him. The first could have something to do with the diamonds his father had left. If he were getting too close, the individual who had them might want to have him watched, or—killed?

That was a sobering thought, more at that particular moment, because of the possibility, than at any other. He might have been killed in New York, or perhaps in Amsterdam. But he wasn't. And that could mean that there had been some hesitation on the part of the individual who had the diamonds. But now?

Julian couldn't even make a good guess. He picked up his wineglass and drained it.

The second reason someone would be following him could be connected to the diamonds he was going to deliver to Legris. But no one other than Lublin and Legris knew about them. Or were others involved? Julian didn't know. If there were—

He suddenly found himself staring at two men. They stopped in front of the café, obviously trying to decide whether to enter it. He realized one of the men was Korditz, his father's friend.

He leaped to his feet, almost upsetting the table. He slapped a handful of bills on the table, grabbed his coat and rushed from the restaurant. In the street, he called Korditz by name.

The two men began to run toward the opposite corner.

Julian went after them, still calling Korditz's name, but before he reached the next corner, Korditz and the other man had vanished into a stream of people.

Breathing hard, Julian stopped. People were looking at him and walking around him. Julian wiped his sweating brow.

He walked as far as the corner, crossed over to the other side and eventually returned to his hotel room.

Unable to calm himself, Julian put through a call to Cynthia. "I had to speak to you," he told her. "I mean, I think—" He took a deep breath and started all over again. He said, "I know this sounds crazy, but I'm really being followed. Not only am I being followed, but someone I know from New York is probably doing it or having it done. I saw him. I was inside a café having lunch. He was outside talking to another man. When I went out and called his name, he and his friend took off."

"What do you mean, 'took off?' "

"He ran away. He and his friend ran away and became lost in the crowd."

"You might have been mistaken," Cynthia suggested.

Julian shook his head. "I could have been. But I wasn't. I really don't know what the hell is going on. But it's something real weird, and I'm part of it. But I don't know which part. I'll be damn glad when this whole thing is over and I can resume my life—my real life."

"If you can, come back tonight . . . Come straight to my apartment."

There was a breathy quality in Cynthia's voice that Julian found exciting, and he told her so.

"I love you," she said. "I love you, and I want to show you the best way I can."

"I'll try to leave tonight," he said.

"I'll be waiting," she responded. "Now try and be calm and please take care of yourself. Promise?"

"I promise," Julian said. Feeling much better, he put the phone down. But the next moment the phone rang. He drew back and looked at it, wondering if it were the person who had called him before. It rang two more times before he could bring himself to lift it up. Clearing his throat, he said, "Hello."

"This is Legris . . . I must change our appointment," he said. "I want you to come to number fifty-four rue de Plateau . . . Get a map of the city and rent a car. There will be a light in the archway of the entrance. Be there at nine tonight."

"Listen, Mr. Legris," Julian told him, "all I want to do is ask you a question or two about my father. I—" There was an unnatural silence on the other end, almost as if Legris had put his hand over the mouthpiece.

"Goddamn it, Legris—"

"I can't speak with you now," Legris said. "Meet me tonight, and I'll answer your questions."

The line went dead.

Julian shook his head and dropped the phone back into its cradle. He was furious with Legris's high-handed treatment of him. He had hoped to take a late-night plane back to Amsterdam; now there seemed little possibility of that. He looked at his watch. It was only three o'clock; he had a six-hour wait before he met with Legris.

He took a deep breath, picked up the phone and arranged with the concierge to have a car and a map of the city available by eight that night. Then he dropped down on the bed, kicking off his shoes and loosening his tie, and said, "Maybe I'll be able to sleep for a while."

But after a few minutes of holding his eyes shut and hoping sleep would come, he gave up and lay staring at the ceiling. Suddenly he began to wonder if he wasn't being set up for something. His heart skipped a beat and began to go like a trip hammer.

Julian stood up and went into the bathroom. He ran the cold water, washed his face and held the inside surface of his wrists under the running water. When he felt slightly less tense, he went back into the bedroom and stood at the window.

The street lights were on and there were lights in the windows of the apartment house across the street. A delivery truck was parked in front of the hotel.

Julian moved away from the window and dropped down into a chair close by. Though the room was in darkness, he could see the reflection of the window and lights of the building across the street in the mirror.

He went over the sequence of events that had taken place during the last fifteen days. Everything that had happened had some connection to his search for his father's diamonds. And anything that would happen, he was sure, would happen for the same reason.

Julian thought about his father's involvement with Guber, Borsky and Korditz. They must have been into something that required his father to go abroad many times a year. Because he had met Spinelli, Julian thought they had been involved in some sort of smuggling operation. Most likely diamonds, though it could have been other things, too. Perhaps drugs? The package Lublin had given him to bring to Legris could just as easily contain heroin or cocaine as diamonds.

Julian went to his valise. He took the package out and hefted it. He couldn't tell anything from its weight. He switched on an end-table lamp. There wasn't any way to open the package without cutting the tape.

Julian put the package on the end table and sat down. He suddenly realized he was being used as a courier among Guber, Lublin and Legris. He was intent on finding his father's diamonds; he had made it easy for Guber to use him.

Standing up, he walked to the window, turned and looked back at the package. Julian resented Guber for taking advantage of him and deceiving him. Now Julian understood why he was being followed: Guber wasn't going to allow any mishaps.

Julian began to pace again. He was determined to find out what kind of operation his father had been involved in, and the only way to do that was to make the delivery at the specified time and place. He was no longer afraid; there was nothing to be afraid of. He was well protected; even Korditz was in Paris to make sure nothing happened either to him or to the package he was to deliver. He felt so confident he decided to take a long walk and have dinner before the rendezvous with Legris.

Korditz and his companion were breathless and perspiring by the time they slowed to a normal walking pace. Neither spoke. They had run along the Champs Élysées, turned down the avenue Roosevelt, then into the grounds of the Grand Palais and finally across the place de la Concorde toward the rue de Rivoli.

"Are you sure it was Dimetrov?" the man asked. He was younger and taller than Korditz.

"Yes. Absolutely sure. He was standing off to the side of the building looking at us."

"I don't understand why you ran."

"Because, as far as he knows, I'm not supposed to be here," Korditz answered.

"But you said he was looking at us."

"That doesn't mean he saw us."

"He may not have seen us, but I bet he heard Julian calling your name . . . Everyone on the damn Champs Élysées did."

Korditz didn't answer. Seeing Dimetrov had unnerved

him. The odds against something like that happening were tremendous; yet it had happened.

"So what do we have?" the man asked.

"You tell me."

"The Ruski is shadowing Julian and so are we. When we take Julian out, we'll take the Ruski out, too. . . . So what's the big deal? Listen, I have two other men with me. They're the best there is for this kind of job."

Korditz stopped under the arcade, pretending to be interested in the goods of a nearby street vendor. "The Ruski makes complications. Two bodies, with one a KGB agent, will make the Russians very angry."

"That can't be helped. If you're that worried, come along and watch it happen."

"No thanks. I'll wait for you back in the hotel," Korditz said, beginning to walk again. "Julian is slated to hand over the goods about nine. He will have to drive past the Parc des Buttes-Chaumont. You can take him out along the route."

"Are you sure he'll have the goods on him?"

"The package will be on him."

"It better be, or he'll be killed for nothing," the young man said. "One of my companions will work with me, and the other will go after the Ruski."

Korditz didn't answer.

41

Dimetrov and Fournier sat opposite each other in a small restaurant on the rue de Temple. Dimetrov had arranged the meeting earlier that day. The restaurant's menu (written on a slate blackboard) changed daily. The waitress was the owner's daughter and the cook his wife. Everything was home-made, including the hot bread.

Dimetrov ordered onion soup and tripe. Fournier preferred the vegetable soup and asked for veal in wine sauce. They shared a house white wine.

When the waitress left their table, Fournier asked, "Are you sure Korditz saw you?"

"There would not have been any reason for him to run if he hadn't."

Fournier broke off a piece of bread and buttered it. "That you weren't trailing Korditz, and yet you managed to see him, only confirms my belief in the role of coincidence in our lives."

"The odd part is that I don't think Korditz and his friend were trailing anyone either," Dimetrov said. "They were walking along in the most nonchalant manner."

"Where were you?"

"Standing against the side of the building. I had just bought a copy of *Le Monde* and had finished looking at the front page. I lowered the newspaper and found myself looking straight at Korditz." The waitress brought the wine and bowls of soup to the table.

"And you're sure Korditz is here to have a man killed?"

"Yes, I'm absolutely sure," Dimetrov answered. He spooned up some of the steaming soup and gave a vigorous nod of approval.

"Are you that man?" Fournier asked, though he had

been told by Avigeor that Julian had been duped into the role of courier.

It had never occurred to Dimetrov that Korditz and his friends might have hired someone to take him out. That he had overlooked the possibility made him frown. There was no reason for him to believe Korditz didn't suspect he was KGB. Marrosov might have told him.

"I asked you a question," Fournier said.

"I hadn't thought about it until you pointed out the possibility."

"What do you want me to do?" Fournier asked. He had finished his soup and put the spoon down in the bowl.

"Pick Korditz up and hold him . . . Have one of your men plant something on him. But hold him."

"And what are you going to do?" He was playing with Dimetrov, hoping to discover something more about his plans that he didn't already know or guess.

"You know I can't go into that."

"I've heard rumors that you're investigating something about the movement of diamonds in one direction and Jews in the other."

Dimetrov couldn't stop the color from rising in his cheeks. "Where did you hear that?"

"Here and there," Fournier answered. "In this line of work, your enemies and friends are interchangeable. Information comes from both sources."

"Will you pick Korditz up?"

"If I do, will you tell me what you're after?"

"I can't do that," Dimetrov said, shaking his head. "And you know I can't."

The waitress brought their entrées.

"Was Marrosov involved?" Fournier asked as soon as they were alone again.

"I'll tell you this and only this. I'm certain Korditz and his friend Begin had Marrosov killed."

Holding a piece of veal on a fork, Fournier asked, "Do you want to take Korditz out permanently?"

"If you can't have it done, I know several people who will do it, including a police detective in New York."

"Consider it done," Fournier said, extending a hand across the table. "I'll have one of my men find out where he's staying."

"He's at the Hotel Angleterre," Dimetrov told him. "He's been followed since he arrived here."

Fournier nodded approvingly. "How did you know he was coming to Paris?" he asked.

"We have ways," Dimetrov answered.

For a while they continued to eat without further conversation. But after the cafés au lait were ordered, Dimetrov said, "I don't want anyone following me. I don't want anyone in my way. I'm very close to the end of the line on this one."

He chose his words carefully, knowing they held a veiled threat. But he had carefully worked out a plan that would bring him face to face with the men he wanted. He was going to stalk the stalkers. At the right moment, he'd intervene. That would throw him and Julian together against the men who would be trying to kill the two of them. He had to gamble that neither Julian nor he would be killed in the first burst of gunfire. Then, as a comrade in arms, he'd accompany Julian to the place of delivery and he'd have his man.

"I understand," Fournier said with a nod. "I think I know how you feel."

Dimetrov didn't answer. He finished his café au lait, shook Fournier's hand and started to take out money to pay for his lunch.

"Please allow me," Fournier said. "After all, you're a guest here."

"Not exactly a guest," Dimetrov answered with a smile. "Next time we meet, I'll pay."

"Next time," Fournier agreed.

Julian drove away from the hotel at eight o'clock. He had gone over the route he'd take with the concierge and didn't have the least doubt he would find his way to the rue de Plateau. The concierge had commented that the area around the Buttes-Chaumont had many fine old houses.

From the map of the city he had looked at earlier, Julian knew his goal was roughly to the northeast. He drove along the right bank of the Seine until he came to the boulevard de Sebastopole, where he turned left. The night was very clear, and people were in the streets doing their Christmas shopping.

Now and then Julian encountered a knot of traffic that slowed him, but never for very long. He reached down to the dashboard and turned on the radio. A woman was singing. He listened very intently, trying to make out the words of the song, but he only understood a few.

He went through a residential neighborhood consisting mainly of buildings several stories high, but not so high as to be classified as tenements. He passed a very poor section of the city and went over a canal. Another few blocks brought him in sight of the park. Here and there a street lamp shone, but for the most part, the park was a huge dark area.

Julian slowed, noting the names of the streets as he passed them. There wasn't any other car in front of him. For a while now, he hadn't seen any people, either. There was a curve in the roadway that followed the shape of the park, which, he had seen on the map, was a crescent. A man was now singing on the radio, easier to understand than the woman.

Julian found himself thinking about Cynthia, surprised by his love for her. A car in the rearview mirror interrupted his thoughts. Even as he looked at it, it suddenly speeded up. Within moments, it was on his right. He glanced at it. There were two men in the front and one in the rear.

Suddenly the car swerved into him. Julian yanked the wheel to the left. The car alongside crashed against him again. Julian lost control of the car and headed into a clump of bushes, where he came to a stop.

Before he could move, a third car came racing up the street, turned and smashed into the rear of the car that had forced him off the roadway. Julian flung open the door.

"To the rocks," a man shouted. "Julian, get to the rocks."

The rocks were off to the right. He took a deep breath, eased out of the car and in a low crouch, he ran toward the rocks.

Two shots exploded.

Julian dropped to his stomach and bellied his way to the rocks. The men behind him were shouting to each other in Hebrew.

"This way," a man called in English from the shelter of the two large boulders that rose up like columns in front of him.

Julian went into a crouch again and dashed for the opening between the two boulders. Another shot exploded, followed by the ping of the bullet as it ricocheted off one of the boulders.

Julian leaped up, ran and was through the opening. A hand reached out and pulled him off to one side.

"Kass!"

"Later," Kass said. He handed him a revolver. "I hope you remember how to use it. The safety is off."

"What the hell is going on?" Julian asked, breathing hard.

"Later," Kass repeated. "They're going to come after us. We've got to make it back to either your car or mine. Are you ready to move?"

Julian nodded. What was happening now was almost familiar. He had lived through similar situations in Nam a dozen or more times. Only there it was in the jungle, and this was happening in a Paris park.

Kass motioned to Julian to follow him. They started to move away from the boulders. Suddenly Julian heard a noise behind him; he whirled and fired.

A man screamed and stumbled.

"To the trees!" Kass said. "Make for the trees." But as soon as he broke from the cover of the boulder, another shot was fired. Kass grabbed his arm and continued to run.

Julian went after him.

A man shouted something in Hebrew.

"You killed one," Julian explained.

"That leaves two," Kass said.

"How do you know that?"

Kass shook his head. "We still have to get to one of the cars." He flexed his arm. "I was lucky. The bullet just grazed me."

Julian nodded.

Kass started off through the woods.

"Where the hell are they?" Julian asked, sweating despite the cold.

"Close by," Kass answered.

The cars suddenly came into view. They were no more than a hundred meters from them, but their headlights were out.

"That's where they are," Kass said. "They're waiting for us."

"How—"

"I'm going to move toward the cars," Kass explained. "But one or both will have to show themselves to fire at me. You have to get your shots off before either one of them gets me." Before Julian could speak, Kass was working his way along the edge of the trees. He kept low but made a great deal of noise.

The two men near the cars suddenly stepped into the opening.

Julian could see them clearly. He raised the revolver, held it steady with two hands and squeezed off three shots as fast as he could.

One man dropped; the other turned and ran.

Kass rushed to the fallen man and put two more rounds in him; then he called to Julian. The two of them got into the car Kass had driven and, with Kass at the wheel, sped away.

Julian opened the window to let the cold air wash over his face. "Now will you tell me what's going on? No, I know what was happening back there . . . I want to know why it happened."

Kass pulled over to the side and stopped. "Let me take care of my arm," he said; "then I will tell you what you want to know." After a few minutes, he stanched the blood from the wound. Using his and Julian's handkerchiefs, he created a makeshift bandage.

"Are you sure you can drive?" Julian asked.

"Yes," Kass answered. He started the car and eased it away from the curb. "Those three men were trying to kill you, as they killed all the other couriers."

"Couriers?" Julian feigned ignorance. "What the hell are you talking about?"

"The diamonds you're carrying."

"How do you know about them?"

"Let me finish . . . The diamonds will be turned over to men who will then make arrangements to have a Jew or Jews leave the Soviet Union."

Julian was very quiet. He asked, after a few moments, "Then I was being followed?"

"Yes."

"And I did see—"

"Korditz, yes."

"You mean from the very beginning, I was set up by Max?" he asked, using the inflection of his voice to make a question out of his statement.

"In a manner of speaking. You were so interested in finding what you were sure your father left that—"

"Max took advantage of it?"

"Yes."

"I might have figured something like that for one of my scripts," Julian said with a bitter laugh. "But to have it happen to me gives it a very different feeling, very different. . . . I know about Max; now tell me about the other two."

"Korditz is part of the three we just met. He was fingering the couriers for his gangster friends, and trying to make it look like it was the Mafia or the East Germans—take your pick."

"And Borsky?"

"He worked with Max."

"And you," Julian asked, "where do you fit into all of this? You're not just M. Kass, are you?"

"Does it really matter?"

Julian shrugged. "I guess not," he said. "I guess the only thing that really matters is that you were there to keep me in one piece."

Kass offered Julian his hand.

Though Julian appeared to have accepted Kass's explanation, he did not. He was sure Kass was not just M. Kass, the good Samaritan. "Did you really know my father?" Julian asked.

"In a manner of speaking," Kass answered.

"What does that mean?"

"I knew a great deal about him."

"How?"

"I'd rather not explain . . ."

"I think you had better," Julian said, pointing the revolver at Kass. "Pull over and tell me how you knew my father."

"You're not going to kill me," Kass said.

"You don't know that . . . Now, tell me about my father."

"He was a courier," Kass said. "No, he was much more. There were times he made all the arrangements."

"Trading Jews for diamonds?"

"Yes, we have reason to believe he organized the entire operation."

"Who are the *we?*"

Kass shook his head. "That I can't tell you."

Julian lowered the revolver. Everything he had found out about his father began to make sense.

"How long was my father involved in the business of trading diamonds for Jews?"

"Eight years, that I know about."

"Eight years," Julian repeated sadly, knowing that it corresponded to the period of time when he had had so little contact with his father. "And how many times did he risk his life?"

"Many," Kass answered. "But he knew what he was doing."

"You admire him?"

"I admire any man who does what he sets out to do."

"You turn at the rue de Plateau," Julian said. "It will be the house with the light in the archway." Julian pursed his lips. There were so many things he would have liked to have told his father, so many.

"Here's the street," Kass said, making a right turn. The street was deserted except for two small trucks that were parked near the house with the light in the archway.

Julian and Kass got out of the car. They walked across the gutter toward the house. Just as they reached the other side, there was a sudden burst of illumination and a voice over a bull horn ordered them to halt.

Both men were blinded by the glare of the lights.

"The American," the voice said, "proceed into the house."

"Fournier?" Kass shouted, recognizing the voice despite the distortion produced by the bull horn. "Fournier?"

Julian remained motionless.

Suddenly Kass pulled his gun and pointed it at Julian. "Fournier, I'll kill him," he shouted.

"There are ten marksmen with their rifles on you, Dimetrov. You'll die the instant you pull the trigger. . . . Throw the gun down and let the American go into the house."

"You double-crossed me!" Kass shouted, "You double-crossed Russia!"

"Put the gun down," Fournier told him. "Drop it into the street where I can see it."

Kass looked around. But the lights prevented him from seeing anything. He tossed the revolver into the street.

Julian ran toward the house. Several moments later, he was inside.

There were four men in the bare room. One of them said,

"I am Legris . . . The other three are business associates."

Legris was standing. The others were seated at a table with a telephone on it. A single light bulb in a ceiling fixture illuminated the entire room.

From the outside, he heard Fournier say, "Shulamith, get the gun and bring our Russian friend to the van . . . Thank you, Dimetrov, for being so cooperative."

The glare of the high-intensity lights suddenly vanished from the window.

"Please," Legris said, "would you give me the package?" Julian reached into his jacket pocket, withdrew the package and handed it to Legris.

"You can leave now," Legris said. "You have done your job." He started toward the table where the three men were seated.

Julian suddenly grabbed hold of his arm. At the same time, he pulled his revolver out. "No one move . . . I was almost killed coming here. Before I leave, I want some answers. Who is Dimetrov?"

"A KGB agent after the men there," Legris said, gesturing toward the table.

"And who are they?"

"Russian businessmen," Legris answered.

"Now tell me who was worth all this."

"A man named Urishensky," Legris answered. "A man your father vowed to bring to the West."

"Did my father know him?"

Legris shook his head. "He knew his father; they were in Auschwitz together."

Julian nodded. Somehow now he could understand how important it was to keep a promise that was made so long ago.

"Now will you go?" Legris asked.

"One last question?"

Legris nodded.

"Who is the man Dimetrov called Fournier?" Julian asked. He remembered that name. It was on a slip of paper he had found among his father's other papers.

"A friend," Legris answered.

"Not good enough! Who is he? I know my father knew him."

Legris turned to the men at the table.

One of them nodded.

"He is your half-brother," Legris said.

Julian tried to speak but couldn't make his tongue or lips obey him.

His fantasy was true. Sam had another family, another son. He had a brother.

"He is also a French intelligence agent with ties to Moscow and to Israel. And now you must leave."

"Will I be able to see my brother?"

"Someday soon he will come to you."

"Tell him," Julian said, forcing the words out of his constricted throat, "tell him I'll be waiting . . . Tell him that Sam must have planned this whole thing to bring us together. Will you tell him that?"

"Yes, I will tell him."

Julian lowered the revolver and walked toward the door. He stopped before he opened it and asked what would happen to Dimetrov.

"Nothing," Legris answered. "He will be held until our business is finished; then he will be released and no doubt he'll return to Moscow."

Julian stepped out into the street. It was absolutely deserted except for the car he and Dimetrov had left there. He crossed the street. His breath steamed in the cold night air. Nothing had turned out as he thought it would. He slipped behind the wheel, started the car and, before making a U-turn, looked back at the house he had just come out of. The light in the archway was already out.

Julian nodded. As he pulled away, he had the satisfaction of knowing he had kept his father's promise. To loosen the tightness in his throat, he swallowed several times. "All in all," he said aloud, "you were a man, Sam—a *mentsh*—and that's about as much as any two sons could want their father to be . . ."